A Tale of Flight and Flame

A Realm Apart

Kristie Price

To all the readers who "hate it here", these realms were my escape. I hope you get lost in Louella's adventures (like I did), and forget about the current state of ours - even if it's just for 300 pages or so.

"If we find ourselves with a desire that nothing in this world can satisfy, the most probable explanation is that we were made for another world."

C.S. Lewis

Contents

PRONUNCIATION GUIDE

Ahitian: ah-HEE-shen

Algonquin: al-GON-kwin

Chester Pala Delphine: CHES-tur PAY-lew del-FEEN

Hana: HAH-nah

Jasper Kele Delphine: JASS-pur KAY-lay del-FEEN

Kaiman: KYE-man

Kapa'a: kah-PAH-ah

Kapu: KAH-poo

Lanai: lah-NYE

Louella Aponi Delphine: loo-ELL-ah ah-PAH-nee del-FEEN

Maka: MAH-kah

Malcolm Dasan Royce: MAL-cum dah-SAHN rois

Molokai: moh-loh-KYE

Poipu: POY-poo

Rowland Calian Delphine: ROH-land CAL-ee-in del-FEEN

Sebastian Ahiga Royce: seh-BASH-chin ah-HEE-gah rois

Theadosia Sakari Delphine: thee-ah-DOH-zhea sah-KAR-ee del-FEEN

Waimea: WAY-may

Wikitian: wih-KEE-shen

ONE

LOUELLA APONI DELPHINE

Castle Waimea, Kapu Island

"Louella! You can't—" Chester's voice is cut off by the whooshing sound of Shea's leathery black wings flapping against the ground as she stomps her feet into the earth below us.

I grip the reins with my left hand while twisting them tighter around my right wrist. Digging my bare feet into the cold metal stirrups that hang on either side of Shea's body, I tighten my thighs along her back to ensure I'm secure while flying.

Suddenly, Shea's feet make three booming bangs as she lurches forward and swoops up into the sky, jerking me back. My instant reaction is to grab the jade horn of the saddle so that I don't slip and fall to my death . . . The last thing I need is for my brother to get his final "I told you so." I can picture him standing above me as I lie dead on the ground, shaking his head, knowing he's always right.

I look down at Chester's tall, imposing frame, which grows smaller as we ascend. He watches us with a scowl on his face, his eyes glowering into mine—so I taunt him with a smirk. Fists clenched at his sides, the muscles in his arms are straining, making the swirling designs of his tattoos undulate. He takes a few steps backward as his shoulders slump in defeat and his head tips back in exasperation from playing this game with me every night. In a final sign of resignation, he throws his hands in the air and walks toward the dragon caves.

With a self-satisfied laugh, I turn to focus my attention ahead of me as Shea deftly and quietly carves through the darkness of the sky, which is punctured with tiny stars. The higher we climb, the brighter they become.

Closing my eyes, I let the wind whip the end of my braid against my back. When Shea levels us out, I unclasp the horn and spread my arms wide as if I were flying all by myself. Goosebumps break out along my arms and legs from the rush of air. Even with my long-sleeved shirt and thick pants, the chill manages to pierce through the weave in the fabric like tiny sewing needles, relentlessly pricking its way through the cotton. For an island that is constantly humid and hot, it's cold above the clouds, especially in the night sky with no sun shining to warm me up, but I don't care—I feel free and alive.

Shea and I have never flown in the daylight. So often on our nightly cruises (and tonight is no exception), while my eyelids are still lightly closed, I envision the layout of the island below us from a bird's-eye view: Images of tall, bristly palms bending under the tropical breeze flash before my eyes. I can see grass, wood, and leaves stacked intricately to form the hut roofs of the hundreds of villagers' homes below. Gravel pathways wind together to lead to the center of the village, which is lined with little shops built of stone and taupe-colored canopied tents. I picture people bustling between the stalls below, shuffling to get shopping done or working hard to trade and make deals.

And just outside the village center, a castle looms up on a hill, with its gray stones and its elegant and lavishly vibrant gardens. On the top of every turret, a flag whips proudly, bearing the Waimea crest: a dragon displayed front and center with intricate Wiki designs swirling around it. Having memorized the details of that flag from an early age, I can see it so clearly in my mind's eye now.

I take a deep breath in, smelling the salt and seaweed from the ocean air as it hits my nostrils. I picture lush grass peppering the rolling hills that stretch as far as they can—until they tumble over into cliffsides or meet a shore-line. The beaches extend around the island, creating a perimeter of soft beige and black sand as cerulean waves gently crash. As quickly as the waves land, they get sucked back into the ocean, picking up rocks as they return. The rocks bump and bash against each other as they fall into the sea, almost sounding like a melody, or maybe a cry that they don't want to leave the island just yet.

The thoughts of Kapu Island bring a tingling sensation up through my body, making me shiver—and this time, it's not from the cool air.

I love my home.

Shea snorts to warn me of the turn she's about to take. I already know it's coming because we take the same route every time we ride. Finally opening my eyes, I grip the horn again, and Shea dips to her right, making a quick turn and leveling out once more. I can see the moon reflecting off the shore ahead of us, and my heart races knowing what my dragon will do next.

When the beach approaches, Shea begins to gradually descend. Once she's out over the water, I swiftly pop my feet out of the stirrups and onto the saddle on Shea's back. Standing with one foot behind the other, like I'm on a surfboard, I hold my balance. Right on cue, Shea dips her legs into the water and glides steadily above it. The salty ocean sprays my face as I carefully lean to the right, dipping my fingers in the water. It's freezing and forceful against my hand, causing me to reach with my left hand and clutch the leather strap of the reins. This is my favorite part of our ride together. The water grounds me while the air liberates me—and melding the two together in this way makes me feel at peace.

After a while, Shea emits a shrill squawk to let me know that it's time to go. She lifts her legs out of the water as I sit back down in the saddle, placing my feet into the stirrups. And just like that, she ascends higher once again and we make our way back home.

As we get closer, I can see the landing grass next to the dragon caves. Chester has returned to where we left him, but now his arms are crossed over his chest and his foot is tapping impatiently. Shea straightens her legs and extends her dark black claws as they sink into the ground below, giving us a soft landing, but she rips the earth to shreds as we come to a complete stop. When Shea's wings settle and the world around me becomes quiet again, my brother rushes over to start in on me like he does every night.

"Louella, you are going to get seriously injured one of these nights. I repeatedly tell you to tighten the reins and grab the horn before takeoff. If you hurt yourself, the chief will never forgive me . . . he may even kill me."

I jump off Shea's back and study Chester for a moment as I consider snapping at him with some attitude of my own. His chest rises and falls with each huff of frustration, the fabric of his black T-shirt taut across his muscles. He's combat-ready in his matching oversized black cargo pants, minus the one thing I always find odd about my big brother: his consistently bare feet. For someone who dresses as if he's poised for a fight, he rarely has shoes on. Right now, he's standing in front of me with his hand out, impatiently waiting for me to dismantle the saddle and bridle so he can put them away in the equipment shed and pretend like tonight's little excursion never happened.

Chester's brows are furrowed so deeply they are almost touching. The wrinkles on his forehead are profound from years of constantly being on edge and never knowing how not to take life so seriously. Regardless of the deep grooves embedded in his chestnut skin, his face has a softness to it because, behind the mask of worry, he's a sweetheart—a hopeless romantic. Chester's dark-chocolate eyes are wide, but right now he's squinting at me, glaring like I'm a puzzle he will never be able to assemble—I always have a missing piece. I notice he's a bit more on edge tonight, as if something else is bothering him. I briefly study the flaring nostrils of his wide nose, which reminds me of my father's. His lips are what I envy the most; his are full, and mine are thin like my mama's . . . I'm not entirely sure how Chester ended up with all the good genes of the family, but he did.

Right as he opens those full lips, I pivot back toward Shea and get to work removing the riding equipment. I've decided not to fight back with him tonight, but I do give him a hard shove when I push the saddle to his chest. After all, he is right. Women are not supposed to ride dragons. Especially not the daughter of the chief—or, as most know him, the king.

Yes, that's right. I'm the chief's precious, dainty daughter—also known as Princess Louella Aponi Delphine of Castle Waimea. In my mind, that's not who I am. I'm a warrior. I'm not dainty at all. I have curves because I love to eat and because I'm strong and muscular to keep up with my dragon. When I'm not sneaking out to ride Shea, I'm sneaking out so my brother can teach me how to fight with a sword, dagger, and bow and arrow. I know how to pierce a man's heart—not by wearing stunning dresses or cooking delicious food, but with a weapon. Preferably a sword . . . I'm still working on the trajectory and aim of my arrows.

Papa and Mama have no idea what their princess has been up to in the early-morning hours, which means they also have no idea what their son, Prince Chester Pala Delphine, does during those hours as well. Or that other women in the village often join me to learn how to fight and fly.

Chester interrupts my thoughts as his voice cuts through the silence of the night. "One of these days, our little secret will be spilled because you're too reckless, and then you will have to go back to your boring life of learning how to be a wife. Do you want that, Louella?" He doesn't wait for my response before continuing, "I know you don't, so make sure you go through all the safety checks I've taught you."

I stalk behind him with Shea's bridle in hand, watching his jet-black braid move across his back as he hustles the saddle to the shed next to the dragon caves.

I really want to push him again, this time from behind so he falls face-first onto the ground (and maybe lands in dragon shit, if I'm lucky). But Shea lets out a thunderous snarl as if she can read my mind. I glance at her, letting my eyes adjust to the florescent-purple lines that run along her spikes. She's raven black, which makes it hard for me to see her with the limited lighting out here. I quickly stick my tongue out at her as she disappears into the darkness of the cave to our right.

I'm assuming she's retreating to rest before she has to train with our military's cavalry unit tomorrow. She doesn't let anyone else ride her but me, so she doesn't need that much rest. Any time a man from our cavalry tries to saddle her up, she bucks and jerks until they finally give up and let her lie under the shade of the willow tree. I snort to myself, thinking about my girl chilling in the breeze while everyone else is grunting, sweating, and busting their asses.

I'm really going to miss her.

Last month, the chief announced that he had arranged for me to marry the young and ever-so-handsome Prince Malcolm Dasan Royce, the next in line as ruler of Castle Hana. It's a power move for both castles—Castle Waimea and Castle Hana—because we both have the strongest dragons in the land.

Currently, dragon crossbreeding is not allowed without joining castles either by marriage or by siege. Our dragons are the fastest and deadliest, and they have the most accurate aim. Castle Hana has dragons with electrical currents that run through the spikes along their spines and wings. These dragons can't shoot electricity—but they can zap prey by touching it with their wings or spikes. Impressive enough already, but when our castles join by way of my arranged marriage, the dragons can then be crossbred into the fastest, most deadly accurate, electrified dragons. Making them the most lethal on the island . . . which, I'm not sure why we need such vicious dragons. Our island hasn't been to war in, like, a hundred years. But I'm not good at the politics of running a castle, so for once, I'll do what I'm told.

There are four castles that rule over their respective villages on Kapu Island, each bearing its own breed of dragons with a special trait or strength. Castle Molokai, on the island's western side, has dragons that can swim underwater for extended periods of time—I've heard that some even live in the ocean, but I haven't seen that for myself yet. Castle Lanai, dawning on the east coast of the island, has dragons that are excellent trackers. They can use their sense of smell and taste to hunt down prey and predator alike. Castle Hana lies to the south, and Castle Waimea is in the north. All four castles of the island circle around Maka Mountain, which is considered a neutral area that none of the castles can truly claim as their own.

Years ago, the four castles went to war in the only battle the island has ever had. Fighting over who would claim the mountain, Castle Hana emerged as the victor in the three-day-long, bloody, senseless Algonquin Battle. But when they tried to fly to the top of the mountain, the conditions were too dangerous. They lost six dragons and their riders before they gave the land up. Not a soul wanted it, so the four castles declared it neutral territory—no one has fought for it since, and I don't think they ever will. It wouldn't make sense to claim the land because the mountain is so tall and steep that you can't build on it or use it for any functional purpose. In fact, Maka Mountain's elevation is so high that it sometimes snows at the peak—even when it's always warm and tropical below, where we are. I've heard that the dragons are the only ones who have been to the summit of the mountain, so they alone know what it's like . . . if only they could speak.

Chester barges out of the equipment shed and slams the door, making me jump. His mood is awful right now, and I can tell he won't combat-train with me tonight since he's all pissed off about something. He's still wearing the same scowl he had on his face after Shea and I landed earlier. He storms past me, leaving me to scurry behind him to catch up.

"Chester, slow down. What is the matter? Why are you so upset tonight?" I'm on his heels, but he doesn't falter, nor does he answer. "I'm sorry. Next time, I promise I will keep my hands glued to the horn, and I'll keep the reins tightly wrapped," I plead.

Chester spins around, and I stop short before I slam into him.

"It's not that. I'm sorry I'm being this way." His face has gone soft, and I can see there is pain swirling in his dark eyes. Chester is my best friend. I know something is getting to him—and if it isn't me, then there's only one other person I can think of.

"Did something happen with Lucas?" I ask. Lucas is one of the dragon handlers who live on the castle grounds. Chester met Luke when my brother became old enough to start learning how to handle the dragons and train our riders. Luke is ten years older than Chester, which makes it a sensitive subject for our family (mostly Mama and Papa, because I couldn't care less). My parents know they are in a relationship but aren't keen on the fact that Luke is thirty-two years old and Chester is twenty-two.

Chester sighs before he sputters through a response. "Kind of, I don't know. Yeah, I mean . . . Yeah."

"You can tell me, you know that." I place my hand on his shoulder, a gesture of reassurance for him to continue.

"I know, and thank you. You already have so much to worry about, what with marrying a man you don't know and all. I don't even know how you're coping and not stressing the fuck out right now. I don't want to burden you with my problems."

"Hey, it's fine. I'm really not stressed about marrying a hot young prince. Plus, Shea can cave with me at their castle. I'm sure it won't be that hard to sneak out at night. I'll figure it out. I may be a salty, stubborn bitch, but I'm going into this with an open mind." I'm actually not sure whether Shea will be able to come with me yet, but I'm just trying to ease Chester's mind. He's worried about me too. That's what older brothers do.

Chester lets out a small laugh as his shoulders drop, letting go of the concern he held in them seconds ago. "Papa informed me today that I will be escorting you and a small selection of the breeding dragons to Castle Hana in five weeks. That means I have to leave Lucas behind, and

I don't know if I'll ever return." He scrubs a hand down his face and then waves it in the air. With a huff, he continues, "This is stupid. I'm not upset; I get to be with you, and you'll be able to ride. Plus, I don't even know if Luke likes me as much as I like him. It's probably just a sex thing, you know?"

"Chester, stop. He does like you like that. You have been together for two years. He hasn't seen anyone else in that time and neither have you. Also, I am excited for you to be coming with me, but my life isn't yours . . . Please don't feel obliged to stay by my side forever. You can say no to Papa. Have you tried saying no in your life, other than to me?"

"I would never think of saying no to the chief. But I guess I could try it." He pauses as he rubs the back of his neck. "Are you sure you'll be all right if we send someone else?"

I pull Chester by the elbow and wrap my arms around his neck. "I will be more than all right. We won't be far from one another, and I'm free to come home to visit whenever I want." Chester wraps his arms around my back in a tight hug.

"I'm sorry you have to marry someone you don't love, Sis."

My breath catches because I suppose I'm sorry too. I've never been in love, so I don't know what it feels like or what to expect. I have met Malcolm twice in my nineteen years of life. I vaguely remember our interactions, but I think of him playing with a couple of friends as they laughed and practiced sword fighting together. That's not what I remember the most, though . . . I remember how devilishly handsome he was. I mean, girls swoon over the mere mention of his name. What's not to love about Malcolm's sun-kissed toffee-colored hair, emerald eyes, dark skin, ripped body that accentuates his Ahitian tattoos, and chiseled jaw? To top it all off, he's actually a really sweet guy, from what I can recall. I don't imagine it will be that hard for me to fall in love with Malcolm.

Long before announcing his plans for my arranged marriage, Papa had brought me along a handful of times to Castle Hana for some negotiations regarding crops and harvesting, which is when I met Malcolm. Papa has taken me with him to one other village, though I can't remember which one. Our castles all trade with each other, so my father is often sailing or flying off to attend meetings and make deals. He tried to get me involved in the politics of it all, but I inevitably ended up wandering off to the gardens or dragon caves . . . I lost interest quickly.

Each castle and its village specializes in a trade, which is then merchandised to the other castles and their villages. Castle Waimea produces fruits, vegetables, grains, and the like. Castle Hana produces beef, poultry, other wildstock, and eggs. Castle Molokai sews and sells clothing, along with furniture goods—anything fabric-related. And Castle Lanai sells the fun stuff: weaponry, dragon bridles and saddles, and—everyone's favorites—booze and bud. You would think our plant-loving people would be the ones to grow marijuana, but the village of Lanai has the perfect position next to the mountain, with just enough light and darkness, along with the right humidity levels and airflow—the conditions can't be beat. Once, while helping (or rather, killing time) in the fields of Waimea, I asked the lead agriculturist why we don't grow bud. After answering my question, she gave me all the details to cultivate the perfect batch of marijuana. It was fascinating.

Chester suddenly steps back from our hug, jarring me from my thoughts. He holds my shoulders while looking into my eyes. "Are you all right? Did I lose you there for a second?"

"I'm fine." I clear my throat as I refocus on the conversation with Chester. "I think I might really like Malcolm. And who knows? Maybe we will fall in love."

Chester nods his head in agreement. "You know, for someone so headstrong, you're terribly optimistic."

"Ches, I have to be . . . I have to trick myself into thinking that there's still hope for me."

"This is bullshit, Ella. I'll be upset for you."

I smile, and Chester quips a small smirk at me. He turns and loops my arm under his. With our elbows locked, we make the trek back up to the looming castle.

The sun is peeking above the ocean horizon now, which lets me know that soon the village below and the castle above will be humming with the vibration of people getting ready for another day of arduous work.

TWO

LOUELLA APONI DELPHINE

Castle Waimea, Kapu Island

That same morning, I roll over in bed a few hours later and check the clock on the wall, which reads five to eleven. Being a princess on Kapu Island means I don't have many duties during the day, so I can sleep in. I've finished my years of homeschooling, and now it's off into the real world of marriage and other shit I've never cared about. Soon I'll begin training with Mama on how to be a chief's wife and what it will entail. I'm not excited about it, but it must be done. I'll bite my tongue and fake a smile until . . . well, forever? Now that I'm being sent off to marry my wonderful, dashingly handsome prince, I'll have to wear a perma-smile until I die.

Truthfully, I hate doing nothing all day. Though I might sleep late, I'm not one to lie around or sit still for too long—so I usually wander down to the village of Waimea to see whether any vendors need help selling, cleaning, or stocking the shelves for the day. Everyone's very kind, and they seem appreciative that I offer my services.

Sometimes, I'll head out to the fields to assist with harvesting and washing the crops for transportation. I enjoy the quietness of the fields, the smell of the dirt, the wind against my warmed cheeks temporarily cooling me as the sweat steadily drips down my forehead and back.

Life can get boring as a princess, and since I'm the only princess on the island, I often feel lost—like no one else endures the daunting repetition of nothingness that I live in. From time to time, a weird wave of feelings washes over me of wondering what my life could be like somewhere else. I daydream about a world so different from my own, where I can train and fight simply because I want to, or where I can have a say in my future . . . But the island stays consistent in its ways of peace and routine; I guess I should be thankful for that.

I flop out of bed and sleepily shuffle into my bathroom, deciding that I will head down to the fields and work until dinnertime. I brush my teeth and undo the sleep-tousled braid in my hair. Rustling my fingers through my scalp, I fluff out the tresses. It feels so good, coaxing a shiver down the length of my spine. I brush my hair to flatten it out a bit, throwing my thick curls in a heap of a messy bun on the top of my head.

One glance in the mirror to make sure I don't miss any pieces, and I'm good to go. I check the sides and the back of my head, but I don't see any stragglers. Looking at my reflection straight on, I give my tanned face a once-over, noticing some blemishes along my chin. I run my fingers across them and think about dabbing on some foundation to hide the redness. Unfortunately, I don't know how to apply makeup very well. The royal stylist has tried to show me, but I'm too impatient to grasp it. I don't have an hour to waste every day staring in the mirror, trying to make myself look more "presentable." For whom? It's certainly not for my sake, and I have no one I want to impress anyway. However, I do have a feeling this is on the list of wifely duties my mama must teach me in the coming weeks.

Mama is the queen (literally and figuratively) of perfection. I've never seen my mother without makeup, even if it is only lightly applied. Her hair is never out of place, and her skirts are never wrinkled. Our culture isn't too fond of makeup hiding our natural skin, but that has evolved—I wish it hadn't, though. I think my mama is effortlessly pretty, and I would love to see her without makeup more often. I do understand that she finds comfort in the feeling of having makeup on—much like how I feel with a braid in my hair—but it has become a habit, a routine that she is fond of, and so I'll be expected to learn and do the same.

I dodge out of the bathroom toward my closet before I let thoughts of the upcoming marriage consume me. I toss open the closet's narrow double doors and head to the back, where I keep my usual daily clothing. Forgoing traditional Waimea dress, I tug my sports bra down over my head, along with a loose-fitting gray T-shirt, then I pull on black cropped leggings. Finally, I shove my feet into socks and sneakers as I race downstairs.

The inside of what our family calls home isn't your typical fairy-tale castle or palace. You won't find grand chandeliers, plush carpets, intricate tapestries, or tacky wallpaper. However, the exterior of our castle is exactly what you'd expect: Light-gray stone creates the massive foundation and high towers—like the ones you read about as a child, where a fictional princess who donned long golden locks tosses her tresses out the tower window for her prince to climb up and save her. Each turret holds a flag of the Waimea crest—our family crest—flying proudly in the sky. Some windows are stained glass, and some are thick frosted glass, which obscures our figures into shadowy silhouettes from curious eyes below. Large arches stand prominently over every entryway, tropical floral landscapes color the grounds around the castle, and a sturdy brick wall encloses the entire complex—keeping would-be intruders out.

But because the interior of the castle isn't outfitted with the usual castle-like décor, that's what makes me love our home so much. We have basic chandeliers that aren't gaudy or spooky looking; the lights are here simply to illuminate the rooms and that's all. Most of the floors are tiled in a beige color, except for the dark wooden floors in the bedrooms, which are designed to reflect our personalities and accommodate our needs. Hanging on the walls are portraits of our family, of generations past and present. The castle feels more like a home than just a place the royal family dwells in. Each room holds sacred memories of the Delphine family: Sharing stories of our days with one another around the dining room table as we stuffed our bellies full of delicious food, especially pineapple cake. The quiet evenings alone in the library when I was supposed to be studying but instead lost myself in the imaginary world of a good book. Chester and me racing down the hallways, jabbing our elbows into each other as we fought to reach the staircase first, and the wooden-framed portraits of our ancestors rattling against the walls from our stomping feet. Their eyes and smiles painted as if they already knew who would win because they've seen this race many times be-fore. Our laughter bouncing off the walls as Mama shouted up at us to behave. These are the moments that make me love our castle—our home.

I make my way into the dining room, where all our meals are served and where most of Papa's meetings are held. My parents are fairly easygoing when it comes to sharing meals, so they don't care if we eat breakfast and lunch on our own—but we must have dinner together as a family every night, with no exceptions.

When I enter the dining room, Papa is sitting at the head of the long wooden dining room table. He looks up from his paperwork scattered around the bowl of fruit that is his late breakfast and gives me a large smile that spans from ear to ear, revealing his pearly white and perfectly straight teeth. He's wearing a dark-blue polo T-shirt that exposes his Wiki tattoos along his arms and neck. The swirling ink comes up to his chin and stops at his jawline. The lone tattoo on his face is a strip of black swirls just below his bottom lip. He has the most tattoos of anyone in the village because he is the king. Tattoos are a tradition in our culture and have several meanings: tribal ranking, strength, heritage, nature, femininity, and masculinity. The tattoo on my left arm matches the one on Papa's left arm, along with many of the other Waimea villagers. This particular Wiki design is a coming-of-age tattoo and an initiation as a Wikitian, meaning you're now part of the tribe and the village of Waimea. Each castle has its own style of tattoo, so when I marry Malcolm of Castle Hana, my right arm will be inked in an Ahi tattoo—making me an Ahitian, as well.

I approach the table, pull out the seat on his left, and sit down.

"There's my Ella-Bella." His tone is soothing, and his smile is proud. My papa is a soft-spoken man, but his voice carries all the way to your soul. Whenever I hear him speak, it makes my heart melt. Papa isn't like any of the other kings I have met (and I've met them all). He's kind and has a huge heart—he genuinely cares for his people, his family, and his dragons. He's also brilliant. He always seems to know what's going to happen before it happens. I've seen him angry only a couple of times in my life, and both of those times were when the life or health of his two children was affected.

"Morning, Papa," I respond as I grab a bowl of fruit sitting idly in the middle of the table, along with a scone.

Papa chuckles, "It's 11:45; it's barely the morning anymore, Ella." He shakes his head and jabs at a piece of fruit. I follow suit and pop a chunk of watermelon into my mouth.

"Eh, I know . . . Couldn't sleep last night," I say as I chew.

"Ella, Queen Theadosia would slap the back of your head if she heard you talking with your mouth full. Plus, you can't fool me, girl. I know what you're up to at night."

I gasp and immediately cough loudly from nearly inhaling the watermelon. I'm shocked, and not because he called Mama by her title, which he so rarely does, but because my cover is blown. I lightly pound my chest to suppress my slight choking situation. I look up at him from my bowl, meeting his large gray eyes with my own. My brother may have inherited most of the good genes, but one thing I'm glad to share with Papa is the color and almond shape of our eyes. Right now though, I can't figure out what's behind his.

"Ehhh, I've seen you on Shea. You're the only one she takes direction from. As a father, I wish you would be more careful. But as a chief and king, I must remind you that you know ladies aren't meant to fly . . ." he pauses, letting the tension linger before finishing, "but we can keep it our secret." Papa places his hand over my idle one on the table and gives it a squeeze. I'm relieved he's not upset with me. In fact, his eyes look glossy, as if he's about to cry. He's been this way since he told me about my marriage arrangement. Papa is not happy about the whole thing, but business is business, and our castles and villages becoming united makes sense . . . to them at least.

I nod my head at him with a sheepish smirk before stabbing another piece of fruit with my fork.

"What are your plans today?" he asks.

Just as I'm about to respond, Chester and Lucas join us in the dining room. I look over at them as they walk next to each other, so close their shoulders brush. They are laughing and talking about something one of the dragons, Jade, did while training this morning. Luke is wearing loose black cargo pants (a near-identical match to my brother's) and a tight black tank top, his muscular, tattooed arms on display. His head shines under the lights of the dining room, and it makes me wonder when he lost all his hair—but baldness suits him. His smile is larger than life, peeking through the salt-and-pepper beard he keeps trimmed and tidy. Sometimes Chester and Luke almost look like father and son when they walk side by side, but I would never tell Chester that . . . I think that's what my parents see also, and maybe that's why it's hard for Mama and Papa to accept them as a couple.

My father's face beams again when he sees Chester, but as his eyes flick to Luke, the happiness behind his smile falters a hint. He recovers, declaring, "Chester and Ella-Bella are gracing me with their presence this afternoon? I'm truly blessed."

Chester pulls out a chair to the right of Papa, and Luke sits down next to me.

Luke nods his head at Papa and says, "King Rowland, good to see you, sir."

The chief responds with a skeptical nod.

Undeterred, Luke looks at the three of us with excitement in his blue eyes. "Hey, did you all hear that one of the villagers realm jumped again?" he asks enthusiastically.

At this, my father releases a heavy, exasperated sigh.

Chester looks over at Luke, his eyes wide as he slightly shakes his head to cut his boyfriend off from talking, but it's too late.

"Not this again. I've told the villagers—specifically the realm jumpers—to stop traveling to places during the full moon cycles." Papa slams his fist on the table, causing us to jump and my half-eaten bowl of fruit to bounce. This is now the third time in my life I've seen Papa so angry.

"Well, sir, I don't know if it's true," Luke rushes out. "The villagers are saying she brought back some sort of candy."

At that, Papa's face turns red, like the strawberry that sits idly on my fork.

"This is madness! She risked her life and our identities for candy?!" Papa has raised his voice now.

I place my fork in my bowl as Luke shifts uncomfortably in his chair. I keep my head down, sneaking a quick glance through my lashes at Chester sitting across from me. He moves his lips into a frown, and I jump as I feel him kick me under the table.

"Ow! What the heck, Chester?" I shout. Now I'm fully looking at my brother, and I realize he meant to kick his boyfriend and not me . . .

I shift my eyes to Luke, and the tops of his cheeks that rest above his beard are flushed with embarrassment. In his hand, Luke clasps his pocket watch, which is attached to the belt loop of his work pants.

"Oh, would you look at the time? I was supposed to start cleaning the dragon caves five minutes ago. Duty calls!" Luke shoves the watch back into his pants pocket. He stands up quickly, pushes his chair in, and hustles out of the room.

Watching him as he makes his exit, I understand Chester's attraction to Lucas. He's tall and muscular, and he's a cheerful guy—but sometimes he's so dumb.

"Well, that was awkward." I shrug my shoulders and look at Papa. He's biting the inside of his cheek, still staring at the archway Luke just passed through. His balled fists are pressing into the table, and he keeps squeezing them tighter as if he's ready to explode again.

"I gotta go help Luke." Chester rises from his seat and slowly tucks the chair back into the table.

"Yeah, do what you have to do, kid." Papa's voice is even again. He shakes his head, and as he watches Chester leave the room, he lets out a choppy exhale.

I stand up from my seat, noticing the anger in Papa's eyes. This is too much for me to digest so early in the morning—er, afternoon. "I'm going to help in the fields today. Do you need me to do anything around here before I head out?" I hesitantly ask, silently praying he just lets me go.

Papa looks up at me and gives me a lighthearted smile, "No, Ella, you go have fun."

Choosing not to linger a second longer than necessary, I head out of the dining room toward the front door to see if I can catch up with Chester and bombard him with questions about the realm jumper.

When I walk out the front door, the blazing sun is high up in the sky and the thick, muggy air rushes over my body, enveloping me in its warmth. I can smell the plumeria trees that line the castle entrance mixed with the salt-misted air from the sea below, so I inhale deeply. That fragrance is a familiar scent that always reminds me of my home.

A few steps into my travels, Chester pops out beside me from thin air just as I exit the gate in the stone wall of the castle. At the exact same time, a rooster clucks nearby, sending up a shrill cock-a-doodle-doo! My heart leaps into my throat and I let out a quick shriek as I clench my hands to my chest.

"Shit! Sometimes Luke is so fucking stupid." Chester has both of his hands on the top of his head, tugging at his hair in frustration.

"Fuck, you scared me! So did that damn fucking cock," I snap.

"Really, Ella? This is serious. Why does Luke always mess shit up for us!" He sounds like a whiny child. I'm starting to get tired of listening to his and Luke's stupid lovers' quarrels.

I wave my hand in the air dismissively. "Oh, whatever. Papa will get over it. It's not like Luke was the one who realm hopped . . ." I trail off and stop walking, forcing Chester to pause too. "Well, I mean . . . Was it him?" I tap my finger on my chin as I consider the possibility.

"No, he doesn't know how to do that stuff," Chester scoffs.

We both resume walking along the gravel path. I'm heading toward the fields, but I think Chester is now as well. He continues to vent to me about how he and Luke were doing so well with my parents coming around to liking him, and now he thinks Luke blew it.

Meanwhile, I'm too distracted with Luke's news. I've heard that certain people on the island know how to, but I don't know the specifics of realm jumping. From what I've gathered throughout the years, realm jumping is when people go through a hole in the air, bringing them to another realm or universe. People do it for various reasons; some want to escape the island, others want a quick vacation, and some bring goods back to trade. I've seen things that people have brought back from the realms—like clothing, alcohol, jewelry, and electronic devices. My favorite relic was an iPod . . . that was cool. Our people know what happens in the other realms, but we have no need or desire to live like them. And if someone does, I guess they never travel back here once they've jumped. Kapu Island has everything you could ever need. It's safe, homes have indoor plumbing and electricity, and the weather is always perfectly tropical. We don't do any large manufacturing, but that minimizes our waste and pollutants. It also means we don't have iPods, though.

I interrupt Chester's babbling to ask, "So how does one realm jump?" I turn to him, my eyes squinted, deep in thought.

"Ohhhhh no, no, no. You aren't going to try and attempt that." Chester lowers his voice, "You already ride a dragon. Which is totally illegal."

"Come on, Ches! I'm just curious about how it works. I don't want to actually do it."

Chester sighs, and I know I've convinced him to spill the details, or at least what he thinks he knows about it.

"Realm jumping, or," Chester uses air quotes, "'realm hopping,' can only take place when shit in the sky is aligned or something. I don't really know. Something about the phases of the moon, maybe. Or the sun?" He tilts his head to the side, unsure. "There's also a specific location on the island where the world 'opens'—people call it a portal or black hole . . . Don't tell anyone I told you this." Chester shoves me in the arm, but I shrug him off.

"Well, have you seen where the world opens?" I ask, with one brow raised.

"No, and even if I had, I wouldn't tell you." Chester huffs out a breath and purses his lips.

"So . . . do the other realms know about us like we know about them?"

"Mmmm, some of the people from the other realms know about us. And I'm done answering your questions. There are books about it in the library. Make yourself useful and go research it for yourself."

I kick a rock at Chester's bare feet, but it swerves to the right. "Thanks, Bro. You should probably go get your man and talk to him before Papa hunts him down for names."

"Fuck. I know. Catch up with you later." Chester veers to the right in a light jog toward the dragon caves. He flinches as he gingerly walks over the sharp stones stabbing into his feet. I don't know why he doesn't just wear shoes.

I continue down the path into the heart of the village, which is alive with the booming voices of shoppers and merchants, as well as crying and laughing children. I carefully trek through the pedestrians walking in and out of vendors' tents and small shops. Friendly faces turn to greet me, along with a few waves. Some people stop to clap and cheer as I walk by them, and a blush creeps across my cheeks. I offer a sincere smile and wave in return, high-fiving young children who run past. They react as if they've never seen me before, but they see me nearly every day. It's an odd feeling being liked and admired by so many people, but I love our village.

I wonder if I will love the village of Hana this much—or if they will love me . . .

My papa is a cherished king, but those few who don't love him are typically scoundrels looking for free handouts, which they will never get from him. Everyone must work and earn their living in our village—including our family. Something I've heard the chief say since I was old enough to remember is, "We are all equals. If one person is poor, then we all are; when one person is abundant, then we are all abundant." It doesn't mean that we ride the coattails of others' successes and wins (or failures). It means that we all work together to help one another. It also doesn't mean that if you are sick or can't work, then he makes you struggle. We never fail to help the less fortunate—they never go without. It's just that some villagers don't like this mentality, even though it's been working since Pop-Pop was in charge decades ago. Why would we change it for a select few who disagree?

I'm almost through to the other side of the marketplace when I see my mama helping at a clothing tent about ten feet away. I can't miss Queen Theadosia—no one can. She's tall, about as tall as Papa, and the sun is perpetually shining on her long black hair with not a single strand out of place. Mama typically wears a stern expression, like Chester's infamous scowl, except hers is accentuated by her chin tattoo. But she's not always as serious as she presents herself to be. It's truly a sight to behold when her hazel eyes dazzle while she laughs and smiles for Papa, Chester, and me during little moments we share at home.

Her slim frame is invariably draped in ankle-length dresses that are usually white, black, or some shade of gray in between and decorated with our family crest—like the flags that stand tall on the castle turrets. Today is no different, but she does have a purple-and-white orchid placed above her ear, adding a splash of color—her version of "fun"—to her appearance.

Before I approach, I already know the tent belongs to her best friend, Tallulah, because she's been selling other-realm clothing for years in this exact location. Tallulah stocks all the trendy must-haves from the various realms, and Mama brings me clothes when she helps out at Tallulah's stall. My favorites are the leggings and sneakers. I loved my first pair of leggings so much that Mama brought me back five more pairs so I can alternate throughout the week.

Tallulah waves me over when she sees me approaching the heavy canopy. Pebbles scuffle beneath my feet as I pick up the pace, making my way toward the tent.

"Hey there, Ella. Where are you off to today?" Tallulah asks me as she places her hands on her hips. Her gray-and-black hair is twisted into a mound of madness on top of her head. She's wearing a flowy red sundress that complements her soft facial expression.

"To the fields to help with the crops," I answer.

"Ahhh, got it. Looking to clear your mind in the silence of the fields?" Tallulah probes further.

My mother stops hanging the clothes on a rack behind her friend and turns toward us.

"No, I just want to do something productive before I'm locked away in a castle all day, every day, as Mrs. Malcolm Royce—you know, normal women things." I shrug my shoulders and frown, staring intently into Mama's hazel eyes. She defiantly lifts her chin and moves to stand beside Tallulah to join the conversation.

The truth of the matter is that I do have conflicting feelings regarding my marriage to Malcolm. I know it's what is best for Waimea because it will guarantee security for our castle and our people for years to come (at least as long as I'm alive). And Malcolm . . . well, he is a gentleman—from what I can remember—and he's strong. Those are the main attributes you look for in a husband, right? Another truth is that I enjoy antagonizing my mama. She's so uptight and rigid. Making her upset in little, annoying ways ignites a tiny fire inside me that is oddly satisfying. I like to ruffle her feathers and watch her squirm as she's rendered speechless by my antics.

"Louella, give it a rest. Marrying the chief was one of the best things that could have ever happened to me. I love your father."

I roll my eyes at her response. "Yeah, yeah, I've heard it all before. You can save it," I snap.

Tallulah lets out a small giggle, and Mama glares at her.

"I would love to stay and chat, but my days of freedom are numbered."

"Ugh, you save it," Mama responds before returning to the rack of clothing behind her.

Tallulah gives me a quick wink and mouths, "See you tonight."

I wave and dodge out of the marketplace.

When I arrive at the fields, I see all the workers picking the crops and placing them in sacks that hang from their shoulders. I walk into the barn and pull one down for myself, slinging it over my shoulder and adjusting the straps for a comfortable fit across my chest. Leaving the barn, I begin my day of harvesting. Today I choose to pick tomatoes so I can squish the rotten ones in my bare hands. It helps relieve my stress.

I bolt upright at the sound of knocking on my door, knowing that it's 2:00 a.m. and Chester is here to wake me up and get my ass moving down to the dragon caves. I sleep wearing my riding clothes, which include a long-sleeved shirt and thick long pants. It can become quite hot to sleep in, but I don't want to waste time fumbling around getting ready—I would hate for Shea and the ladies to have to wait for me.

Any night we train, before Chester comes to knock on my door, he does a once-over of the castle grounds to make sure the night watch guards are changing shifts and their barracks are empty. Frankly, the barracks aren't supposed to be completely empty at any point, but the guards have grown lax since there haven't been any threats on the castle in a long, long . . . long time. I can't complain, nor will I ever tell Papa of the guards' negligence since this gives me enough time to slip past their quarters and race down to the caves without being seen. On my way back from riding, the guards temporarily leave their posts for the morning meeting in the front garden. Not very smart—but it works for me as I sneak back in through the rear patio and all the way into my room. I've never been spotted. Sure, there have been some close calls, but I think even if I were caught, no one would question it because Chester's with me. They know I'm safe.

As I approach the caves, I see the others gathered in a circle, chatting quietly and laughing under the dim lights surrounding the shed and caves. Tallulah is the tallest of the group, and her silver strands glow in the lights. Tallulah's sister, Camilla, stands next to her, talking in a low voice with her usual mischievous smirk on her face.

There are about fifteen women here tonight, more than we've ever had before. Apparently, the ladies of Waimea are starting to grow tired of their usual "duties," and they want adventure and excitement like they've never experienced before.

This all began a couple of years ago, when Tallulah caught me training one night with Chester. We thought for sure our nights of sneaking out to fly and fight were over when she spotted us. To our surprise, she had no interest in blowing our cover and instead asked if we would be willing to organize a training camp with more women from the village. When we answered with a look of disbelief, Tallulah informed us that she and her sister met up for a reading group with other women once a week. During one of their meetings, a discussion started about the castle dragons, and the women were seriously interested in learning to ride.

At the time, Chester had blurted out a quick no, and Tallulah had understood. For months, I begged him to reconsider. Every time I would bring it up to him, he would hush me and walk away. One early morning a little over a year ago, while practicing foot placement during sword fighting, Chester had stopped to get a drink of water. He stood with his back resting against the weaponry shed, staring out at the first rays of the sun rising over the sea as dawn approached. I had given up groveling before him, but out of the blue, without even acknowledging me, he announced, "Let's train these women. You're in charge of communications, and I'll teach."

I dropped my canteen of water as I excitedly jumped up and down, clapping my hands and letting loose a low shrill from my lips. After Chester told me to calm the fuck down, he gave me the conditions—which I knew were coming because there are always conditions with Chester, it's just how he operates.

Chester's conditions:

1. No one is to know about what we are doing. If there's even a whisper around the village or the castle, he's shutting it down.

2. Everyone needs to listen to his directions carefully; we can't afford any injuries.

3. I have to shovel dragon shit from the caves for a year (because that's what brothers are for).

That third condition led to one of the longest and smelliest years of my life. There were days I took three showers because of how the stench clung to my clothing and hair. I'm thankful that my time of poop-scooping has since come to an end—I guess it's all part of working your way up.

Each time I look around at my newfound family of the strongest women I've ever known, it amazes me that this group was inspired by me . . . Sneaking around and forming a militia of ladies who can fly and fight? That's pretty badass. We've broken away from the repetitiveness of the life we were assigned, and it invigorates us—we feel truly alive.

Of course I feel bad for going behind Papa's back, but when will it be our time? We don't want to sit idly by anymore. We want the opportunity to join the cause and fight for what's ours . . . even though there's no looming threat to fight against as of right now.

The men of the island are born to become warriors and fight for their respective castles. They begin combat training and dragon riding at the age of fifteen. Even though Kapu Island is currently enjoying a time of peace and there is no need for an active military, I've overheard Papa stating that their training helps a boy become a man.

Whatever.

I guess I'm a hypocrite since I'm being married off to Malcolm and giving in to becoming a wife, but that's not my plan once I get to Castle Hana. I'm still going to fight and fly, and being queen will allow me to shake things up. Change the rules . . . maybe.

I approach the group, taking my place next to Brynlee, already feeling as small as a mouse next to her impressive stature. Brynlee is the strongest of the group. She's a bit taller than I am, but she's solid muscle, and I don't think I've ever seen her smile. She keeps her dark-brown hair in a tight braid running down the center of her head, and both sides of her scalp are shaved to expose her Wiki tattoos. She's a person of very few words, but she's not mean.

Still, I would not want to mess with her.

When I sidle up next to Brynlee, she glances at me and grunts. I return her grunt with a nod. Sometimes it's nice being in her presence because she never asks questions or engages in small talk, and every once in a while, that's nice.

The women grow quiet when they notice I've arrived. I barely wait for the silence to fully settle before calling out, "Ladies! Chester should be here soon; he stopped off to grab the bows and arrows to use for our lesson today. You know the drill: we don't have much time, so let's make it count. Today, we will be learning how to shoot accurately while riding."

The women respond with various noises of grunts, claps, and sighs.

I continue a little impatiently, "If you don't want to join us—then don't."

A hush engulfs the crowd.

"That's what I thought. Let's head to the equipment shed and prep the dragons until Chester arrives."

The circle disperses as everyone moves toward the shed, forming a line to enter. I am first to go in and grab Shea's saddle and bridle, then I walk into the cave to fetch her. Lanterns line the cave walls, casting low light, but it doesn't matter. I have trouble seeing Shea in the dark, regardless of how often I've done this. Luckily, I've memorized exactly where her den is located.

When I arrive at Shea's den, she's already sitting up and staring intently at the opening of her shadowed nook. Her icy-blue eyes twinkle with excitement as she watches me make my way to her side with the equipment in hand. The violet spikes crack along her back, like she's popping her knuckles to loosen up.

I hoist the saddle onto her back and make haste to secure it. It doesn't take me too long since I've done this so many times—I'm confident I could do it with my eyes closed. Our dragons are big, but they aren't massive—they average about the size of two horses combined. Their leanness is what makes them so quick and stealthy. Hence, another reason why saddling up isn't too strenuous.

After slipping the bridle over her snout, Shea gives me a small squawk to let me know she's ready for flight. She lets me lead her out of the caves, and I see my brother strolling in our direction on his way to saddle up his own dragon, Zeus. Chester is smiling tonight, so that must mean he and Lucas reconciled.

"Hey, Bro, you ready for training?" I ask.

"As ready as I'll ever be. I swear, you chicks have aged me drastically."

I give his shoulder a slight shove with my free hand; the other is still holding tight on Shea's reins.

"Ow! Rude!" Chester shouts.

I laugh and shake my head. "You're weaaaaaak," I drag out.

My brother ignores me and walks closer to the group of women that has formed behind me.

I spin to face them, guiding Shea around with me.

"Good morning, ladies," Chester practically shouts.

A hush falls among the women. I glance around to double-check the riding equipment and ensure the saddles are secured correctly on each dragon's back. We had a couple of mishaps at the beginning of our secret sessions due to improperly fastened saddles . . . Thankfully, those incidents were nothing fatal and only short drops from the air, which resulted in no injuries.

I dodged that arrow.

Chester continues, "As I'm sure Ella informed you already, today, we will be learning how to shoot with accuracy while riding. This is a skill that has taken some warriors many years to perfect. How this will work is I will send you up one at a time. Once you are airborne, Zeus will be racing toward you with a fake hay-stuffed rider attached to his back. You have five chances to hit the dummy rider. If you fail to hit the dummy, I will send you back up until you get one in. The number of times I have to send you back up is the number of times you will sit out of riding in our next lesson."

The women erupt with complaints and gasps: "What? Is he joking?" "How am I going to hit a moving target on the first try?"

I step forward once more. "Ladies, think positive. We can do this. Let's mount and ride!"

My brief pep talk doesn't seem to have inspired confidence. The women look deflated already, but they scurry to their dragons nonetheless. And then we begin the training.

After a couple of hours, we are finishing up for the night with two riders left. Nearly everyone has passed the training, but it's taking some of the riders a few tries—Camilla being one of them.

Jewel takes off into the air one last time with Camilla on her back. The dragon's skin is a pearlescent white, making her shimmer even in the predawn darkness. Once they are in the air, I turn to Shea to dismantle her saddle. As I finish unfastening the last buckle, I hear Chester scream from behind me. I whip around to see Camilla and Jewel ten feet in the air, with Camilla hanging off the side of Jewel, gripping her reins as she squeezes her eyes shut, holding on for dear life. I rush to Chester's side to try to prompt Camilla to open her eyes and get back on her dragon, but before I can say a word, Camilla's hands slip down the leather straps. Her body falls fast and hard onto the ground below, landing with a loud thud. Chester runs toward her, and I follow behind. She is gasping for air as her chest heaves up and down, working hard to catch her breath.

"Camilla! Camilla, are you all right?" Chester kneels to the ground and scoops her head into his lap.

Her eyes are open and she's nodding her head yes, but she still can't seem to calm her breathing enough to speak.

"Are you hurt anywhere? Did you land on anything?" I ask as I kneel beside her as well. I place my hand lightly on her arm.

Camilla nods again and attempts to lift her left leg in the air but lets out a loud gasp. The grimace contorting her face tells me the pain is radiating through her body.

Chester moves his hands down her leg, not noticing anything until his fingers graze her ankle. Camilla jumps and her eyes bulge, round and wide. My brother observes her ankle, and from where I'm positioned, I can see it has already begun to swell.

"I . . . think I . . . broke it," Camilla says in between breaths.

Chester moves it ever so delicately to see how much motion she has, but Camilla yelps in agony.

Tallulah appears next to me, so I make room for her to get to her sister's side.

"Camilla, oh my goddess! Are you all right?" Tallulah looks shaken up.

"Yes, I'm fine . . . but . . . I think I broke my ankle," Camilla replies thickly.

"We will get you better," Tallulah reassures her. She looks to Chester and me but directs her words to Camilla, "We need to take you to the village healer." She bends to lift her sister in an attempt to get her up and into her arms.

Chester locks eyes with me, and I can tell what he's thinking. The concern is written all over my face, and I can see it all over his. We are both thinking that we are fucked.

The healer is required to send their patient records and injuries—along with the cause of the injury—to Mama. It's a duty that was appointed to her by the chief because she wanted to be more involved in the well-being of the villagers—and it's really coming back to bite us in the ass now.

Chester breaks eye contact with me, and I watch as he attempts to slow Tallulah down. "Let me get her," he offers. He begins to place his arms under her body but then stops.

My pulse quickens, and I can feel my heart beating in my ears. It's so loud that I can't hear what's happening around me. Questions are racing through my head: How are we going to get out of this? What will happen to us? What am I going to do? But before I can think of a plan, Papa is in my line of sight, prowling his way down the hill toward us. I look over to Chester, who is already rushing toward our father to try to intercept him. Chester tries to slow Papa down, but the chief easily brushes past him, continuing on his way toward Camilla, Tallulah, and me. I stand and brush off my legs, stepping to the side and bowing my head. Papa kneels beside Camilla and lifts her up and into his arms.

"Are you hurt, Cami?" he asks. His voice is gruff but full of worry. Without waiting for an answer, Papa starts his descent to the village carrying Camilla.

"I think I broke my ankle, but I'm fine. It was all my fault. I was being careless and stood while riding," she rushes out nervously. She must be worn down from the number of times people have checked to see if she's all right.

"Papa, wait!" I call after him.

He stops and slowly turns to face me.

I rush up to him and close the gap between us. "I'm so sorry. I didn't mean for this to happen. Please forgive me, Papa, please?" I plead.

He looks down at Camilla. His eyes soften, but a scold is embedded on his face.

"Louella, you crossed the line. Sneaking out and riding dragons with your brother is one thing, but you are forming a militia behind my back—and a militia of women? You know that's illegal. Your punishment will be no more riding. Your duties as a future wife and a future queen begin tomorrow. You will be on twenty-four-hour surveillance, and you will be escorted around the castle grounds at all times." His voice is dripping with disappointment, and I know that he's no longer speaking to me as my papa but as the chief.

"Papa, no! Please! Don't take this away from me. I love Shea; I love this too much!" I attempt to beg and reason with him just once more.

"Too late, Louella! Camilla is injured, and all you can think about is yourself. Your punishment is final. Go back to the castle and straight to your room. I raised you better than this."

I glance at Camilla as embarrassment floods my face. I can feel my cheeks growing red.

Camilla frowns and mouths, "I'm sorry," as Papa marches away.

My knees buckle and I hit the ground. My sobs flow fiercely from my chest, and my hands shake. I punch the ground as hard as I can. The sting from the hit does nothing but make me cry harder. I feel a hand on my shoulder, and through the blurriness of my tears, I can faintly see Chester offering his other hand to help me stand. I turn away and look up at the castle, unsure if I'm ready to begin my fake life of fake happiness with my fake husband—but it's now or . . . now.

THREE

LOUELLA APONI DELPHINE

Castle Waimea, Kapu Island

"No, Louella, you're not following my lead. A good wife follows her king to the dining table and waits until he is seated first before she takes her own seat. You must wait for me to sit, then you can sit," Mama stresses for the second time as she settles into the chair at the head of the dining table.

It's been a month since Camilla's accident, and true to his word, Papa made me start lessons with Mama the very next day.

I puff out an annoyed breath, blowing a single curled strand from my face that somehow has come loose from the tight updo my hair has been slicked and sprayed into since six this morning. The spray holding my hair in place is sickly sweet and giving me a headache—it's made by the royal healer from an obscure concoction of sugar, alcohol, and at least three different flower oils. It's disgusting. I'm tempted to run my hands through my hair and mess it all up, but I place my elbows on the table in a slouch instead.

My mother clears her throat and I immediately sit up straight, drawing my elbows to my sides.

I've come to despise training to be a wife and queen—especially when Mama's the one training me. She's a perfectionist down to every single breath that I breathe. There's nothing Mama takes more seriously than her rule as queen, and it's exhausting.

Even though Papa is the chief, he always let Chester and me have fun and be kids while we were growing up. Mama never failed to make comments about our hands being dirty, or that we were eating too much pineapple cake, or we were not being respectful enough, but Papa would argue with her, saying, "Just let them be kids, Theadosia." She would relent back then, but now she has full control. In these lessons, there's no Papa here to tell her to go easy on me, and even if he were, he wouldn't say a damn word because he's still angry with me—and Chester.

I work a finger through the tight, pinned curls to try to relieve some pressure from the updo pulling at my scalp. And my top is so tight that it feels like it's bound to me and restricting my lungs. The only comfortable aspect of a queen's daily ensemble is the skirt because it's flowy.

"Mama, can I take a break? We've been at this for two hours now," I whine.

Before she can respond, I glance to my right and see Pop-Pop entering the dining area. I can't control the smile stretching widely across my face when I see his soft smirk. His long silver hair is forever staticky and messy, and he tries unsuccessfully to tame it in a bun at the nape of his neck. His thin frame holds a slight hunch as he walks due to his old age, but his arms still swing jubilantly with each slow, deliberate stride he takes.

My grandfather is the ray of sunshine in the castle, with his warm smiles and sarcastic jokes. He understands me—almost as much as Chester does. Pop-Pop is easy to talk to because he incessantly shares stories about love and hope, and you can't help but feel happier after being around him. He is constantly boasting about how he's proud of me even though I haven't really achieved anything in my life just yet . . . he still reassures me his pride is real. And his warm hugs are all-consuming—the kind you sink into and forget about the world, if only for a short while.

"Theadosia, make sure you take care of my Ella-Bella," Pop-Pop says to Mama as he winks at me.

Mama huffs in reply, "Yes, Jasper, I'm being as kind as I can be, even though your granddaughter has trouble listening." She sneers at her father-in-law as he approaches.

Without warning, she jerks her chair back and it screeches across the floor. I follow suit because that's what you do when a woman gets up from the table.

I guess I did learn something.

Pop-Pop pulls out the chair beside me and slides into the seat.

"Oh, stop, Theadosia! You're being too hard on the girl. The formalities aren't the same as when you were a young queen. Not everything is as rigid as you. Let her breathe," he replies, waving a hand in the air at her.

Mama sighs. "This is why you drove Ada crazy—you never take anything seriously. You and Rowland are exactly the same."

Pop-Pop laughs soundlessly and shakes his head, nudging my elbow. "That's what makes us fun," he whispers to me.

Ada was my grandmother, but I've only ever known her as Gam-Gam. She passed away from a progressive illness when I was a baby. Rumor has it, Mama and Gam-Gam were very similar. From the stories I've heard my family tell over the years, I'd have to agree.

Mama lets out another loud sigh before she turns on her heels and exits the room.

"Ughhhhh," I groan, dropping into my chair and placing my head in my hands. "This is terrible. I hate this! Why me?"

Pop-Pop places his hand on my back, and I look up at him. The dark skin around his eyes is wrinkled, and his gray eyes are warm and welcoming—just as much as the man they adorn.

"Louella, you are the best person for the job. I can't wait to see my granddaughter as a queen. You are smart, cunning, strong—I could go on forever, you know." He pauses, checking to see whether he's convinced me. "Just do what your mama says, and then you'll be on an adventure of love and power . . . And if you want to run away, you can. I won't tell anyone." He slaps my back lightly as he bursts out in laughter. Although his words weren't all that reassuring this time, I feel a bit better.

I beam at him and shake my head. "I love you, Pop-Pop. What will I do without you?"

"Ohhhh no, you aren't getting away from me. I'll be at that castle every week!" he declares.

My chest blooms with warmth, knowing that my family will still visit me in my new life.

"Are you all ready for the trip tomorrow?" Pop-Pop asks.

"Um, what trip?" I retort.

"The trip to Castle Hana. You are meeting with Prince Malcolm—an informal get-together so that you two can learn more about each other. He's going to show you around and introduce you to their staff. No one told you?" Pop-Pop twists slightly toward me, drawing his head back into his shoulders with confusion.

My fingernails scratch across my palms as my heartbeat picks up.

Why did no one tell me?

"No, my lovely parents must have forgotten to inform me about the trip I will be taking."

"Eh, don't get upset about it. It's a simple day trip," Pop-Pop reassures me. He turns back to the table as the staff walk in, bringing our lunches.

I push my chair out and stand. "I'm not hungry anymore. I'll see you later, Pop-Pop. Love you," I hastily say, hurrying out of the dining room. I suddenly feel anxious about this trip—and hurt that my parents never told me about it.

The ship sways beneath me as it enters the homestretch of our journey to Castle Hana. I look down at my traditional tribal outfit, consisting of a matching two-piece dress made of pink-and-white cloth with the Waimea crest in a repeating pattern, and try to embody the princess I'm supposed to be. I run my hands over my skirt for the hundredth time to rub the sweat off my palms from the nerves that are building inside me. Trying in vain to cover my exposed belly, I tug on my top, which wraps snugly around my chest.

I'm not dreading this visit with Malcolm—he's an attractive guy and I'm, well, an intrigued girl. He's kind—I remember that also. The thought of him makes me a bit weak in the knees. My memories of the last time I saw him, so tall and handsome, cause my stomach to flutter with anticipation. Carefully, I scratch my scalp from under the floral crown that's garnishing my braided and pinned hair. The nervous sweat gathering at my brow and the noxious hairspray mingle into a terrible combination that makes my skin burn. I'm not used to this costume yet.

No one else accompanied me on my voyage except for the crew aboard the ship, who will serve as my royal guard once we arrive. With everyone busy manning their positions, it was a long ride with only myself to talk to.

Finally, I can tell by the change in the air that we are approaching the village of Hana. Compared to the village of Waimea, it's much more arid on this part of Kapu Island. Just as I start to fixate on how oppressively hot and uncomfortable it feels in this new climate, the docks come into view ahead and I can see the Royce family standing in a line, waiting for my arrival. At first sight, the group is a blurry mass from how far out we are, but they are quickly coming into focus the more we press on.

Normally, the king would be standing front and center, but Prince Malcolm is in his place instead. His stature is the giveaway; Malcolm is taller than both of his parents and most of the guards surrounding them. The prince's posture reads as if he's already king, but he has stood like that since before the day I met him. Today, I'd swear he stands a bit straighter because this day is all about Prince Malcolm meeting his docile bride-to-be and showing that he is ready to take over the throne.

As the ship inches closer to the docks, my eyes drink up all six feet plus of Malcolm's body. He's like no man I've ever seen before . . . His eyes are a piercing emerald, which contrasts beautifully against his deeply tanned skin.

The vivid colors of crimson-red and amber-orange flowers intertwined with the green grass of his crown make his eyes pop, and I notice them in a way I never have before.

Draped over Malcolm's shoulders is a tribal-patterned shawl, with the ends of the fabric hanging loosely down his arms, leaving his sculpted chest and tattooed arms exposed. Right where the chiseled V lines on his stomach point to, a knot is twisted into a length of cloth to hold it together and form the traditional skirt-like outfit he is wearing. I tear my eyes away when I begin to wonder what's under that cloth. My throat is tight but my mouth is watering, so I have to force back a swallow as this weird feeling takes over me, creating heat between my thighs. I never doubted that I would be physically attracted to Prince Malcolm, but I remind myself that it's what lies beneath his looks that truly matters in a marriage.

Once the ship is docked, I am escorted by my guards to the pier. I keep my eyes down as I'm ushered toward Malcolm and his parents. Though my hair is secured in an intricate updo with no loose strands to be found, it doesn't stop me from continuously motioning to swipe hair behind my ears. I take a deep breath, adjusting my shoulders and standing taller to finally look up as I stop a few feet from my betrothed.

Malcolm's face is stern as his eyes cut into mine and hold my gaze intently. I shift uncomfortably, breaking eye contact as I take in his form up close. His height is intimidating, his tattoos are dark and deep on his skin, and his toffee-colored hair is short, wavy, and delicately styled to be pushed back and off his forehead.

The prince clears his throat, and my body jerks to attention, my eyes snapping back to his face. A playful grin tugs at his lips, and it looks hot as hell but also frightening. His face resembles a dragon's before they lay claim to their prey.

"Princess Louella Aponi Delphine, welcome to Castle Hana." Malcolm's voice is deep and almost seductive.

My pulse starts racing, and I can feel a thin layer of sweat forming on my forehead—and this heat I'm feeling has nothing to do with the sun high in the sky.

I bow my head and curtsy, reciting a polite salutation, "Prince Malcolm. Thank you for having me."

I keep my head bowed and look up at Malcolm through my lashes. Heat floods my stomach when I see his hooded eyes as he sucks on his bottom lip. If Malcolm realizes he's frazzled me, he doesn't show it. Slowly I adjust myself to stand tall before him again.

He holds out his hand and I don't hesitate to place mine in it. Then he turns and stands beside me so that we're now in front of his parents. They are both wearing scowls on their faces, which leads me to involuntarily pinch my eyebrows in confusion for just a moment before I realize that is not proper princess etiquette. Quickly, I smooth my facial expression into a shy smile.

"Lou," Malcom acknowledges, and I gulp down my dislike for the nickname—I hate that he calls me that, but I bite my tongue instead of correcting him—"you remember my parents? Chief Victor and Queen Maribeth."

I curtsy before the king and queen and say simply, "Sir, Ma'am." After I bow my head low in a show of deference, I rise to my full height once again.

Their faces have not changed as they continue to look down at me with their heads held high.

"Louella, so nice to see you again," Queen Maribeth says facetiously, her words not matching the look on her face. The queen's hair is the same color as Malcolm's, but instead of a casual style like her son's, hers is pulled back tightly in a severe bun atop her head, which is adorned with a floral crown twice the size of mine. Her crown is so massive that I'm surprised her slender neck can even hold it up. Queen Maribeth is an inch or two shorter than me and she's thin, with barely any muscle mass.

I nod just as she turns to ascend to the castle, which is facing us, sitting on a hill farther off in the distance, away from the docks. I'm feeling a little confounded because this marriage arrangement was what they wanted and they planned. So why are they acting so cold toward me?

My eyes flick to King Victor, who offers me a small smirk. His eyes are black, holding no warmth in them. He's a bit shorter than Malcolm, but unlike his son, his hair is as black as his eyes. The king's headpiece resembles the queen's, but his is embellished with a ruby-red crystal in the center of the flowers—it screams, I'm the motherfucking chief.

Malcolm clears his throat again, and King Victor turns on his heels to catch up to his wife.

"Well, that was a warm welcome," Malcolm nervously chuckles.

I would press him for answers regarding their behavior, but I don't know him well enough yet. I shrug off the interaction but store it tight in the back of my mind to probe my parents about when I return home.

I glance up at Malcolm and see that his cheeks are flushed pink. Still clasping his hand, I softly rub my thumb across his knuckles to ease the tension. He stays facing forward but gives me a brief side glance—I immediately stop moving my thumb and look ahead as he guides us toward the castle.

So he's the kind that holds in his feelings . . . This should be fun.

***

After nearly four hours of touring Castle Hana's grounds, we finally make our way to the dragon caves. My stomach is hollow and my feet are killing me, but this is our last stop before Malcolm takes me inside for dinner. If I weren't so excited to meet the dragons, I'd have begged to skip it in exchange for the chance to sit for a few minutes.

Malcolm has shown me every inch of the castle grounds, leaving no stone unturned. Mama told me to take notes on what Malcolm "fancies," things that he likes to do, eat, laugh at . . . But I still know nothing about him. I haven't learned much about Malcolm, what he likes to do, or who he is as a person; all he speaks of is the future of Castle Hana and what King Victor and Queen Maribeth want to see from us. He's passionate about his parents' outlook on their people and castle, but he has no true passions of his own.

I think I'm catching the slightest glimpse of who Malcolm truly is as he shows me the dragons. We're deep in the caves, standing at the den of a gnarly-looking beast named Maverick, who Malcolm introduced as his mount. Maverick is a deep-scarlet red with black-tipped spikes along his back—he's terrifying and formidable. The flesh along his back is covered in scars, which are obviously the result of other dragons gnashing at him. I'm sure he has left some nasty-looking scars in return, what with the two large, pointed horns as black as a starless night jutting out from his head. But all that doesn't frighten me one bit. No, it's his face that is truly a sight to behold. He has a long, narrow snout with sharp teeth that protrude even when his mouth is closed, giving the impression that he's always smiling. His chilling sneer makes the hairs on the back of my neck stand at attention.

What really pulls the whole ominous look of Maverick together is the violent swirl of amber and crimson coloring swirling around the slits of his pupils. If I didn't know any better, I'd swear I have fallen down deep and am face-to-face with the goddess of the underworld herself.

Maverick stands stoically in his pen, keeping his eyes locked to mine as Malcolm moves about the caves, rustling tools and equipment as he carries on explaining other abilities their dragons have dawned. I'm entranced by Maverick's appearance and how rugged he is compared to his rider. They are complete opposites in looks, but maybe Maverick is a sweet dragon on the inside.

Malcolm is in the middle of telling me how their dragons' electrical currents can't burn you, nor can they kill you, but they can immobilize you temporarily. That's when I decide I want to feel the electricity of Maverick. I slowly stalk toward him with my hand outstretched—Malcolm is too preoccupied talking to notice what I'm doing, so I hope he doesn't mind. I look away from the dragon's eyes, knowing that I will chicken out if I keep my gaze focused on his. When I get close, he gives a low growl as a warning, but I can't resist. Maybe I'm a glutton for punishment, or maybe I want to feel the rush of something exciting—who knows?

Right when I place my shaky hand on the largest spike atop Maverick's head, Malcolm turns to me and tilts his head in confusion. Then it happens.

The spikes along Maverick's back make a crinkling noise, like crumpling paper. Tiny lights reminding me of fireflies twinkle from the middle of his back and up to his head, right underneath my hand. I jump back as the sparks pulsate through my fingertips.

Sucking in a breath, I hiss, "Ouch!" as I clench my hand to my chest.

"Lou!" Malcolm rushes toward me while Maverick proceeds to crinkle and crackle, emitting a low, maniacal growl. When Malcolm reaches me, he takes my hand and inspects my fingertips. "Are you all right?" His tone is soft, but I can tell he is trying to mask his annoyance.

I snatch my hand back and inspect it myself, forgetting I am in the presence of a prince—soon to be king. Surprisingly, there is no wound or mark, just a weird sensation pulsating where my fingers met Maverick's spike.

"Yeah, I'm fine. Thanks," I respond.

"What were you doing?" Malcolm asks, his mouth forming a frown.

"I was wondering what the electrical currents felt like."

Malcolm squints his eyes at me, and I can only imagine the thoughts and questions swirling behind those green eyes.

He thinks I'm utterly insane.

To relieve some of the tension billowing out of him like smoke filling the air around us, I offer him a timid smile, clasping my hands in front of me.

"Sorry, I had a childish impulse—seeing something and needing to touch it. My apologies, Malcolm." I let out a small giggle and return to the perfect-princess demeanor I've been taught to maintain. Suddenly it dawns on me, and I recognize this situation for what it is. I know that I have to admit my mistake, because men like Malcolm are always right and, of course, women are always wrong.

After my confession, his face relaxes. Abruptly, he starts walking back the way we came. "Let's head back to the castle for dinner, shall we?" he asks from over his shoulder as he marches ahead.

On our way out of the caves, we pass a den I hadn't noticed before. Inside, a gray dragon with purple spikes across its back—much like Shea, but in a shimmery, smoky hue instead of her jet black—is sleeping in the corner. It's a beautiful creature, and I ask Malcolm for the dragon's name. All the excitement and happiness that had been there when he was showing off the caves mere minutes ago now drains from his face. Without answering me, Malcolm ushers me to the exit. I tell myself to remember this small show of emotion.

As we continue our walk, I observe how the castle staff interact with Malcolm. There are no pleasantries or jokes. Just curt nods or ducked heads as they scurry by. It is all straight-faced and serious business, which is not how I was taught to interact with our royal staff.

Castle Waimea and Castle Hana seem to be totally opposite on, well, everything.

My eyes go round when we enter the castle. Craning my neck, I follow the long gilded beams stretching across the ceilings in each room. I find the several large, gaudy crystal chandeliers hanging every few feet from the beams hard to ignore as they twinkle in the golden light of early evening. The floors are pristine, sparkling like calm water, without a ripple or nick on them. Castle Hana is the definition of extravagant, seeming much more like a palace than a forti-fied castle—but nothing about it makes me feel welcome. It feels hollow and lifeless . . . like there has been no laughter, playing, not even sadness here—like this is all for show.

King Victor and Queen Maribeth are seated at the dining table but stand when Malcolm steps into the room . . . an outdated tradition our family no longer performs. Their expressions are still harsh and cold, leaving me yet again to keep my head and eyes down as I stand behind my seat next to Malcolm, who is taking the place at the head of the table. Unfortunately, the king and queen are both standing across from me, making it hard to avert my eyes.

"Mother, Father. Thank you for joining us. I wanted to share this dinner with you both so we could all get to know Princess Louella," Malcolm says rigidly as we all sit down.

"Yes, I am just dying to get to know you," Queen Maribeth echoes, mimicking her son's stern tone, but her comment suggests she's being condescending.

I nod in response, a polite gesture that hopefully shouldn't warrant another mean remark.

"Louella was telling me that she's dabbled in archery and weaponry, and she's spent some time helping in the dragon caves back at Castle Waimea. She also informed me that she has quite a green thumb. I think we should carve out some space on the grounds so Lou can grow her food and things. Wouldn't that be nice?" Malcolm asks as he grins widely at his parents.

I look at the profile of his face. My heart swells at such a kind suggestion and how proud he appears right now.

"Mmmm, archery and dragons? Those aren't exactly hobbies fit for a girl . . . ," King Victor glares at me from the other side of the table just as the waitstaff lay bowls in front of us, which are filled with a thick orange soup or maybe stew—I can't tell.

Malcolm ignores his father, picks up his spoon, and begins to slurp down the orange liquid.

"I do love the idea of the garden, though. We could have her grow our supply of food for the castle. If she's truly as good as she says she is, we could try growing our vegetation for the whole village . . . cut back on some costs." King Victor's features relax as he speaks directly to Malcolm now.

The prince sips his soup and shoots a look at his father that I can't quite read.

"Actually, the soil on this side of the island wouldn't be beneficial for growing in large quantities. Sure, some things we could grow in bulk, but it wouldn't be enough to stop the trades you have with Castle Waimea," I pipe up before I indulge in a spoonful of soup.

"Hm, says who?" Queen Maribeth questions.

I dab my mouth with my napkin and place it back in my lap before explaining. "Says Castle Waimea's lead agriculturist. I often work closely with her, and she's taught me all about growing conditions. Unfortunately, Castle Hana has some of the worst conditions and soil because it barely rains on this side of the island."

Looking into Queen Maribeth's gelid eyes makes me feel uneasy. I can tell she doesn't like me, and the feeling is mutual.

"Well, aren't you a plethora of knowledge?" she responds. "Are you this knowledgeable about being a queen? Running a castle? Going to battle? Being a wife? Bearing children?"

I blink a couple of times as her words sink in. Knowing full well that she's baiting me but refusing to back down now, I sit up straighter in my chair, shifting uncomfortably before I answer, "I think so."

"That's enough, Mother." Malcolm keeps his head over his bowl of soup as he raises only his eyes to look at the queen.

She picks up her spoon, and I watch as she swirls the bowl's contents around but never actually brings the spoon up to her mouth.

That's the last thing I say for the rest of our "getting to know Louella" dinner.

Instead of trying to have a civil conversation with my hosts, I opt instead to give all my attention to the delicious-ness placed on the table before me. Our main course is a Kapu Island signature dish called kalua pig. It's a whole hog that has been wrapped with banana leaves and smoked underground, which makes the meat extremely tender and smoky. Tonight, the kalua pig is served with a side of rice.

As I savor each morsel, I know one thing is for certain: the food at Castle Hana is incredible, even if the company isn't.

King Victor and Queen Maribeth quickly finish their meals before Malcolm and me, and as soon as they are done, they excuse themselves from the table without even saying goodbye.

Once they have left the room, I let out a deep sigh, inadvertently grabbing Malcolm's attention.

"Louella, please ignore my parents. They only want to make sure that this is the best decision for our people before handing over their reign to me and my new bride. I'm sure this is scary for you—it's scary for me too."

I shake my head. "No, I understand. I just want to be able to fit in and make you happy . . . But sometimes I fear I won't be as good of a queen and wife as my mother or Queen Maribeth." I look Malcolm in the eyes, hoping to find reassurance and not the same judgment I see in his parents' eyes when they look at me.

Malcolm gently places his hand on top of mine on the table before us. At his touch, I relax my pinched eyebrows, and from my concern and worry bloom admiration and desire.

"You'll be perfect." Malcolm's voice has become gravelly and hungry, like he's desperate for me, for this, for us—and at this moment, I foolishly want to believe him.

FOUR

LOUELLA APONI DELPHINE

Castle Waimea, Kapu Island

It's been three days since I returned home from Castle Hana. Everyone has been rushing around to meetings and making arrangements for my upcoming nuptials, and Papa has been taking his dinners in his study. As a result, I haven't been able to speak to my parents or Chester alone about King Victor and Queen Maribeth's attitude toward me. Tonight, though, Papa has called a family dinner to discuss my trip, so I can finally talk to them about everything.

Mama woke me up this morning and told me the castle staff were going to start packing my room today, but I begged her to let me do it. I want to have the final say on what happens to all my stuff. She's allowing me to do the packing, as long as I finish by the end of this week. I didn't hesitate to tell her we had a deal.

I've been going through my belongings all day, but no one would be able to tell, judging by the state of my room. It looks like a hurricane came through and blasted clothes everywhere. I've been creating piles for what I'm taking with me, what's staying, and what can be donated, but if you were an outsider looking in . . . it's utter chaos.

I check the clock hanging above my dresser and realize that it's ten minutes until dinner. I glance around at the piles filling my room, pressing my lips into a line as I debate whether I should keep going after dinner or resume tomorrow. Being honest with myself, I know it will probably be the latter.

I jump up from the current heap of clothing I'm buried in and run to the bathroom to fix myself up, and then I make my way to the dining room.

When I enter the room, Papa, Pop-Pop, Mama, and Chester are all seated around the table and laughing with one another. I pause at the entryway as I attempt to capture this scene in my mind because I know the Royce family won't be the same as mine—things will never be the same once I become a Royce. There will be no more laughing at the dinner table, no inside jokes, no heart-to-heart conversations . . .

Pop-Pop notices me first and our eyes meet, like he knows what I'm thinking without me having to say a thing.

"Come on, Ella-Bella, we've been waiting for you!" he shouts over the laughter.

A smile spreads across my face and I hurry over to take the empty chair next to Mama. Barely in my seat, I waste no time snatching a pillow-soft roll from the basket in the middle of the table and begin to pull it apart over my plate.

"All right, Sis, you're up. Spill all the Castle Hana secrets," Chester manages to form words between the giant chews of bread he just shoved in his mouth.

"Chester, that's not funny. This isn't a spy mission; this is your sister's future," Mama scolds firmly. "And don't talk with your mouth full," she adds for good measure.

My brother freezes mid-chew, mouth open and eyes wide, staring at Mama. "I was joking! C'mon, Mama, you know that!" he pleads.

I toss a small piece of bread at Chester over the table. My aim is true, hitting him in the cheek and falling into his lap.

He grabs the chunk from under the table, shrugging before popping it into his mouth. This time, he chews with his mouth closed, and Pop-Pop and Papa chuckle at him.

"But really, Ella, how was it?" Papa asks.

I make myself look busy as I slab knifefuls of butter onto the torn-up pieces of roll on my plate. How do I accurately portray the Royce family without sounding like I'm complaining? After a moment of thinking, I finally respond.

"Malcolm is such a gentleman—he's great. We had a wonderful time together touring the castle grounds. He knows everything about being a king." I shove a bit of bread in my mouth and chew nervously.

"Good." Papa nods in approval. "Were King Victor and Queen Maribeth present?" he adds.

This is where I need to choose my words carefully. I clear my throat and take a sip of wine before I speak again. "Um, yes."

"How were they?" Mama questions. I look at her before I answer, and I can see a fire burning in her eyes . . . Or maybe I'm projecting, seeing what I want to see, and it's something else shining behind them—perhaps genuine curiosity?

I slowly place my glass down in front of me and release a heavy exhale. "They were not very nice to me, actually."

Waiting for a reaction, I look around the room. But it seems as though everyone at the table is motionless, and the silence is deafening.

Papa puts down his roll and looks me in the eyes as he presses, "How so, Louella?"

I'm being put on the spot, and I'm not even sure it's worth telling them about my experience. Maybe I should brush it off.

Too late. I opened my big mouth.

"Well, they were very cold toward me, and they weren't very nice to Malcolm either . . . They said snide remarks to me, and overall, it seemed as though they weren't happy about Malcolm and me getting married. Which is weird, since I thought this was what they wanted."

Mama and Pop-Pop glance at each other before looking at my father. Papa steels his spine and his nostrils flare. My three elders pass glances among themselves for several seconds, and I look to Chester to gauge his expression. He narrows his eyes at me and then furrows his brow as we both grow impatient.

"What in the world is going on? Are you going to tell us or just leave us in this awkward silence?" Chester blurts out.

Mama nods at Papa as if she's giving him the go-ahead to share their secret.

"Your mother and I were worried about this because we don't have the best history with Castle Hana. They've always had a small vendetta against us . . . But then again, Queen Maribeth and King Victor are very traditional, serious people. It could have simply been their personalities that made them seem mean," Papa says diplomatically.

"You're being too nice," Pop-Pop murmurs.

The waitstaff enter the dining room and delve out plates of salad to each one of us. When they leave, Papa continues.

"We don't speak often about our history with Castle Hana because it's something we are not proud of, nor is it something we even believe to be entirely true. But many years ago, your great-great-great-aunt Princess Althea Aponi, much like you," Papa nods his head in my direction, "was arranged to marry Malcolm's great-great-great-uncle Prince Leo Royce. Sadly, shortly before their marriage was supposed to occur, the Algonquin Battle began.

Althea's brother, who was your great-great-grandfather, Prince Jasper Aponi the First, was a true warrior and one of Castle Waimea's strongest riders and archers fighting in the war. On day three of the battle, it was raining hard, which created tough visibility for the cavalry. Arrows were speeding through the air in rapid fire, knocking our men off their dragons and sending them plummeting to the ground. When Prince Jasper spotted the enemies, he swiftly shot down each rider one by one, leaving no one left." Papa pauses, looking over to Mama before resuming.

Chester and I are both so entranced by what the chief has to say that we haven't moved. We stare at him with eyes wide, anticipating what is to come next.

Papa looks between Chester and me, then he resumes his story, "One of the warriors Jasper shot down was Prince Leo Royce. Jasper had no idea he had killed the prince until Jasper was back on the ground. When word got out that Castle Hana's beloved Prince Leo had been slain by none other than his bride-to-be's brother, we retreated and so did the other two villages, leaving Maka Mountain to Castle Hana. Even though Jasper had no idea whom he had slain, Castle Hana never let it go. They have believed for decades that it was a targeted attack—an assassination to prevent the marriage. If Jasper had known it was Prince Leo, he never would have shot those arrows." Papa sits back in his chair and focuses on me. "With this problematic history in mind, your mother and I were wary at first when the king and queen approached us with the idea of you and

Malcolm marrying each other to join our castles. But they were so excited and friendly toward us. They made a treaty with us that no war was to happen again, and our castles would move forward as a united force . . . and I still believe that."

"Wait! You still believe that even though Ella is basically telling us they lied to you?" Chester is outraged, and he slams his hand on the table.

"Calm down, Son. What makes you think they lied to Ella?" the chief volleys back calmly.

"They were unkind to her. That's a huge red flag!"

"That's just who they are as people. We can't assume anything based on one interaction."

I look between the two of them as they go back and forth. My veneer of calm indifference is splintering; I can't take it anymore, and now I slam my fist onto the table as well. Everyone jumps, and all eyes snap to me.

"STOP!" I shout. "If they signed a treaty, then they can't go back on their agreement. Plus, Malcolm won't let anything happen to me. That I know for a fact."

Chester heaves an exasperated sigh. "You're being naïve . . . I thought Mama was teaching you how to act and think like a queen. You're not being very queenly." He finishes his sentence by taking an aggressive bite of his salad.

"And I thought you were a warrior, not a little bitch," I snarl.

"Children—enough," Mama says fiercely, and the table goes quiet—except for the clinking of silverware against our plates as we eat. The rest of dinner follows with minimum chatter, except for the occasional comment from Pop-Pop about how tasty the meal is.

The silence from Papa is making me grow uneasy. I have no idea what is going on in his head or what his story means. This is my future, and the new information he dropped in my lap tonight has me unsettled. I'm scared I'll be trapped in a dungeon in Castle Hana and locked away for the rest of my life for something my great-great-grandfather unknowingly did before I was even alive.

Papa finally speaks again, and I release a deep sigh I had been holding inside me. "We will go through with the marriage, but we expect weekly correspondence from you, Louella. I'll also send one of our guards with you so that you are protected at all times. If they see or hear anything suspicious, they will alert us or get you out of there. If anyone in the Royce family touches you or makes you do anything outside a queen's responsibility, then I will be on the first dragon over there bringing you back home myself."

My throat has become dry, and I'm finding it hard to breathe. I nod my head at my father to acknowledge his instructions to me. I've barely eaten and I no longer have an appetite, so I excuse myself for the rest of the evening to finish packing, leaving my pineapple cake untouched on the table—which is a bummer because it's my favorite food on the entire island.

***

Hours later, when I'm about ready to call it a night, there's a light rap on my door.

"Come in!" I shout from across the room.

To my surprise, Papa slowly peeks his head in before pushing the door open and gently closing it behind him.

"Wow, you're almost all done." He looks around, taking in all the sacks and chests stacked around the room.

"Yeah, I had a lot of time to think after dinner, which oddly made me more focused on packing." I shrug and stand, walking over to my bed and plopping down on it. I'm so exhausted I could melt into the mattress. Papa follows suit, taking a seat next to me.

He clears his throat anxiously, and it puts me on edge a bit, making me tense my shoulders.

"Listen, Ella, I don't want you to worry about that silly story. You go and have fun, fall in love, be the best queen this island has ever seen—I'll take care of everything. Even though you will be married and another man will be taking care of you, you will forever be my little princess. You know that, right?"

My eyes sting, and I bite the inside of my cheek to hold back the tears. I notice my father's eyes are glossy, and I can tell deep down he's regretting this whole marriage situation . . . but it's too late now. I reach out and wrap my arms around his torso, embracing him in a tight hug. He returns the embrace and lays his cheek against the top of my head, twisting to press a kiss to my hair. I try to etch the warmth of his hug and the familiar smell of him in my memory. I'm not sure I'll ever get hugs this sincere again.

"Thanks, Papa," I whisper.

We stay like that for a few heartbeats, until he breaks away first. He places his hand on my shoulder and looks me square in the eyes.

"Take our girl Shea out for one more ride tonight, will ya?" he says in a hushed tone, giving me a conspiratorial wink.

"Are you serious?!" I whisper-shout.

He nods with a pleased grin.

I can't contain the smile that lights up my face as I jump off the bed and do a little dance. After a beat, I pause and look back at Papa.

"Thank you, thank you, thank you. I love you so much!" I say, leaping into his arms to hug him once again.

"Ohhhh, now you love me. All I have to say is 'Shea,' and I get an 'I love you,'" Papa teases.

I giggle at his response.

"I see everything, Ella. I knew the barracks were empty during the guards' shift change and that's how you were sneaking around before. After Cami's accident, I had a conversation with the head of the night watch to make sure no posts were ever left vacant again." He pulls back from me, his strong hands cupping my cheeks, and gives me a no-nonsense look. "But, since I'm allowing you to fly one last time, I'll let the guards off for the night. It can be only this once, Ella. I can't reprimand our staff and then turn around and let them do what I just told them not to do. I'll have Chester meet you down there in case anyone asks questions. Don't hurt yourself either—please be careful."

I give Papa a solemn nod to show him that I understand, and he releases me. Then I dash to the closet to throw on my riding clothes, wasting no time to get to my girl.

I stand in front of Shea, pressing my forehead to her nose. She gives me a loud snort, and her breath comes out warm and wet against my chest. She closes her eyes as I rub the side of her snout, taking in the small bumps and grooves of her soft skin. I don't have to talk to Shea for her to know what I'm thinking—she can feel my grief.

Chester informed me that he will not be escorting me to Castle Hana, but Lucas will take his place. They're both fine with this new plan because Luke will be returning to Castle Waimea after a few months. Turns out, Mama made the final decision because she wanted one of her kids to remain at the castle . . . I've often suspected she favored Chester over me—he's the "good" child between the two of us, and I've always been the troublemaker, the child she could never tame.

I'll be traveling to Castle Hana with my permanent guard and two other riders. Much to my surprise, considering her stubbornly disobedient demeanor, Shea will be going as well. She and the other two dragons will be part of the crossbreeding arrangement with Castle Hana's dragons. Unfortunately, Lucas made it clear that he will not allow me to have nightly visits with Shea at my new home, so this will be my last flight.

So much for me shaking things up and changing the rules.

"All set," Chester announces as he approaches me.

I stand back and slide my hand down the center of Shea's nose. She opens her large round eyes and keeps them steady on mine. Looking into those endless icy-blue pools used to scare me and put me on edge—now, it sets my heart on fire. I love Shea; we have a bond that will never be broken.

I walk around to Shea's side, but before I hop on, Chester grabs my hand.

"Ella—wait," he calls.

I turn to face him. He's looking at the ground and his posture is slumped.

"What is it?" I ask.

After a few seconds, he lifts his eyes to meet mine. "I'm sorry for what I said at dinner. And for being such a pain in the ass over the years. I love being your big brother. Even those times when you've acted more like the older sibling than I have."

I embrace Chester, wrapping my arms around his neck tightly.

"Don't choke me out," he coughs.

I laugh and stand back, holding him an arm's length away from me. "Ches, you are the best big brother. You're my best friend, and that's never going to change."

At that, he grins and nods his head, like he needed the reassurance of my words. "Now . . . I wanna fly!" I fling my arms out, and he shakes his head and laughs at me.

"Get going!" Chester urges, landing two small pats to Shea's hindquarter.

I slide my foot into the stirrup, swinging my body over my dragon and holding the leather straps as I adjust myself in the saddle. She stands and gives a loud caw into the night sky. I look down at Chester and wink, knowing he'll be nervous that someone heard the noise and will spot me. To my surprise, he's still smiling as he shakes his head once more.

Shea begins to take her three giant steps, and I clutch the reins harder. Remembering what my brother taught me, I clasp the jade horn at the front of the saddle for more stability as she takes the last step, swoops her wings ferociously, and lifts off into the night sky.

We take our usual route, and I savor the experience of being so high in the sky. I let go of the reins and spread my arms out beside me, indulging in the sensation of flying on my own for a few luxurious minutes.

Shea stays up high instead of banking toward the water, and I assume it's to let me enjoy the air a bit more. I grab the reins again to prepare for her to turn, but she never does. We are headed straight for Maka Mountain. I give her a small nudge to redirect her toward our normal route, but she doesn't budge. I pull the right strap hard against my body in hopes that Shea will turn in that direction and bring us to the sea, but still . . . nothing. I have no idea what she's doing.

Fear starts to creep into my thoughts, but I calm my mind by reassuring myself that Shea has never led me to danger, and she knows what she's doing (even if I still don't). I ease up on the reins a bit and slouch back as I wait for her next move. My dragon gives me a loud warning squawk as we approach the edge of the mountain, so I hold the straps tight once more and she lifts us toward the mountain's peak.

My body jolts back, and I clench my thighs tight and my hands tighter. Shea's heading straight to the top of the mountain, and I can't stop the fear this time as my heart begins to beat out of my chest. My palms are sweating now, and the leather straps slip through my grasp. Luckily, they are twisted around my wrists for added grip. I can feel the sweat like ice cubes rolling down my back and face as the air gets colder and colder the higher we ascend.

"Shea!" I shout her name now, praying she will understand that I'm scared out of my fucking mind.

But she doesn't falter. If anything, Shea starts to fly faster, straight ahead into nothingness. My braid whips wildly behind me, and my eyes are watering from how fast she's going, the cold air slicing right through me. It's all becoming too much, and I wish she would level out and turn back.

As soon as I feel as though I may pass out, the world around me goes completely black. Everything falls still for a single second, but it seems like a whole hour has passed. There's an odd pressure making my head feel as if it's going to pop and air will blast out of my ears. I want to grab my head but also my chest since I feel like I can no longer catch my breath—but I keep holding on.

Just when I resign myself to giving up and succumbing to the darkness—and just before my hands slip from the reins and the rest of me goes completely limp—my body jolts upright, straight in the saddle, as Shea finally levels out. I snap back to reality, sensation returning in my body and shaking the fuzziness from my head.

"WHAT THE ACTUAL FUCK, SHEA?" I holler through the wind around us.

She snorts loudly in answer and finally turns us back toward the castle.

As Shea descends, I notice that the village below us isn't the village we left behind. I rub my eyes, trying to clear away any lingering haze from what just happened, but all I see are tiny lights all over the island. I squint to get a better look, and I'm in shock. There are buildings everywhere, tall and short ones the likes of which I've never seen before, and long stretches of dark pathways with strange-looking orbs of light zooming by. Coasting lower in the sky, I catch smaller movements: people. Lots of people everywhere who look like little ants from above. At this height, I cast my gaze out and notice that this place looks like Kapu Island . . . but it is not Kapu Island. I can faintly see coastlines, rolling hills, fields for farming—but this is not my home.

Where the fuck am I?

Shea is heading straight toward the dragon caves—or, geographically, where they would be—and as we are getting closer and closer, I notice that it's a dark forested area with no lights or people. At least we will be well hidden and tucked away until I figure out where the hell we are.

Approaching the clearing, I notice that it isn't as large as the one back at the castle and the trees surrounding it are densely clumped together. I glance at Shea's wings as she scrunches them closer to her body. She's rocking side to side now, and I can tell this is not going to be a smooth landing. I try to replicate her body position by hunching in on myself as tightly as I can, bringing my chin to my chest. I can hear the branches battering Shea's wings, and I close my eyes in fear of getting smacked in the face. My body jerks a bit as the trees slash at my legs, leaving behind rips in my pants. Some of the branches grab at my hair, like hands trying to pull me back, ripping strands from my scalp. Begging for this to be over, I uncurl slightly from my defensive position and squint my eyes open a fraction to see that we're so close to the clearing. Right when Shea bursts through the tree line, a particularly aggressive bough lands one final blow to my ribs. A loud grunt escapes me, and my shirt is tugged backward, stuck on the rogue branch. But it's no match for my dragon. Tearing free in an instant, I feel a burst of cool air across my now-bare belly.

As soon as we land in the forest clearing, I jump off Shea and stand in front of her, seething. "Where the hell are we, Shea? What have you done?" I'm whisper-shouting because I don't want anyone to hear us.

I can vaguely see her from the light of the full moon, which is now descending below the treetops. Twigs and leaves stick out from Shea's bridle, and I gently remove them while checking her for injuries. From what I can make out, she looks relatively unscathed. I glance down at my body, inspecting my skin through the holes in my clothing. Besides a handful of superficial scratches and an ache in my side, I am whole. But I'm so scared. I knew I should have flown with a weapon, but this was supposed to be a quick trip. Now I'm unprepared and could be killed at any second.

Shea blinks her pale eyes in response to my panicking as if she's completely unfazed. She lies down in the brush and begins to lick her talons and clean her face.

I remain standing in front of her, foot tapping nervously and arms crossed over my chest. "Well?" I demand.

Like I expect a dragon to talk to me . . . Actually, at this point in the night, after whatever just happened up there, I wouldn't be surprised if she does respond. Shea continues to ignore me and curls up into a ball on the ground, closing her eyes to get some rest.

"Oh, that's just great. You fly me to goddess knows where, and then you take a little nappy-pooh! Awesome,

Shea, that's fucking great." I throw my hands up in frustration.

What am I going to do? It's nearly pitch-black and I have no idea where I am. I need to find my way back home, but how?

I nudge Shea's leg with my foot, "Get up. You are taking me back NOW!" I say firmly.

She opens her eyes and glares at me, then she jerks her head to the right as if she hears something.

My eyes shoot to where she's looking, but I can't see anything. I drop to the ground and crouch beside her. I should have kept my mouth shut, but I didn't think I was being loud enough for anyone to hear me over all the sounds coming from the village . . . At least, I think that's what it is.

The sound of cracking branches reaches me, followed by voices not too far from us.

Shea's breathing becomes more measured. She perches her body, getting ready to pounce on our visitors. I don't stop her since I have no idea what to expect.

The rustling and snapping suddenly stops. We sit silently as I try to assess the situation, but the only sound I hear is the pounding of my own heart. When I think we are in the clear, I take a step out from beside Shea, but then I hear a voice behind me.

"Holy shit, dude!"

I whip around to see who it is as Shea lifts herself up, raising her wings high, poised to attack. Two guys are standing before me, mouths wide open and eyes bulging from their heads as they take in the sight of my dragon.

"Don't move!" I shout.

Their eyes dart to me, and they raise their hands in the air to show me they come unarmed.

"W-w-we saw a black shadow land over here while we were riding our bikes and, and, and we just came to check it out . . . Please tell that thing not to hurt us. Please, we don't want to start anything." The one speaking is shaking and stuttering like crazy. I can see the outline of his fingers vibrating from how scared he is right now, and I feel the same way.

I take in the sight of them both from the remaining moonlight, which is scattered by the trees. They're the same height and look to be about my age. The one speaking has close-cropped hair with a short dark beard on his perfectly round face. He's wearing a T-shirt with the sleeves cut off, along with cut-off shorts and sneakers.

My eyes flick to the other stranger; oddly, he doesn't look nearly as scared. His hands aren't shaking, and his mouth is now closed. He looks . . . amazed. Not frightened, but curious. He puts his hands down slowly, and at that instant, I realize I haven't moved.

Shea pulls her wings back, still tense and defensive, and I hear the bearded guy whimper quietly.

I watch the second guy a little longer and try to focus on his features through the shadows. He has long dark hair that matches his dark eyes. His lips are full as he gives them a small swipe with his tongue, and I don't miss the motion. He too is wearing a cut-off T-shirt, exposing his muscular arms. Moonlight glints off the rings he's wearing on his fingers, and I notice beaded bracelets on his left wrist. His pants are black with slashes in them, which expose his knees and parts of his thighs. Now I find myself licking my lips, and I can tell he doesn't miss the motion either, despite the darkness, as he gives me a knowing smirk.

Shea lets out a gnarly roar aimed at the strangers in front of us, making us all jump. Her mouth is peeled back to expose her teeth, and saliva is dripping from her fangs. It reignites my fear that we have landed in an unfamiliar place and I could be in grave danger. I can't let my guard down.

"Where am I? And who are you?" I try to ask firmly, but my voice trembles a bit at the end.

"Nah, what the fuck is that?" the bearded one asks me as he points his quivering finger in Shea's direction.

"Don't be stupid, dude. It's a dragon," the guy with the long hair responds for me.

"No way, man, dragons aren't real."

"Well, that looks pretty real to me," long-haired guy snarks.

Shea gives a low warning squawk, and that grabs their attention again.

"Answer my questions," I rush out.

"Okay, okay. You are in Kailani Bay, which is on Gemcove Island. I'm Knox, and this is Lloyd." The long-haired guy hitches his thumb to Lloyd next to him. Knox's voice is low and calm, even though he rushed through his introductions. "We aren't going to hurt you or your dragon. Are you all right? Do you need help?" he asks me.

"I'm fine. This is my dragon. I don't need your help," I snap as I slowly step back toward Shea.

Shea sits on her hind legs as she becomes more relaxed around Knox and Lloyd, deeming them to no longer be a threat. It's almost as if the air has cleared and she has accepted them being here. The anxiety in my shoulders eases a bit, and they drop away from my ears.

"Are you even from here?" Lloyd interrogates me.

I start to wonder if maybe I just ended up landing on another part of Kapu Island I have never been to before. But I survey their clothes again and realize that if I were still on my island, the villagers would wear clothes like my people's. The outfits these two are wearing don't look anything like our usual clothes. I've seen things like what they've got on in Tallulah's tent in the market—hell, I have some T-shirts of my own from her stall . . . But that would mean . . . Nah, it can't possibly mean . . . I realm jumped? I glance at the setting moon and then back to Lloyd and Knox.

"I'm definitely not from here . . ."

"Where are you from?" Knox asks as he inches closer.

Shea moves her wing out in front of me as a shield, and I grab on to it.

"I'm not going to hurt you. We need to hide your dragon and get you somewhere safe."

Knox is standing a few feet away from me, and I can see his features clearer now. His skin is a soft russet color, except for the sporadic tattoos decorating his arms. He's intimidating the longer I look at him, but I don't feel scared—if anything, I want to get nearer to him. I want to run my hand across his skin, ask him about his tattoos, and brush my thumb across his dark eyebrows . . .

Lloyd clears his throat, bringing me back to the present as I look in his direction.

"Uhh, yeah, we should probably get going. The sun will be rising soon enough, and people are going to see this big-ass dragon and a girl who looks like she just came back from war," he says.

It hits me then how disheveled I probably look after our rough landing in the forest. I pull my braid over my shoulder, but it's frayed and coming apart . . . and full of leaves. I remember the large gash in my shirt and instinctively try to bunch the fabric together, covering my exposed stomach. Sheepishly looking down at myself, I realize that I'm standing barefoot because I don't ride with shoes.

"Oh shit, I look terrible," I laugh to myself.

Knox gives a small chuckle, "I wouldn't say that."

My head jerks back to him, and I can't help the way my heart squeezes as he gives me a slight smile.

"You're right, I've got to hide Shea. If you fuck with me, I will slice you into a million pieces and feed you to her," I scowl at both Lloyd and Knox, hoping they don't call my bluff and figure out I'm weaponless.

Lloyd puts his hands up and shakes his head from side to side. "Whoa, just here to help lady," he mutters.

"I'm not your lady. My name is Louella. This is Shea."

They both nod and approach Shea carefully.

"Louella, there are some caves about a quarter of a mile that way. Let's get Shea in there to hide during the day. I can take you back to our place, where you can clean yourself up and get some food," Knox offers. I get the feeling he's treating me like a rabbit cornered in the woods and he thinks I might bolt at any sudden movement.

He's not entirely wrong.

I glance at both guys, wondering if this is a good idea. Maybe if Shea and I hurry, we can head back up the way we came and get out of here. I just need answers to what is going on—and I need sleep, and food, and home.

I really want to go home.

I examine the horizon and notice that the moon has all but set, casting us in near-total darkness. If we're going to get home anytime soon, Shea will need rest after what we've been through tonight. I look back at Knox and give him a nod in agreement. I have to hide Shea; if I lose her, I lose my one chance of getting out of here.

FIVE

CHESTER PALA DELPHINE

Castle Waimea, Kapu Island

I waited for Louella to return for two hours, but she never came back. I should have known she was up to something because she was a little too eager to get up in the sky. I had watched Shea fly their typical route for a while, but then she veered off course. They rarely head toward the mountain, but I didn't think anything of it, assuming Ella was enjoying what would likely be her final flight. When they never returned, I cursed myself for not hopping on Zeus and following them.

It took all the courage in me to race to the castle and tell Papa that Louella was gone. He was so angry with himself for allowing her to fly, but he also struggled to believe that she would just take off and never come back. He sent out a fleet of dragon riders from the cavalry to locate her in case she had fallen and was injured, but after searching well into the morning, they had yet to find any trace of her.

Our castle sent out correspondence to the other three castles to be on the lookout for Louella within their villages and surrounding areas. She'll be hard to miss because Shea is with her, and I'm certain those two won't be easily separated. In daylight, Shea's dark coloring flying against a bright-blue sky couldn't be more conspicuous. Under the cover of darkness, however, her fluorescent-purple spikes are the only way to spot her if anyone can get close enough.

Papa waited until the absolute last minute to inform Mama of what happened. He was so nervous to tell her because he's the one who permitted Louella to fly one last time. My father values honesty and doing what's right, which means he is taking responsibility for this incident—plus, Louella will always be his little girl. He could never place the blame on his beloved daughter.

It has been twelve hours since Louella and Shea disappeared, and I'm standing off to the side of the dining room near the doorway as I watch Papa break the news to Mama and Pop-Pop. They're all seated at the far end of the table, and I'm using every scrap of self-control not to pace the length of the room to expel some of my anxiety. My arms are crossed over my chest, and I have been intently focusing on Mama's face. The air in the room is thick, and it makes me uncomfortable. Shifting my attention, I can see

Papa's mouth moving, but he's talking in such a low tone I can't decipher what he's saying.

Mama remains stoic the entire time Papa speaks. It's the kind of silence where you can see her body vibrating and you just know that at the slightest provocation, she's going to rage, turning the whole place upside down with how pissed she is . . . but she doesn't move.

After several moments, Papa's voice increases enough for me to hear, and he presses his palms together in front of his chest as if he's praying.

"Please, Thea. Please forgive me," he begs. "I will find her and bring her home. I know how upset you must be, but I will fix this. I will find our girl."

Finally she speaks, and her words are flat and shaky as she tries to control her tone, "You'd better find her before Victor and Maribeth do."

Mama rises abruptly from her seat, prompting the men to stand as well, and she takes her leave of the dining room. Brushing past me in a blur of motion, she shoves open the double doors, which slam shut behind her.

My father and I lock eyes across the room, both of us stupefied temporarily. Pop-Pop seems unbothered as he sits back down and picks at the grapes in a bowl on the table.

"I told Ella-Bella I could have helped her run away . . . She should have come to me," Pop-Pop mumbles innocently.

The chief looks over at him like he's going to strangle his own father.

I can't take being inside anymore, so I turn away from this mess and set out for the private shore next to the castle grounds to clear my mind.

After walking several feet onto the sand, I plop my ass down and cradle my head in my hands. I sit for a while like that, breathing deeply—until I feel a gentle touch on my shoulder. Shielding my eyes from the sun with my hand, I find Luke gazing down at me with sadness and concern in his light-blue eyes.

"Hey," I say unenthusiastically.

"Want some company?" Luke asks.

My instinct is to say no, but when I look up at him, his sympathetic expression makes me second-guess that answer. He's wearing his usual black cropped pants and a black tank top, which exposes his large arms covered in Wiki tattoos. I pat the sand next to me, giving him permission to join me in my worry.

He wraps a bare arm around my shoulder and yanks me to his side. In response, I place my head on his shoulder. I thought I needed to be alone, but this feels nice. Having someone to take my worries away for a bit is maybe exactly what I needed.

"Do you think she's all right?" My voice is barely audible because I'm afraid to ask questions and receive answers I can't bear to hear.

"Louella is just fine." Luke squeezes my shoulder. "She's strong, she's a fighter."

I want to cry, but that's not who I am. So instead, I pinch my lips between my teeth as I try to focus on what I can do to help track down Louella. I can't think of the worst possible outcome right now. I must hold out hope for my little sister; I must have faith that she will come back to us.

Luke is right—Louella is fine.

"This could cause a war, you know?" I say more to myself than to Luke.

"I know, but our warriors are strong, and our dragons are ready." Luke sounds so assured of what he has spoken. He doesn't seem nervous at all.

I think about what a war would be like between Castle Hana and Castle Waimea. I wonder if the other castles would join and which side they would stand on. Would Malcolm want a war over his bride-to-be? Would he think it to be worth it, or would he just do whatever his parents wanted?

"Someone is going to have to take a trip to Castle Hana and try to pacify the Royces while we search for her," I announce, implying anyone but me.

"I know. I suggest we fly down on the dragons and bring some guards with us, and maybe some weapons . . . just in case," Luke proposes.

"I agree."

We sit in silence until a thought pops into my mind. "Remember about a month ago when you mentioned that someone in the village had realm jumped for candy?" I lift my head from Luke's shoulder and turn toward him questioningly.

His lips curve downward at the memory. "Yeah, I remember. The chief was not happy with me," Luke replies, shaking his head and giving me a guarded look in return.

"Do you think Louella could have done that? She asked me a lot of questions about it . . . . I'm wondering if she found out how to do it—she does like to read a lot. Maybe she really did want to run away." My brows are pinched together as I study his reaction.

He pinches his brows together too, mirroring my unease. As he thinks, his lips scrunch together, moving back and forth across his teeth. "That's a possibility, but they don't have books on how to realm jump," he finally says.

"Do you think you could bring me to that villager?"

Luke breaks our physical contact as he unhooks his arm from around my shoulders. Now facing the water in front of us, he hesitates. "Eh, I don't know Chester. I don't want to get anyone in trouble."

"I won't tell my father. I will keep this between you and me . . . and the villager." I grab his hand that's resting on his thigh as I attempt to plead with him.

Luke turns toward me and scans my face. Grimacing, he bites his lower lip, and I can see the reluctance burning in his eyes. After several seconds, he responds, "All right, but this must stay between us. And if we have to realm jump . . .," Luke lowers his voice, "no one can know."

I smile at him, the all-consuming dread easing off me a fraction. "Thank you for helping me try to save my sister."

Luke squeezes my hand. "I would do anything for you, Chester."

***

When I return to the castle later that day, Papa is still in the dining room as I walk past.

"Chester, a word." His voice is severe and a bit frightening.

I stop in my tracks, and immediately my heart is beating wildly in my chest. I inhale sharply, clenching my fists as I about-face and trudge into the dining room. Stepping through the propped-open double doors, I see my father sitting at the head of the table with multiple maps spread across the surface and papers scattered about. It's weird to see him looking the part of a military strategist, but that's part of the job.

I clear my throat and ask, "Yes, sir?"

Papa looks up from the document he was reading, his face stern. "I'll be sending you, Lucas, and three others from the cavalry to Castle Hana to discuss the disappearance of Louella. I know we alerted them already, but I need you to gauge their reactions and try to calm them if they are upset. I'm not asking you to do this; it is an order. You leave in two days."

Fuck.

I knew there was a possibility I would have to go since I'm one of the captains in the military, but I fucking despise Maribeth and Victor. I visualize punching a wall, and then I take a deep breath.

"Yes, sir," I say with a sharp nod.

"Let's try and ensure harmony with the Royce family. I know you aren't very fond of them, but when Louella comes back, she's going to be a Royce."

I nod once more. "Yes, sir."

"You are dismissed." Papa looks back down at his papers without another glance my way. This is the angriest I've seen him in my life . . . and I hate it.

I do as I'm told and walk out into the hallway to head to my bedroom, where I can ruminate over this until dinner.

Six

Louella Aponi Delphine

Kailani Bay, Gemcove Island

"So, you really have no idea what a restaurant is?" Lloyd asks while he stuffs his face with scrambled eggs. His brown eyes are wide with disbelief.

"Nope. I also have never seen bacon like this. It's so weird and . . . and stringy." I hold up the strip of bacon with my thumb and forefinger and dangle it before my eyes with my lip curled in a disgusted sneer.

Sitting across from me, Knox gives me a soundless chuckle and shakes his head.

I place the disturbing meat back on my plate, feeling a little deflated and exhausted.

Knox has remained quiet through most of our breakfast and it's unnerving. He keeps looking at me like he doesn't trust me, but for some unknown reason, I feel like I want him to trust me. As if some strange part of me wants him to acknowledge me and befriend me—but I'm getting the impression that may not happen anytime soon . . . And I should be thinking about other things, like getting the fuck out of this place.

After hiding Shea in the nearby caves early this morning, Knox, Lloyd, and I rode to their house on their motorcycles (or "bikes," as they call them). It had taken some convincing to get me on one of those precarious machines. But after what I had been through—and with a little coaxing from Knox and Lloyd claiming that "it will feel like flying on a dragon . . . kind of"—the fight in me was gone, so I finally gave in. At the house, I washed away the worst of the grime from my journey with soap and water. I freshened up to the best of my abilities, re-braiding my hair, scrubbing my face, and gargling with a swig of mouthwash.

Knox loaned me some of his clothes since mine were ripped and muddy from the crash landing in the woods, and Lloyd was kind enough to let me borrow a pair of sandals. His feet are smaller than Knox's—or so Knox claims, and I was not about to argue. I had held the footwear in my hands and wondered how the hell these were going to work. They are what Lloyd calls "slippers," but they look like the flimsiest, floppiest sandals I've ever seen in my entire life. Two measly straps attached to a rubber sole, and that's it! That's the shoe. No durable leather like we use back home, no laces to tie securely around my calves, nothing.

But I had no other footwear, so this was my best option. I slid my feet in and shuffled my way out of the bathroom.

Carefully and slowly, I made my way down the small hallway and back to the kitchen to find Lloyd and Knox. I was too on-edge to sleep in an unfamiliar place, so I sought to fulfill my next most-pressing need: food. While I was washing up, they had both realized there was nothing to eat in the house. Before I could panic, Lloyd reassured me we would find food—even at 5:30 a.m. At that point, I had no choice but to believe him, so the three of us headed out and ended up at a small place with tables and people and food . . . I guess it's a restaurant.

I tried to explain to Lloyd that Kapu Island doesn't really need restaurants because the villagers prepare all their own meals in their homes and the royal families receive their meals at the castles. I mean, we have pubs, but nothing like this. This is an assault on my senses: the clanking of plates and silverware; the incessant chatter surrounding us; the cloying scent of so many meals cooked at once, some sweet, some savory, all mixing together; the way everything on the table is a little bit sticky . . . This is far from the innocent banter and comforting atmosphere of my family's dining room table.

"Okay, here's what we know: you have seen some things from our island before, but you aren't from this island or this world?" Lloyd is chewing and speaking at the same time, and it grosses me out. Some of the jiggly yellow egg that's stuck on the tines of his fork flops off and tumbles down his gray shirt with cut-off sleeves, landing in between other various stains, which he seems to not notice, just like the egg. A white paper napkin is draped across his dark-blue shorts, but I can't seem to understand the placement since he periodically wipes his greasy hands on his pants . . . next to the napkin.

I glance over at Knox, but he keeps his attention on his plate, completely engrossed in the toast and yolk he's eating. He's wearing a black shirt with the sleeves cut off, but the front has some sort of design on it and is vacant of any stains.

As I shift my gaze between Knox and Lloyd, I wonder what happened to their clothing and why their sleeves and pants are always torn instead of sewn into a smooth hem. I quickly take notice of the other men in the restaurant, and a lot of them don the same look . . . It must be how they typically dress in this realm.

Knox takes a sip from his white ceramic coffee mug, and it draws my eye. He's very meticulous about the way he eats—almost like he has manners. Knox also has a white paper napkin draped across his black shorts, but unlike Lloyd, he wipes his hands and blots the corners of his mouth with his napkin.

I never thought I would admit this, but maybe Mama isn't wrong for being so strict about etiquette.

I heave a sigh. "Yes. I don't know how many times you must ask me that, Lloyd. I'm not from here. I think I realm jumped or something. I don't know." I shove my plate away

and slam my back into the seat cushion behind me, slump-
ing my shoulders in defeat.

"I've heard of that," Knox says calmly as he leans forward
and rubs his fingers together over his plate to clear any
crumbs from the toast he just finished.

"You have?!" I practically shout, and the patrons around
us look over but it doesn't bother me since I'll never see
these people again. I immediately perk up. If he knows
anything of use, then we can figure out how to get me back
home.

"Mhmm, yeah. I read about it in a book about faeries
and mermaids and shit I borrowed from the library. It was
fictional, meaning not true, so I don't think it will help you."

"Well, what the fuck?" I snap. "Why would you get my
hopes up?"

"I'm helping you enough. Besides, seeing you get upset is
kinda cute," Knox replies with a sly grin.

I can feel the heat rushing up my neck and into my
cheeks.

Lloyd rolls his eyes. "You flirting is charming and all, but
we do need to help her get out of here. Plus, dragons kill
and eat people, bro. We gotta get that thing fed too so it
doesn't annihilate the entire island," Lloyd says around the
half-chewed food in his mouth as he looks to Knox beside
him.

"He's right, but Shea hunts at night. She will feed off wild
animals, birds, and things like that. She knows the rules;
she won't kill any humans, and she will stay on the ground."

"So, she won't eat people?" Knox asks.

"No, she doesn't eat people," I reiterate. "I rode her here and I'm a person," I say, my tone flat as I gesture to myself to illustrate my point.

"Riiiiiight," Knox draws out, seemingly unconvinced. "Does she breathe fire?" he asks.

"Negative. Dragons on our island don't do that," I answer simply, balling up my napkin and tossing it on my plate.

Knox squints his eyes at me like he doesn't believe a single thing I've said.

"Let's just get to the library, grab that book, and maybe we can dig up some information in there. I mean, I know it's fiction, but it's worth a shot?" Lloyd suggests, turning to his friend for confirmation.

"All right, let me grab the check, and let's head out," Knox agrees.

I watch Knox intently as he pulls out a brown leather wallet from his back pocket. He's so handsome in the daylight, it's unfair. I spot a silver ring looped through his bottom lip. I didn't see it in the dark when we first met, but I watch his tongue slowly move the ring back and forth as he concentrates on counting out his money. My eyes trail down his arms, catching how the veins in his arms flex, making his tattoos pop as he grips his wallet and shuffles the bills around. It's such a simple movement, but it's oddly satisfying. I bite my lip and look at his face to find him now staring at me, his expression dark as he raises an eyebrow.

"See something you like?" Knox's voice is smoky, almost sultry.

My stomach clenches, and I press my legs together as I look away. I snatch the clunky plastic cup from the table and gulp back some water to hide my face. Placing the cup back on the table, I clear my throat. "No, just curious as to what a check is." I shrug nonchalantly, trying to make it look like I wasn't just marveling at him.

Lloyd takes one last bite of toast and abruptly gets up and strides toward the exit.

Knox rolls his eyes as he tosses money on the table, then closes his wallet and slides it back into his pocket. He doesn't answer me. He simply stands up and follows Lloyd out the door.

It takes me a moment to get my legs moving since I'm still processing what the hell just happened between us. I shake my head, clearing my thoughts, and slowly rise from my seat to go meet them next to their motorcycles.

Knox places an ugly black helmet in my hands—the same one I wore on the way here—and I gently put it on over my braided hair. He swings one leg over the bike, taking a seat, then he turns a knob in between the handlebars and twists one handle. Suddenly the machine roars to life. I jump a bit because I'm not used to the loud noise it makes yet. I slide onto the bike behind him, intentionally maintaining some distance between our bodies as I hold on to the strap attached to the seat in front of me.

***

The entire ride to and from the library is one of the toughest I've ever been on, and that's including the first time I rode Shea. My body was so tense trying to be careful and not touch Knox but also not fall off. I am so grateful when we return to the boys' house that I honestly could cry tears of joy.

Knox guides the bike toward the garage, and I release my grip from the strap.

It's just the two of us since Lloyd left the library and went to "run errands"—I pray that includes getting food for the house. Without him here, I feel flustered with Knox, which is weird because I don't even know these guys.

I rip the helmet off my head and hand it to Knox before he can even dismount his bike.

"I'm beat. Can I get some sleep before I return to Shea?" I blurt out, trying to disguise how uncomfortable I had been sitting behind him.

Knox nods and steps off the bike. Awkwardly, I stand off to the side, twisting my hands together as I wait for him to remove his helmet and place them both on the handles of the bike. He moves toward the door that leads into the house from the garage, and I follow. He opens it and stands back as I walk inside, but I stop and press myself to the wall so he can enter and lead the way once more.

Knox storms through the doorway, pointing to the left as he says, "Here's the kitchen, but you've already seen that and the bathroom." He then points to the right, "Here's the living room, but you probably noticed that too."

I quicken my pace to keep up with him, but I'm unable to get a full view of either of the rooms he just indicated. We walk down the familiar hallway, and I recognize the bathroom at the far end with its door ajar.

Pausing at the first door on the right, Knox turns to face me. As his glaring stare roams my figure (in total distaste, I might add), I focus hard on schooling my features as the smell of the house smacks me in the face. It's not a terrible odor, but it's not all that enjoyable either: a mix of fresh marijuana and stale ale, along with some sort of zest-like scent . . . like orange or lemon.

Blech, what a bizarre smell.

"You can sleep in here," he says as he twists the knob and the door swings open. "We only have two bedrooms in the house. This one's mine, and the other is Lloyd's." Even though this is a nice gesture, his tone has turned cold, as if he hates every second of this.

"Perfect, thanks." I smile as I run my hands down my braid and tuck a wayward strand behind my ear.

"Yeah. If you need anything, I'll be in the garage." Knox pushes past me and walks back the way we came.

I step fully into the bedroom and gently shut the door. The white walls are littered with posters ranging from motorcycles to surfers on massive waves and, my personal favorite, women who are nearly naked sprawled across sandy beaches. I study the women and then look down at myself. Maybe that's why Knox doesn't care for me. Maybe I'm just not what he considers pretty . . .

I shake that notion from my head. I've never been the type to worry about what men thought about me, and now is the worst possible time to start. With a sigh, I kick off my sandals and stand at the end of Knox's bed, hesitant to crawl across it and under the big blue blanket on top. But I can't fight sleep any longer. My eyes are heavy, and the bed looks so inviting. I place my knees on the mattress and shuffle my way up to the pillows, stopping to bounce a bit to test the comfiness.

It'll do.

I tug the blanket down and slide underneath. Nuzzling into the pillow, I take in the smell of Knox enveloping me. The funk of the rest of the house doesn't reach me here. In his personal space, it's the scent of the ocean, a campfire, and an odd aroma of sweet vanilla or almond maybe . . . But before I can decide which, the room goes black.

A soft rapping on the door wakes me. I take in my surroundings and panic when I have no idea where I am. Jolting up, I look around the unfamiliar room, blinking hard to remember what happened—and then I hear his voice, and it all comes back to me.

"Louella, it's Knox. It's going to be dusk soon. We should probably get to Shea."

I clear the grogginess from my throat, "Ah, yeah, be out in a minute."

Slowly, I crawl out of Knox's bed and move to the door. Before I turn the knob, I check the mirror hanging on the back of the door. I quickly fix my borrowed clothes by running my hands down the front of my shirt and adjusting the baggy shorts so they are on straight. I open the door, and Knox is leaning on the frame with one arm above his head. I nearly crash into him but yank my head back in surprise just in time, keeping my feet planted. Our faces are only inches apart, and I can feel his breath on my forehead.

"I did some research about realm hopping—" he starts in a low voice.

"Realm jumping," I interject to correct him.

"Yeah, whatever," Knox grunts as he leans back and rolls his eyes. He takes his warmth with him, and in that instant, I long to feel it again. He flicks his lip ring with his tongue, as if he's bored with this conversation already and needs something else to do. "Come check it out when you're ready. I'm in the kitchen." His arm drops from the doorframe and he walks away without another look, leaving me alone in the doorway with this longing inside.

Before I can think too much about what that might mean, he returns with a towel in his hands. "Feel free to shower—you may need one," he says as he gently pushes the towel to my chest.

I take it from him, avoiding his gaze, and he's gone again. Mortification fills my gut as I consider his words, wondering how bad he thinks I look right now. My braid came undone while I was sleeping, and I can see the loose tresses out of the corner of my eye. I flip my hair back behind my shoulders in a feeble attempt to hide the frizz and realize that he must think I'm a frazzled hot mess. I lift my arm, giving my armpit a small whiff, and nearly choke on how putrid I smell. Unwilling to spend a second more in my current state, I leave Knox's bedroom and jog to the bathroom.

Feeling a little more put together after a decadently hot shower and with my unruly hair tamed as best as I can manage, I meet Knox at the table in the kitchen and take a seat next to him. He is staring at a rectangular device very intently, and its bright glow illuminates his profile. He has a book spread open on the table and papers scattered about, which look like handwritten notes.

"Want a drink?" he asks without looking up.

"Please," I mumble.

Knox is out of his chair in an instant, startling me, and he opens the door of a large, white (and quite loud) chest. He grabs a clear bottle from inside it, kicks the door closed behind him, and twists the top off before placing the bottle in front of me. I'm a little overwhelmed by all the unfamiliar things I've encountered in my short time here, but I'm not about to admit that to him. I pick up the bottle and look at it in my hands. The label reads, "Purified Drinking Water," so I take a big swig. The water is so cold that I can feel it run down my throat—it's incredibly refreshing.

"Okay, here's what I found online about astral myths and realms and all that shit."

I twist the cap back onto the bottle and set it down on the table in front of me. "What is 'online'? And what's that you're looking at?" I can't help but ask.

Knox looks up at the ceiling deep in thought, and I can tell he's formulating a response. After a moment, he taps the rectangular device in front of him. "This is a laptop—it's like a pen and paper, but digital. And 'online' . . . it's like a big network that you can connect your laptop to, and it has information and music, and you can connect with other people—all at your fingertips," he says as he wiggles his fingers, his hands hovering over the device.

"Wow, all right. So, like a library on your laptop?" I say, trying to understand.

"Yeah, I guess so. Anyway, here's what I found. Based on what the web says and our handy library book, Mystikal Times, it seems as though realm jumping can take place only during a new moon in a fire sign or a full moon in a fire sign. Which means," Knox ruffles through the stack of notes surrounding him and then pulls one out before continuing, "you came here last night, when there was a full moon in Leo, and you can realm jump again . . . let's see here . . ." He trails his finger along the piece of paper, stopping abruptly. "Hmm, September twenty-fifth is the next full moon in a fire sign. Aries, to be exact." Knox sits back in his chair and crosses his arms over his chest.

My heart starts beating loudly, and my ears are ringing. "I have to stay here for six fucking weeks?! This is insane!" I stand up and pace the length of the kitchen, biting my thumbnail as I wonder why Shea would do this. Or does she even realize what she's done? "Are you sure there's no other way around this? Are you absolutely sure?"

I stop pacing and look at Knox, who hasn't moved. In fact, he's got a scowl on his face, with his brows pinched together as if he's angry about this, like this is somehow my fault.

"Six weeks?" I state, more than ask, hoping he read something wrong while researching.

He rolls his eyes—which I'm getting pretty sick of by now. "Look, I don't want you here just as much as you don't want to be here, but I'm sure the six weeks will go by fast and then you can just go home."

"It's not that simple!" I start pacing the kitchen again.

Knox throws his hands up. "Explain then," he fires back.

"I'm getting married in a week and a half; I'm becoming a queen! If I'm not there and I just casually miss my wedding, there could be a full-on war. There must be another way home . . . or a loophole or something."

I stop and stare at Knox for answers, but nothing comes out of his mouth. We watch each other, neither of us moving except for the flexing of his jaw muscles as he grinds his molars together and the rapid rise and fall of my chest as panic grips me.

Knox finally slams the laptop shut, grabs his keys off the table, and stands. In a few long strides, he's at the door. But before he leaves through it, he turns and says, "I'll meet you in the black car outside. We are going to see your dragon."

My eyes are wide in shock, and I'm staring at the door he left ajar. But with no other ideas as to what the hell I should do now, I follow him to the car.

We ride in silence as the road curves and we're driving toward the setting sun in the distance. The small sliver of light still sitting above the horizon is piercing through the window and into my eyes. I turn away, and my vision is filled with spots. I carefully study Knox while he flicks switches, turns the wheel, and lays his hand on the knob that sits between us as he jerks it around with purpose. The car is loud, just like his motorcycle, but the music playing throughout the vehicle is kind of sweet—which is the opposite of what I expected. I guess I assumed he would listen to something raucous like the motors he seems so fond of, but a ukulele fills the air, accompanied by a soft, crooning voice. He must feel my stare because he flicks his eyes my way but keeps his head straight forward. I quickly avert my gaze to the right and look out the window.

For the rest of the ride, I try to think of ways to get out of here. Maybe I could do some research of my own . . . but I wouldn't know where to even begin to look. I make a mental list detailing the pros and cons of being stuck in this world.

Cons:

1. I'll miss my wedding day and becoming a queen . . . and potentially instigating a war.

2. I'll miss my family.

3. Shea won't be able to fly, which means no flying for me either.

4. I don't know anything about this world, and I'm stuck with two strangers, one of whom doesn't seem very fond of me.

Pros:

1. I'll delay getting married and becoming a queen.

2. I'll get to explore a new realm.

3. Knox's motorcycle is kind of like flying, just not as fun.

4. The stranger who seems to hate me is kind of hot . . .

No, stop it. That shouldn't be a pro.

Selfishly, I can't pick which list outweighs the other, and it's too late to decide now because we are pulling over to the side of the road, at the edge of the forest. After Knox turns the car off, we both hop out and I follow him into the wooded area, through the clearing, and back to the caves where we left Shea early this morning.

Relief floods me when I spot my dragon—she wasn't discovered, and she didn't take off and leave me here. Instead, she's outside the cave, chomping on something as we approach. The purple spikes along her spine are raised in warning, meaning she senses that someone is near. Shea whips her head around, and blood drips from her chin as she bares her teeth. When she notices it's me, she snorts and turns back to her meal. I can't quite tell what it is she's caught, but by the look of the coarse white fur, I would guess a goat.

"Ugh, that's fucking nasty," Knox says in disgust.

"Dragon's gotta eat. If you don't like it, then you can wait for me in the car," I snap.

"How can you watch her? Doesn't that gross a little princess like you out?"

"Mmmm, nope. I've seen worse things than this back home. Shea is relatively tame while eating, unlike some of the other dragons. One of our boys prefers organ meat, so he guts the animal before working on the rest of the carcass. It's quite disgusting, but who am I to yuck someone else's yum?"

"Wow, I've never known anyone to be immune to witnessing something like this, especially not a girl," Knox muses, trying to provoke me. "You really are from a totally different world."

"Yeah, I totally am."

I notice Shea is still wearing her harness and bridle, so I gently tap on her hindquarter to get her to lie down. Now that she's at arm level, I can reach the buckles to remove the riding equipment. As I work the saddle off her back, Knox watches intently.

"Is the man you're marrying a warrior?" he asks with a hint of irritation in his voice.

I huff out a laugh. "Malcolm? Yeah, he is. All the men are trained warriors by the time they turn eighteen. I mean, unless they have an ailment that prevents them from being able to fight or ride. Then they take on another role within the military. For Castle Waimea, Papa ensures that everyone in the village has a role—I bet it's not that different at Castle Hana, where Malcolm is from."

Knox clears his throat before pushing further, "Do you want to get married and be a queen?"

I pause while I consider how to respond. Do I keep my answer vague? Or do I divulge all my thoughts about my arranged marriage to someone who's hardly more than a stranger, the expectations from my family and Malcolm's, and the significance of this treaty between our castles? Resuming my task of removing Shea's bridle, I choose vagueness.

"I guess. I'm not really sure. I don't know Malcolm that well, and I love my freedom—but Malcolm's easy on the eyes, and I think he will respect me, for the most part."

I walk Shea's riding equipment into the caves and tuck it

away. When I come back out, Knox is wearing the same repulsed expression he had when Shea was eating.

"Wait—so because he's hot, you're fine with marrying him? That's fucked."

I stop and cross my arms. I'm uncomfortable with this conversation. No one has asked me how I feel about marrying Malcolm, and I honestly haven't told anyone . . . well, other than Chester.

"I don't have a choice. It's an arranged marriage between Castle Waimea and Castle Hana—a power move, and I'm just a pawn in the game. Good princesses do what they are told, or something like that." I shrug my shoulders, hoping to end the discussion.

"Are you really the good-girl type, koa?" He flicks his lip ring, and the motion causes me to bite my bottom lip.

"What do you mean?" I ask, befuddled.

"Let's get this show on the road. We should probably grab you some clothes that fit if you are going to be staying here for six weeks." Knox begins the walk back to the car, ignoring my question.

I turn and give Shea a good pat. As many times as I have seen her eat, I will confess (to myself only) that it is kind of gross—so I avoid giving her snout rubs.

"I'll be back tomorrow, girl. Keep a low profile. We have six weeks here, so let's not get caught until then. You're still in trouble for this."

Shea turns to me as she licks her face clean. Her pale eyes blink at me and it almost looks like she's smiling, but dragons don't smile . . . I know that. She nods in acknowledgment and gets back to her meal. I can hear her tongue lapping against the goat carcass, and an involuntary shudder of revulsion courses through me.

The sun has fully set by the time I make it back to the car where Knox is waiting, and we leave Shea for the night.

SEVEN

CHESTER PALA DELPHINE

Castle Hana, Kapu Island

I can see the stone structure of Castle Hana approaching as Zeus soars above the water, hugging the coastline. There are five of us—three guards, Luke, and myself—flying in a V formation on our way to discuss the news regarding Louella's disappearance with the Royce family. Luke is my wingman, flying to the right of Zeus and me, while the remaining three guards are dispersed behind us, two on my left and one on Luke's right. This will be an uncomfortable conversation at best. At worst, well . . . the five of us are equipped to defend ourselves in case things really take a turn and we need to make a swift exit. Unfortunately, I decided to sacrifice the size of our weaponry to make it harder for their royal guards to detect, but that means we have less to work with. Most likely, they will outnumber us because their military is probably on high alert, but at least we won't go down without a fight.

From above, I look around the grounds for Castle Hana's dragon caves. I know from our caves at Castle Waimea that there is usually a large clearing nearby for takeoffs and landings. Once I spot them, I signal Luke with my fingers to the area where we can land. He nods and then swirls his hand in the air to grab the other riders' attention, then he points to the landing spot.

As we descend closer to the open field, I notice three figures hustling out of the castle. We sent word that we would be coming, but I assumed they would at least let us land before they bombarded us with questions.

By the time my boot hits the ground, the king is already standing only inches away from me.

Hardly waiting for me to turn and face him, Victor starts his inquisition. "Where did she go? Malcolm and Louella are getting married in a week." His voice is shrill and grating.

Holding Zeus's reins in one hand, I clench my other fist at my side since I already want to knock Victor out. Glancing around him, I notice the queen and the prince are rushing up to join him. Malcolm's handsome features are filled with worry and doubt. Maribeth's thin face is filled with disgust, as if she can't bear the sight of us being on her land or in her presence.

From behind me, I hear Luke whisper, "On guard," and the dragons stomp their feet against the ground as they obey his order.

Maribeth lifts her lip and sneers at the command. She reminds me of an agitated dog, ready to bite at any moment.

"Castle Waimea is bringing word that Princess Louella Aponi Delphine has been reported as missing. We have search parties in every village, forest, sea, and sky, as you have heard, but nothing has been reported on her whereabouts in two days," I announce. My heart stutters a bit as I speak, realizing that she's gone—it's more real once I say it out loud.

Maribeth scoffs in disbelief; Victor throws his hands in the air. But Malcolm remains unreadable and a bit distant.

"We already heard. We want to know what Castle Waimea will be doing for us since our arrangement has fallen through," Victor says in a condescending tone.

I look over to the prince again to see if there's any solution he can offer. After all, it's his bride who went missing. His face slumps into a frown, which surprises me. I thought for sure he would be relieved not to have to marry a stranger.

Malcolm notices me observing him, and he steps forward, placing a hand on his father's shoulder.

"Papa, I think we should give it more time. I think Lou will be back. Maybe she just needed some time alone to think. This is scary for both of us." Malcolm's voice is gentle as he speaks but also reassuring, as if he believes in what he is saying.

Victor wiggles Malcolm's hand off his shoulder and his face flushes to an unnatural shade of red as he rounds on his son, leaning closer to Malcolm's face. "I am still the king, and you will treat me as such. Do not disrespect me or my authority," he hisses through clenched teeth in a failed attempt to be discreet while threatening his son.

Malcolm steps back a foot and lowers his head in submission.

I open my clenched fist, palm flat and fingers pointing down, giving the men and dragons behind me a warning that this may escalate.

Victor turns back to us as Maribeth hastily walks forward to close the distance she initially kept between him as she takes his side.

"This isn't good enough. We are giving Castle Waimea two weeks to bring us Princess Louella, and if she is not standing before me in that time, then we will have no choice but to seize your castle, your land, and your dragons," Victor states as spittle flies from his mouth.

Maribeth juts out her jaw in agreement, fully supporting her greedy little husband. She finally speaks: "You should be grateful for the opportunity to make this right. Our offer is more than generous, considering we'll almost certainly need to rearrange the wedding . . . if you even find her."

The queen's callousness shouldn't surprise me, but it does somehow. I can't stand to watch her exaggerated facial expressions any longer, so I shift my gaze back to her husband without acknowledging anything she's said. Staring into his dark eyes, I can't stop the feeling of utter loathing bubbling up inside me. I want to spit on his cheek and punch that smug look off his face—but instead I adjust my leather vest and banish the thought from my head.

I clear my throat to make sure that my dislike for the Royce family isn't present in my words before responding, "She will return, and once she does, she will be walking down the aisle with your son. I will deliver the message of your terms to Chief Rowland."

Victor lets out a self-satisfied humph before pivoting away to trudge back to the castle with his dutiful wife kissing his ass behind him.

Malcolm, however, is still standing in the same place. He finally lifts his head and glances over his shoulder to ensure that his parents are not within earshot before he looks me in the eyes.

"Is she all right?" he asks.

I don't know how much I can tell him because I don't know where his heart truly lies—with his parents or with Louella.

"She will be. Just keep an eye out and let us know if you hear anything." I give Malcolm a quick smile of comfort, even though I can't be sure of the words I just spoke.

The prince—my sister's fiancé—watches us prepare to take off, and I don't turn to see how long he stands in that clearing after we've launched into the sky.

During the entire ride home, I can hear nothing but my pulse rushing in my ears. I knew there was a chance of war, but now it's official and it's terrifying.

"Are you sure you want to do this?"

It's the third time Luke has asked me on our walk down to the village. Immediately after we landed back at Castle Waimea and I delivered Victor's message to the chief, I forced Luke to take me to the realm jumper so we could speed up the process of (hopefully) finding Louella.

Luke has fallen behind me on the path since he's still unsure about revealing the villager's identity to me. I'm stomping ahead anyway, because I have no problem knocking on every door until I find the person I'm looking for.

"I can't believe you keep asking me that when there's a very real possibility that we will be going to war." My tone is clipped, but his question is starting to get on my nerves. It's as if he doesn't understand how important this is to me, to my family, to our village.

"Yeah, but there's also a possibility that Louella didn't realm jump, and we are wasting our time," he argues.

"Well, if she didn't, then we can check it off the list after we've at least explored the possibility," I counter.

"Plus, I'm not even sure they are going to tell you how to do it because you're the prince."

I let out a low, frustrated growl as I spin around to face Luke, halting him in his tracks.

"Stop it, already! Just let me do this." I'm practically shouting. I don't wait for his response as I turn on my heels and continue to walk.

Luke collides with my shoulder as he lengthens his strides to pull ahead of me since I truly have no idea whose house we are going to.

"Fine," he grumbles barely within earshot. After that, we exchange not another word or look as I follow him closely.

We walk in silence as we approach the end of the main gravel road. A quaint home sits quietly on the edge of one of the shortest pathways in the village, which is convenient—some of the pathways extend up to eight miles, and I don't have time for that with my patience evaporating by the minute. As we approach the home, I notice dim lights shining through the small windows, and a sense of déjà vu strikes me. I eye the building, racking my brain trying to recall if I've been here before.

No, it's not possible. I hardly ever go to the edges of the village . . .

Luke steps up to the threshold and, without hesitation, gives the solid-wood door two quick knocks. But before the door swings open, it dawns on me that I have been here before.

Tallulah Belmonte wrenches the door ajar and stands at the threshold, but her initial welcoming smile fades into confusion. She looks from Luke to me as our eyes clash. Her hair is in a messy bun atop her head, which she's wrapped with a scarf covered in Wiki designs. She's wearing her usual color of vivid red; this time, it's an embroidered top with a long embroidered skirt to match. The lights from inside cast her in shadow, making it hard to see her facial features clearly—but they are imprinted on my brain just like any other loved one I know because she's like family to me.

"Ch-Chester! Lucas!" she stammers. "What brings you here?" Tallulah looks over at Luke, no doubt wondering why the two of us are on her doorstep, and if she's in trouble.

Luke just shrugs, offering her no hints as to what this visit will entail.

Now I understand why he asked me so many times if I was sure about this. He was afraid I would be upset learning that the Belmonte sisters are the rebellious realm jumpers my parents aren't very fond of. Truthfully, I couldn't care less. As long as they give me the information I'm seeking so I can follow this lead and hopefully save Ella, then they can rest assured that I will keep their little secret.

I step forward, bringing myself shoulder to shoulder with Luke. "Luke told me that you may have information on how to realm jump, and I want that information."

Tallulah hesitates as she searches my eyes, clearly debating whether it's safe for her to answer. We stare at each other for several seconds before she slowly starts to close the door in our faces, but I kick my foot out to prevent her from shutting it all the way.

She lets out an exasperated sigh, cracking the door open once more. "This isn't a good idea, Ches. If Camilla and I get caught spilling realm-jumping information to the prince, we will both be exiled from the village, and we can't afford that—we would have nowhere to go."

"I'm exhausting all possibilities while I search for Louella, even if that means crossing the chief and the queen to find her. I'm not leaving here until I get what I need."

Tallulah taps her thumb on the door as she contemplates her decision. She looks down at her feet, and I can almost see the wheels turning in her head. I know she's going through all the things that could go wrong with letting us in and sharing what she knows with me. Tallulah is Mama's best friend, and she would never betray her—but she also loves my sister and me like we are her own children. I know she would do anything to help find Louella.

Finally, Tallulah looks up at me. With a frown on her face, she names her conditions. "You have to promise that if you get caught or your parents ask where you got this information, it wasn't from us. Swear to me that you'll tell them you read about it somewhere."

"You have my word that you and Camilla will be safe. I won't let anything happen to you both," I state firmly. I will not let Tallulah and Camilla go down for what I'm about to do. "I'll pay you both for the information, if that makes this a fair trade?" I ask.

Tallulah sighs, "I don't want your money. I never have. I just want to make sure I don't lose my family and friends over this."

"Please help me, Tallulah." My plea is almost inaudible. I'm desperate now; I need to find Louella. Not only because she's the key to stopping the potential mass destruction of our village, but also because, selfishly, it feels like a part of me is missing and it's killing me. I want to find her to make sure she's not . . . gone forever. My eyes begin to burn, but I swallow down the emotions I've been keeping inside, blinking back the tears.

After several more seconds of contemplation, she opens the door fully and gestures for Luke and me to enter.

I hastily step through and Luke follows, ducking to avoid hitting his head on the low doorframe. Once inside, I scan around to see where Camilla is, but I don't spot her. Tallulah shuts the door and saunters over to the kitchen.

"You boys want some tea?" she asks as she bustles around.

"Sure, I'd love a cup," Luke responds as he pulls a chair out from the kitchen table and plops down.

I follow suit and take a seat next to him. As I slide my chair in, he lightly places his hand on my forearm, grabbing my attention.

"I'm sorry," he whispers, leaning in close. He offers me a sympathetic smile, and I can't really stay mad at him now that I understand why he's been so cagey about all this.

"Me too," I whisper back with a gentle smirk.

Tallulah slams the teapot on the stove, interrupting our hushed moment, and strides over to the stairs. "Camilla! We have guests!" she shouts, causing the two of us to jump.

Luke slaps his hand over his heart and shakes his head. "Fuck, that startled me."

I can't help but laugh at his reaction.

"Oh, sorry. I forgot how loud I can be." Tallulah turns from the banister and heads back toward the stove. I can hear footsteps from above, but they are slow, and it sounds like Camilla is dragging something along with her. She appears at the top of the stairs, her raven-colored hair is always cut short and sits just below her jawline. Like her sister, Camilla also wears a sleeveless, strapless embroidered top, but hers is an amber color paired with matching embroidered cropped pants. I pause when I catch sight of her ankle covered in a wooden contraption resembling a cast—and then I remember the accident.

"Do you need help?" I ask her, but she shakes her head.

She staggers down the stairs and grips the railing the entire way, stepping with her uninjured foot first and then placing her bandaged foot next to it. Once she's on even ground, she hobbles over to the kitchen and drops down in the chair facing me.

"What are you two troublemakers doing here?" she asks with a childlike grin. Camilla is a tiny lady, but her personality packs a punch—Ella loves that about her. Even though Camilla is the older sister and, based on my personal experience, I'd assume she would be the serious, no-nonsense sibling, she was always the "fun" aunt when Ella and I were growing up . . . and it makes sense that she would be a realm jumper. She's headstrong and wild, the complete opposite of Tallulah . . . sort of like Ella and me.

I hear water pouring from the kettle, and a moment later, Tallulah spins away from the kitchen counter with two teacups and places them in front of Luke and me. She walks over to the empty seat next to her sister and slowly sits down.

Luke and I look to Tallulah as Camilla's eyes dart among the three of us.

No one has answered Camilla's question yet. Her smile fades as her brows pinch together. "Did something else happen at the castle?"

Luke finally speaks up. "Castle Hana is threatening to seize everything we have if Louella does not arrive within two weeks to go through with the wedding."

Camilla's frown twists with confusion and she looks at me. "What does that have to do with us?" she questions, pointing between herself and Tallulah.

"I need to know how to realm jump. There's a possibility that Ella may have traveled to another realm by accident or intentionally to run away," I explain.

Camilla shakes her head, "Oh fuck no, I'm not telling you shit." She crosses her arms over her chest and looks to her sister.

Tallulah sighs, "Camilla, if you don't tell them, then I will, and that could go badly since I don't know all the ins and outs like you do."

Camilla doesn't respond as she bites her bottom lip and her nostrils flare.

All of a sudden, Camilla shoves her chair back and hastily limps over to the kitchen counter. I'm about to jump up and stop her from leaving us, but instead, I watch as she opens a drawer and pulls out a stack of books, along with a few pens. She makes her way back to us and slams the books down. Picking up the thin notebook on top, she tosses it in my direction and then rolls a pen along the table, which comes to rest against the spine of the notebook.

"You'll want to take notes," Camilla deadpans.

I scramble to open the book and grab the pen, eagerly waiting for the Belmonte sisters to begin their lesson on realm jumping so that I can find my sister.

EIGHT

LOUELLA APONI DELPHINE

Kailani Bay, Gemcove Island

It's been a week since Knox and Lloyd found Shea and me in the forest. According to Knox's findings regarding realm jumping, I'm trapped here for roughly five more weeks. The boys don't have a single calendar in the house, but since I last spoke to Knox about it all, I've been counting down the days.

That first night after Knox and I visited Shea, he was kind enough to take me to a market to grab some new clothes and necessities for the duration of my stay. He kept calling the market a "store," since I guess that's what they're known as here. It was one massive room with the most garish lighting I've ever seen, but it was full of all sorts of goods—more than anyone could ever need. I was very overwhelmed the minute we walked in, but Knox helped me find some clothes, and I got leggings in all different colors, which made up for how hopeless I'd been feeling . . . at least a little bit. I've been finding it hard to smile since I landed here, but small things like fresh clothing, a toothbrush, and a much-needed hairbrush helped alleviate some of the added stress I'd been carrying. I'm thankful to Knox, even though half of the time I get the sense that he hates me. Still, he paid for everything, and, in his own unique way, he's done a lot so that I could at least try and feel somewhat comfortable while I'm here.

Being at the market made me understand just how out of place I am in this realm. I've never been somewhere and not known what basic things are or how they work. Knox found it quite enjoyable watching me jump and flinch at the loud people and blaring gadgets all around me.

While I waited for Knox to pay for the goods, I took the opportunity to observe the people in this realm—and they are so unlike my people. Everyone seems to be in their own heads without a care for anyone else around them, which is not how almost everyone on Kapu Island behaves. The girls my age are wildly different here too. When I looked around at the other girls, they all seem so . . . so beautiful. Next to them, I feel so bland, with annoyingly frizzy, crazy hair and pimples on my chin.

Aside from the otherworldly gorgeous girls, I did notice that I can blend in with the crowd—which is nice, considering I'm stopped and spoken to wherever I go back home, being the chief's daughter and all . . . but part of me misses the interactions, the smiles, and the pleasant banter from a stranger. Life here seems all hustle and bustle; everyone's in a rush.

Our trip to the market was the last time I spoke to Knox. He has been very generous, letting me sleep in his room while he crashes on the couch, but we never cross paths. He gets up before me every morning, and I'm usually awoken by his car or motorcycle roaring to life as he heads out for the day. He doesn't return until I'm back in his room ready for bed . . . but I've been sneaking to the bathroom in the middle of the night to see if I can spot him on the couch.

For the past five nights, I've crept the short distance down the hallway and peeked into the living room to find that Knox sleeps on the couch closest to the door to the garage. I think because it's longer than the other two in the room, and he can stretch his legs out fully. His face is peaceful, with his eyes lightly closed and mouth slightly agape as his chest slowly rises and falls with his breathing. He usually has one arm resting on his belly and the other slung over his head. I don't stare too long—I'm not a creep . . . I don't think. It's just comforting to know he's there and I'm not alone in the house—or that's what I tell myself.

My days are mostly spent pacing the house or sitting in the backyard on a rickety metal chair with a scratchy blue-and-white woven cushion, watching the ocean in the distance as I wonder what's happening back home. I hope they are searching for me and they know in their hearts that I didn't run away intentionally.

Reminiscing about my whole family together and how it felt being surrounded by people who knew me and cared about me brings on pangs of loneliness. But I can't deny the relief that clouds my mind knowing I'm not trapped inside with Mama all day learning how to be a queen in a tight ensemble with sticky hair and a greasy, makeup-caked face. The thought makes me shudder every time, and I shift my focus to the ocean again, enjoying the rumbling sound of the waves and my ass on this itchy chair—I'll take this over that any day.

I attempted to read the Mystikal Times novel to see if I could uncover something Knox may have missed, but after hours of reading about faeries and ogres—and a tiny bit about unrealistic dragons—I came up empty-handed. Lloyd, who has been endlessly patient with me (unlike his housemate), tried to show me how to work the laptop and search for more resources online, but that didn't last long. I kept getting too frustrated trying to click and type and all that weird stuff, so I gave up. Knox's research is the best (and only) information we've got, leaving me no choice but to endure the days ahead of me here on Gemcove Island.

Surprisingly, Lloyd has been a bright spot for me. He is super helpful and kind, and he keeps offering to introduce me to new things—that is, when he's not busy working as a clerk at a shop in town. A couple of nights ago, after his shift, he brought home a bunch of food from the market and attempted to show me around the kitchen. He cooked me a grilled cheese sandwich and heated up some soup from a tin can with a red-and-white label and the word Campbell's printed across it.

Watching Lloyd empty the contents of the can into a pot, I nearly lost my appetite. It came out like thick sludge until he added some water to it. Much to my surprise, the soup was actually tasty. Since then, I've had my fill of grilled cheese sandwiches and canned soup.

Goddess, I miss the food at Castle Waimea.

Every night after he is done working and we've had dinner, Lloyd has taken me to check on Shea. Tonight, I'm already sitting in Lloyd's silver-colored car, ready to go, when he slides in behind the wheel. He turns the key to start the engine, and a thumping beat blasts through the vehicle. I'm taken by surprise and slap my hands over my ears at the sound. My reaction seems to fluster Lloyd, and he immediately twists a knob to make it quiet again.

"Sorry about that," he says sheepishly, like he feels bad.

"What was that?" I ask, still a little shaken.

"It's called hip-hop—it's a style of music. I swear it sounds best when it's loud like that."

My eyes widen and I give him skeptical look. I'll have to take him at his word.

With the music low, just enough to fill the comfortable silence, I settle in for the drive. I'm learning that I enjoy being in Lloyd's presence. He's always joking and trying to help me feel more at ease, and it's working. On our trips to see Shea, he fires off questions for me to answer, such as what it's like to live in my realm, what the history of the island is, what I do as a princess, and what the dragons are like. I tell him everything, including all about riding a dragon, and he is enthralled by my life. It's nice to talk to someone about my home—pride blossoms in my chest, but I also yearn to get back to Kapu Island.

"So, what's your favorite food back home?" Lloyd asks as he pulls the car off to the side of the road. We park in the same place every night, and I've learned the way through the forest to the caves where Shea hides out.

I smile and tap my finger on my chin as I think about what I'm craving from the castle kitchen right now. "Pineapple cake," I answer easily, beaming at him.

Lloyd chuckles, "We have a lot of that here. I'm sure we can grab a slice after this, if you want."

"Oh my goddess, yes! Yes! I would love that." My voice is so high pitched, I'm shocked the glass windows haven't shattered. I clap my hands together because I can't contain my excitement.

"Wow, okay. Note to self: pineapple cake makes Louella happy."

"Ugh, yes. It makes me very happy," I agree. "No offense, but I'm starting to get sick of soup and grilled cheese."

Lloyd jerks the lever between us into the "P" position, and I know that's my cue to unbuckle the strap across my chest, just as I've seen him perform this action every night this week.

Neither of us talk as we climb out of the car. Lloyd jogs to the front of the vehicle and flicks on a light in his hand so we can carefully navigate the path in the woods.

As I close the door, its hinges make a crunching noise, but I don't say anything. I move to join him and we set out on our walk through the forest.

Lloyd's car is not as sleek or flashy as Knox's, but being able to chat easily instead of awkwardly listening to the roar of Knox's car engine is a nice change. Weirdly though, I find myself missing Knox and his noisy machines . . . I'm drawn to him. My attempts to deny his pull on me have been pointless. Without trying, he has an unusual way of enveloping me in an odd sense of familiarity; it's like I know him and we are old friends. He reminds me a lot of Chester, and their personalities are comparable: they take no bullshit, they're brutally honest, and they make you feel safe. That thought makes me grin, and suddenly the idea of asking Lloyd questions about Knox is at the forefront of my mind. I often wonder how Knox fills his days, and I'm positive that his best friend and housemate would have to know.

I break the silence. "Can I ask you a question about Knox?"

"Oh, here we go," Lloyd mumbles to himself ahead of me.

I stumble slightly at his hushed comment, and he notices.

"Girls always want to know about Knox," he says over his shoulder. "He's all mysterious and sexy, but the truth is, I don't know much about him. Honestly."

I wish I could study Lloyd's facial expressions as we walk, but from the tone of his voice, he almost sounds exasperated, as if Knox is all he talks about when speaking to women. With my eyes focused on the ground before me, attempting not to trip again, I nearly miss a low-hanging branch. But Lloyd is there to catch it, swooping in to pull it away before it smacks me in the face.

"How? I mean, you live with him . . . You must know something about him. Like, what does he do all day? What does he do at night? What's his family—"

"Whoa, whoa, whoa, young lady," Lloyd cuts me off, sidling up next to me to walk side by side. "That's a lot of questions. I'll tell you what I know, but what do I get in return?"

I gently slap Lloyd's arm, and he laughs.

"You get a gourmet grilled cheese sandwich and a bowl of hot tomato soup. Also, you can't be that much older than me to be calling me 'young lady.'" My smile is mischievous, and he flashes a wide grin my way.

"Well, you just seem so little, being lost in this world 'n' stuff. It's cute—really. And I'll take you up on the grilled cheese and soup! The young padawan has learned the way from the Jedi master," Lloyd says in a mock-serious tone.

"Uh, suuurre," I drawl, confused over whatever he just said.

Lloyd sighs, "Yeah, never mind. I forgot you wouldn't know anything about Star Wars."

"Nope," I say, popping the p, and I lift one brow toward my hairline in utter confusion.

"Moving on then! Where do I begin with Knox Campbell?" Now that Lloyd is beside me, I can faintly see him squint his eyes, thinking hard.

"Campbell . . . like the soup?" I interject.

"Hmm, guess I never noticed that before." He pauses before shaking his head and starting again, "We met about five years ago at Dave's Garage. I brought my car in for an inspection, and Knox was the mechanic who took it back into the garage."

I hold my hand up for Lloyd to stop talking, and he does.

"Wait. What's a garage and a mechanic and an inspector?"

"Oh yeah," he says as realization hits him, "I have to explain these things. It's an inspection. The car we rode in has to get an okay to be driven on the road legally, so I take it to a garage, which is a building where cars get worked on, and a mechanic, or someone who specializes in fixing cars, will check it out. They approve the car for driving, give you a sticker, and send you on your way."

"Ahhhhh, all right. So Knox is a mechanic? He works on cars? And please, can you tell me why you people say 'oh kay'? What does that even mean?" I shake my head and roll my eyes in frustration. I've noticed that Lloyd and Knox are always throwing the words oh and kay in each sentence they speak.

Lloyd chuckles, "It's just another way to say 'all right' or 'very well' or 'okeydokey' . . ." He lifts his shoulders like he's out of comparisons and I should be understanding him by now.

I let out a snort. "'Got it' would have been a good one to use for your explanation, but okeydokey," I say with a tinge of sarcasm, "I understand."

"Anyway, to answer your questions, yes, Knox is a mechanic. Hence why he has a Pontiac Trans Am with a sick custom paint job of a frickin' eagle on the hood . . . and I have a Nissan Versa with creaky-ass doors." He lifts his shoulder in an apathetic gesture.

I don't comprehend the difference between the two cars, but I don't really care about those details.

"Like I was saying, when I brought my car in, Knox and I got to talking while I waited and watched him work. I told him I grew up in Kailani Bay and live in a house that my grandparents left me when they passed away a few years ago. That's when he asked if I knew anyone who had a place available for rent—" He catches himself before continuing, "Uhh, you know, like when you pay someone to live in the house they own? Anyway, the buddy he was staying with was moving, and Knox had to be out by the end of the month. I figured I would offer him my other room. He seemed like a nice guy, and I needed help paying the mortgage—which is kind of the same thing as rent—so it was a win-win."

"Oh, well, that was anticlimactic." My posture hunches with disappointment as I think about how little Lloyd knows about Knox.

"Well, as I said, Knox is mysterious. He doesn't say much. He mostly works all day and then sleeps. But when he has free time, he usually works on his bike or car. Sometimes he surfs, and sometimes he comes out drinking with me and my friends—but only on Wednesdays. That's typically when he picks up a lady and brings her home for some fun."

I frown, but Lloyd can't see my expression in the dark. "Oh? What kind of fun?"

He bursts out into laughter, and my cheeks flush as I suddenly comprehend what he was insinuating: sex. "Some fun" means sex.

"You know, like doin' it? C'mon, don't tell me you've never, you know, had sex before . . ."

I remain quiet for several seconds as I follow Lloyd's lead along the uneven wooded path. My face is hot and red with embarrassment. I should have paused to think before I spoke.

"Erm, no. I have to wait for marriage where I'm from," I answer in a hushed voice. I'm ashamed to acknowledge my inexperience even to a stranger.

"Wow! That's old school. Well, that's kind of outdated around here," Lloyd replies—loudly enough to carry through the stillness of the trees.

His comment sends my heart plummeting into my belly, making me feel ill. A frown forms on my face while my mind floods with images of Knox having "some fun" in bed with someone—the same bed I'm currently residing in every night. The visions keep coming and I can't stop them: Knox kissing another girl, touching her, smiling at her . . . but they finally vanish when Lloyd speaks up once again.

"Back when we met, Knox told me he had been on his own for about a year already. He lost both of his parents when he was younger, and something about a brother too, or maybe a sister? I dunno, but he decided to relocate and start a new life. I thought that maybe he was wanted for a crime or something, but I think that whatever happened to his family has caused him to become a shell of himself. Not to be sappy, but I think he forgot what love is, or he's just one of those guys who doesn't fall in love. I don't know. It's not something we talk about, nor do I think about it often. I've got my own shit—ya know?"

I'm no longer jealous of random girls, as my jealousy is replaced with sadness. I could never imagine my life without my parents or Chester. I think of how lonely and hollow Knox must feel without anyone in the world to love or to show him how to love. Admittedly, I've never been in love with someone romantically . . . so maybe I don't know what that is truly like. I give Lloyd a small hum to acknowledge that I'm still listening to him as I ponder the complexities of a boy who is all about me one minute and then wants nothing to do with me the next.

"Anyway, he kind of just keeps to himself. I do most of the talking, and Knox just listens. It works for us," Lloyd says as we finally approach the caves.

We both stop and scan the area for Shea, wondering why she's not in her usual spot. At this time of night, she's taken a liking to hunkering down to the right of the cave entrance—I assume it's so she can watch out for any unwanted visitors and make an escape if necessary.

Lloyd slowly points the beam of light around, illuminating the rocky cave entrance and the nearby trees, but she's nowhere to be found.

"She's probably in the little cave back there," I suggest, pointing over to the rock formation I hid her in the first night we landed here. We walk over cautiously, but as I make my way inside, Lloyd doesn't move. Instead, he just shines the light into the hole from where he stands.

Hmph, scaredy-cat.

I still can't see her fluorescent-purple spikes or her icy-blue eyes.

I exit the cave a bit bewildered and see Lloyd standing rail straight. His eyes are wide in terror, and the light is trembling in his hand. I dip my chin to hide my chuckle when I see Shea hunched behind him. Her nose is about an inch from the back of his head, and she's puffing out a loud snort with each release of her breath.

"Wha-what is it doing?" Lloyd whimpers as he squeezes his eyes shut.

"She's just trying to scare you," I say as a little laugh escapes me.

"It's not funny. Tell it to stop." Lloyd has found some courage now, his voice loud, though he looks like he may cry.

"Cut it out, Shea," I command lazily.

My stubborn dragon gives one last snort followed by a small, shrill squawk into Lloyd's ear.

Lloyd hikes his shoulders up high and squeezes his eyes closed even tighter.

"She's not going to hurt you."

Shea bows her head to the ground and skulks around him. Her cold eyes stay trained on me. I can tell she's bored and looking for a little fun, but she can't be seen here and she understands that. Shea comes to a stop in front of me, raises her head, and sits back on her hind legs. It's incredible how agile dragons can be yet how stoic they can remain, to the point where you can't even see their chests moving while they breathe—she resembles a statue, like she's not even real. She takes a deep breath while the purple-lined spikes along her back flex and twitch like fingers as they stretch out and then curl in, making little clicking noises like cicadas on a hot summer day.

"Blech!" Lloyd retches like he's going to be sick. "What the hell is it doing with those spiky thingies?" he asks.

I step toward her and gently run my hand down her neck. I love the texture of dragon skin: it's smooth yet bumpy, reminding me of a favorite well-worn leather-bound book. Her black skin feels so familiar beneath my fingertips, and it's comforting to me.

"She's just letting you know that she's the boss."

"Ugh, she can be the boss. She's like Knox in dragon form."

I cackle at that, but he's not wrong. In the little time I've known him, I would have to agree that Knox is a bit like a dragon—always appearing calm on the outside, but an intensity rages and swirls within his eyes and you wonder whether he will consume you or leave you be.

***

Lloyd keeps his promise and takes me to grab a slice of pineapple cake after we visit with Shea.

We're at another restaurant, and this one looks like a tin box with bright, glowing lettering on the front that reads "Diamond Diner." The inside is so . . . fun. There's upbeat music, laughing people, neon-colored photos on the walls, and bright-red glittery seats. Again I'm reminded how loud everything is in this realm, even the colors. But for the first time, I find myself enjoying the experience.

Lloyd and I are ushered to what he told me is a booth. We're sitting across from each other, but I don't even notice him because I'm still taking in the sights and sounds of the diner ever since we entered through the door five minutes ago. I glance at the people in the booth next to ours, and my mouth drops open when I see the stacked plate of food set before them by a woman wearing a powder-blue dress and white apron—the same woman who placed the clear plastic cups with straws in front of Lloyd and me just after we sat down. I've never seen so much food for one person in my life. My stomach rumbles, and I'm tempted to tell Lloyd to forget the pineapple cake and give me that, but my thoughts come crashing to a halt when Lloyd breaks the silence.

"Hey, Knox is here!" Lloyd practically shouts. He waves his hand frantically, and I twist my neck to see Knox for myself.

I try to hide the anger in my eyes when I spot him and a blond-haired girl sitting together in a booth at the far end of the restaurant. They are closely snuggled up to one another, sharing the same bench while the one across from them remains vacant.

The girl has her long, bare legs draped over his lap as Knox holds the side of her thigh with one hand. His fingertips are grazing the edge of her short skirt. He looks up at Lloyd with a smile and nods, but when his eyes flick to mine, his expression switches to menacing—like he's pissed that I even exist.

I whip back around to face Lloyd. "Let's just get the cake and leave," I say quickly.

"Oh . . . yeah, yeah. We can take it home and eat it if you want?"

"Yeah, let's do that." I vigorously nod my head, suddenly desperate to get out of here.

"Cool," Lloyd agrees.

When the woman in the powder-blue dress returns, Lloyd orders two slices of cake "to go."

My neck prickles with the sensation of someone staring. I know it's Knox, but this weird pull I feel toward him, though intriguing, is starting to frighten me. I know nothing about him, he's not even that nice to me when we see each other, and yet I want him. I want him to hold on to my legs. I want to know him more than I want to know Malcolm . . . and that's alarming to me because soon enough, Malcolm will be my husband and my king.

I can't have Knox, and that makes me want him even more.

Turning my head and resting my chin on my shoulder, I try to make myself less conspicuous as I peer at them from the corner of my eye. But Knox catches the movement, and I can see his smirk.

Dammit—I failed.

I keep watching to see what his next move will be.

He gently dunks his finger into the white froth in the tall metal glass in front of him. When he pulls his finger out, it's dripping with the creamy substance, which is sliding over the giant ring he wears and down onto his palm. Knox winks at me and then locks his gaze on the girl beside him, bringing his finger to her lips. She opens wide, taking his entire finger into her mouth, along with the white cream, and I can see her cheeks hollow as she begins to suck. With a light touch, she wraps her hand around his and slowly moves his finger in and out of her mouth. When Knox finally tugs his hand away, he turns back to me and slowly runs his tongue up the same finger that was just in the girl's mouth.

I inhale a sharp breath, and before I can stop myself, I bite down my bottom lip and start sucking on it.

Knox bares a wide grin that stretches from ear to ear.

Embarrassed, I look away again and stare at the tabletop in front of me, keeping my head ducked as I clench my legs together. The pressure creates an odd friction that feels good, which makes me writhe in my seat. I clear my throat at how uncomfortable I am with all of this.

"Ready to head out?" Lloyd asks, and I'm startled by his voice. He's strumming his fingers on the lids of two containers, each with a cake slice inside, and I have no idea when they got here. In the moment, I had forgotten that Knox and I weren't the only ones in the diner.

"Yup," I say, jumping out of the booth in a rush to get to Lloyd's car.

The entire ride home, I am fidgeting in the seat. The nerves at the apex of my thighs are so sensitive that every vibration from the engine or bump in the road sends a tiny spark of pleasure jolting through my entire body. I have pent-up tension inside me that makes me want to scream, but I also want to laugh.

When we arrive back at the house, I burst through the door and hurry straight to Knox's room—leaving the pineapple cake in Lloyd's hands.

I need to be alone.

I slam Knox's door by accident, and I hear Lloyd shout from the kitchen, "'Night, Louella! The cake is in the fridge!"

This feeling used to come sometimes at night when I imagined Malcolm and how he had looked sparring on the training grounds, his built body glistening with sweat from the sun above. He would swipe his hand through his short toffee-colored locks, making his muscles flex. After our engagement was announced, I would touch myself in my bedroom to that exact daydream of him. I would imagine our first time together as I brought myself over the edge with pleasure, pretending that my hands were Malcolm's . . . And now I want to replace him with Knox.

I sit at the edge of the bed, realizing that rushing to Knox's room was a terrible idea when all I can smell is him and all I can picture is his tongue flicking his stupid fucking lip ring. I don't know why I wasn't jealous watching that girl suck his finger. Instead, it . . . it turned me on.

Warmth rushes to my clit as the memory of his finger in her mouth flashes back to me, and I can't take it any longer.

I lie back and slide my hand along my stomach, just below my navel. I hesitate, knowing that this is dangerous. Touching myself while thinking about another man who is not my fiancé? What a horrible idea. But my nerves are pulsing as shivers break out along my body . . . and I've never been one to follow the rules.

I slip my hand beneath the waistband of my leggings and to the wetness between my thighs. My breath catches as my finger swirls around my clit. It's so sensitive and plump—this won't take long at all. I close my eyes and imagine that my hand is Knox's; I picture the veins in his tattooed arms bulging as he works his fingers in and out of me. I bite my lip hard, almost drawing blood, as the tension builds low in my stomach. I fist his blanket with my other hand and pull it to my nose, breathing in the smell of him—sweet vanilla, campfire, and the ocean blending perfectly together—and that makes my heart flutter in my chest.

I wish this were real.

I imagine him kissing me between my thighs, his fingers replaced by his tongue. I wonder if I would feel his lip ring while he kissed my clit, and that thought makes my nipples harden as they rub against the fabric of my bra. I can't fight the sensation that's building inside me, so I stroke myself faster and harder until pleasure erupts throughout my body. The orgasm shatters me with both ecstasy and cruelty—knowing it feels so good, but this fantasy won't ever become a reality.

I muffle my heavy breathing with the blanket as the euphoria starts to fade and is pushed aside by guilt. Silent tears stream down my temples and into my ears with the full realization that I just betrayed Malcolm. I feel so out of control being here in this realm, like I don't know who I am anymore.

As I remain lying on the bed in my guilt, I hear the door to the house open and close. Music begins to play, but I can still make out Knox's voice drifting down the hall as he talks to someone.

"I said tonight's not a good night. I'll catch up with you next week."

His words make my heart race once again. I wipe the tears from my face and listen for him to say more, but it's quiet now. Turning on my side to face the door, I take a deep breath and close my eyes. Feeling safe and comfortable knowing that Knox is home—and alone—sleep comes quickly.

NINE

Chester Pala Delphine

Castle Waimea, Kapu Island

"Now we just have to determine which dragon you will take through the portal," Luke wonders—mostly to himself—as he paces the floor of his home. There should be track marks in the wood by now since he's been at it for a solid twenty minutes. His figure passes in and out of my field of vision as I watch the last rays of the sun fade from the sky through a window across the room. My eyes move to Luke, roving over his usual attire of a black shirt and matching utility pants. Worry deepens the lines on his forehead as he evaluates my options.

Luke lives in a small cabin on our castle grounds. As the lead dragon handler, he needs to be close because he's on duty at all times. And he's reliable; my family trusts him to keep an eye on the grounds . . . Plus, this arrangement works for me since I get to see him whenever I want.

His home is cozy, which seems odd for a man of Luke's stature. He keeps his space tidy and organized, but it still feels lived in . . . not cold or unwelcoming at all. Being that it's meant for a single occupant, there's only one bedroom, one bathroom, a small kitchen, and, true to the quaint theme, a small living room with a desk for the nightly paperwork Luke fills out. The castle receives a report at the end of every day detailing all dragon-related information, such as their health, temperament, flying time (including the rider's name and rank), meals taken, and any other notes that Luke thinks he should share with the chief and the heads of the castle staff—which includes me. His intimate knowledge of everything related to Castle Waimea's dragons affords Luke some say on how the caves are managed, so sneaking out with a dragon should be fairly easy.

"I'm thinking we take Gabriel because he's a deep-brown color that will blend into the darkness of the night sky. He's also from the same bloodline as Shea, so they'll be able to use their echolocation to find one another," I say, giving voice to his thoughts and knowing he'll agree.

I'm sitting behind Luke's desk in his living room, lightly tapping a pen on an open page of the journal Camilla tossed to me the night we visited her and Tallulah. It's been nearly a week, and I've been analyzing my notes over and over, trying to construct a plan of how to surreptitiously get from the castle to the caves, to the landing grass with a dragon in tow, and then fly through the portal without being spotted by anyone at the castle or in the village.

"Mmm, excellent thinking," Luke nods. "Dark colors will limit your chances of being seen by the guards and any villagers out and about when you jump. He's also our stealthiest while flying, so he'll be hard to hear as well." And with that, he resumes pacing.

We stayed at the Belmonte sisters' home for most of the night as they explained in detail how to realm jump. I hastily scribbled while Camilla spoke, and Tallulah chimed in here and there, grabbing the pen from me in an attempt to make my handwriting legible and underlining important reminders—or, more accurately, warnings. Camilla also drew maps of where I needed to go and how to return once I got to the other side.

She explained to us that there are two portals within the village of Waimea: one is on the ground at the back of the fields, and the other is about a thousand feet up in the sky, alongside Maka Mountain, directly across from the dragon caves. The two portals lead to two different realms, which means I need to know exactly where Louella was heading that night to be able to enter the correct realm.

I reassured Camilla and Tallulah that I am certain it was the portal in the sky because she disappeared while flying. I had turned my back on Shea and Ella to walk to the caves, but I saw them moving straight toward the mountain, which was different from their usual route.

I'm rereading my underlined note at the bottom of the page for what must be the hundredth time ("BE CAREFUL!") when Luke asks a question.

"Isn't it crazy that there are portals all over the island? I mean, it's crazy that there are portals to begin with, but I wonder where they all lead and if some go to the same place . . . ," he trails off, lost in his thoughts again.

Luke has been so immersed in all the information we've gathered and the planning we've been doing. But his presence settles my nerves. I am uneasy about realm jumping alone; the number of mistakes I could make is staggering, and I have no idea what it will be like on the other side once I jump . . . but I push the nerves away with the hope that I could save my sister and our village if I find her.

"Yeah, crazy," I reply halfheartedly. I let out a deep sigh, and at the sound of it, Luke stops pacing and pivots toward me.

"Hey, what's wrong?" he asks.

I rap the pen against the notebook a couple more times, reluctant to say what's been gnawing at me. With a wince, I ask cautiously, "How did you know that Camilla and Tallulah were familiar with realm jumping?"

Luke casts his eyes to the floor. After a beat of silence, he raises his head, pursing his lips together before he finally answers. "I, um . . . Well . . ." his voice is barely above a whisper and he's stammering, unable to form a complete sentence.

"You can tell me," I say with an apathetic chuckle. "Nothing seems to surprise me anymore."

Luke nods his head and blurts, "I helped Camilla realm jump." Before I can say anything, he explains, "Only the first couple of times, though. I told her that she would have to do it when one of the backup guards was on duty because I felt like I was betraying you by carrying this secret around."

I break eye contact with him and focus on my hands as I spin the pen between my fingers.

"She said they do it because the other-realm items sell the best at the stall, and they need the money. You know those sisters would never take any kind of handout from the chief."

He's right about that. But his involvement is incredibly risky. Papa would release Luke from his castle duties, likely banish him from the village, and undoubtedly forbid me from ever seeing him again. But what should I do now that I know?

Pushing duty and my parents' expectations aside, how do I feel about him withholding something like this from me? Behind it all . . . there's nothing. I'm not upset, nor am I hurt—at this point, it is what it is. Truthfully, I can't say I wouldn't have done the same thing.

Hell, I basically am doing the same thing.

I look up at Luke, who now has little beads of sweat accumulating at his temples as he waits for my reply. His eyebrows are pinched in concern, but I softly smile at him. "Lucas, next time, just tell me."

Luke's body sags as he relaxes. "You aren't mad at me?"

I shake my head, "No, I'm not. I just want you to feel like you can tell me things."

"I'm so sorry," he pleads, and I believe him. But it doesn't quite settle the unease that's budding inside me regarding the super-secret, super-dangerous mission ahead of me.

"Is something else upsetting you?" he asks hesitantly.

I toss the pen onto the desk in front of me. "There's a lot at stake here. So many things could go wrong." I lean back in the desk chair, sliding my hands through my hair and interlocking my fingers. Elbows out wide, I stretch my chest and feel my spine crack as a result—a sure sign of my mounting anxiety.

"You will be fine. Just remember what Camilla said: 'Hang on tight to the reins, keep breathing, and don't pass out.'" He offers me an unconvincing smile.

"Wow, that all sounds so easy. Especially the part about not passing out." My tone is clipped as I reach forward and slam the journal shut.

"Listen, Chester, I'm sorry, but you have the chance to get Louella back. You've gotta think positive, or else something bad will happen."

Luke is right, and if Louella were here, she would say the same thing.

I sigh heavily, "I know. I'm acting like a brat."

Luke snorts, "Well, I wasn't going to say that." He moves around the desk and kneels in front of me, taking my hands in his. Our clasped hands are resting on my lap, and we gaze at each other. After a moment, he says, "Want me to realm jump with you? Would that make you feel a bit better?"

I look down at our hands, contemplating whether I should accept his offer, but I can't run the risk of losing Luke as well. If I get caught, my punishment won't be that harsh, but if Luke gets caught, we will never see each other again.

"No. I'll be fine." I attempt to give Luke an honest smile, but I think I've failed as he returns my tight-lipped expression.

Luke stands up and places a hand on either armrest of the chair, caging me in. He's hovering mere inches away from me, and his breath fans across my lips. Leaning forward, he places a soft kiss on my cheek, his stubble prickling my skin. I turn my face slightly and close the gap between us as our noses and mouths clash. Luke's lips are warm, which sends tingles racing down my body. I shamelessly grunt as his tongue pushes between my lips and connects with mine. I grip the back of his head, and he places a hand on my side. Luke snakes one arm around my neck, gently holding me there.

Our kiss deepens as we pass moans to one another, and I can feel my cock pulsing. He works a hand down my body and cups the bulge in my pants. I hiss, lifting my hips with how good the pressure feels. Grabbing his hand, I lead him below my waistband so that his bare hand is on my cock. I let out a satisfied growl as he wraps his hand around me and slowly pumps. We are both breathing heavily, making it hard to continue kissing—but we keep our mouths locked together as it turns sloppy. Luke's grip tightens and the pleasure intensifies, but his hand can only move so far with my pants still on. Without thinking, I break our kiss and thrust my pants down to my ankles. Luke looks at me for a moment and then kneels, taking my cock in his mouth.

"Fuck," I groan. The heat from Luke's mouth and the tightness of his lips escalate the tension that's already building. I grasp either side of Luke's face, working his head faster. I release a guttural moan that fills the quiet of the tiny cabin.

Luke's hand on my leg tightens as he begins to moan also, sending vibrations through my cock.

"Fuck, fuck!" I shout as I buck harder into his mouth. My orgasm erupts throughout my body. I squeeze my eyes shut, and in that moment, I've forgotten the world around me, what my name is, and why I'm so stressed out. When I finally come to, my body jerks and I open my eyes again.

Luke is staring up at me with hooded eyes and a smug look on his face.

I wipe the corner of his lip with my thumb. "Thank you," I say breathlessly. The worry is temporarily exchanged for bliss, and it feels nice.

"There has been no word of the search parties finding tracks belonging to Shea anywhere. She would have had to come down from the sky at some point to eat and rest, which should have left some sort of trail for us to follow, but it's like the two of them just vanished," the chief announces.

I can see the frustration radiating out from him. His muscles are tight, constricting in his back with each breath he takes. We are standing in the dining room, where we have most of our discussions, and he's facing the window that looks out onto the village below. Watching his profile, I notice his deep frown, and the wrinkles on his forehead are pronounced—he's definitely not happy. Louella being gone has taken a toll on his spirit, and I haven't seen him smile since her disappearance. The deadline to present Louella to Castle Hana is looming, and the realization is sinking in that we might fail to deliver.

"Papa, I know, but as I have told you, we only have one more week to bring Ella to Castle Hana or we will be attacked. We need to create a perimeter of guards along the borders of our land. We also need to ready the cavalry so that when the Royce family arrives, we are prepared if they come to besiege us."

"No," he states firmly, his voice an octave lower. "I think we should let them in peacefully. This is all a misunderstanding, and they will know that once I have a chance to talk this through with King Victor face to face." He remains standing at the window, refusing to look at me, like looking at me is going to make this mess more real.

Papa has been in denial of the Royce family's ill intentions since our last dinner with Louella, when she expressed her concern regarding Victor and Maribeth, and I've grown exhausted trying to explain to him that Louella wasn't wrong. I could tell by the brief interaction I had with them—and despite what my father may think, they won't understand.

I'm giving this one last try to convince him that we need to protect ourselves. "Papa, please, just trust me on this." My voice comes out strangled and pleading.

Papa faces me after several seconds of silent contemplation, his eyes boring Into me. Releasing a sigh of resignation, he announces, "Prepare the military. Send word to construct the barrier for the guards along the borders, and alert the cavalry to protect the skies." His brow is furrowed, and he continues in a booming voice, "If Castle Hana is seen, I want them to be let in unharmed . . . unless they strike first."

"Yes, sir." I give Papa a nod before I turn on my heels and head to the training grounds to inform the soldiers. With these orders, a small weight lifts off my chest. I'm glad I convinced Papa to come to his senses.

Now, I need time to orchestrate my plan, and I can't realm jump for another two and a half weeks. Camilla informed Luke and me that realm jumping is possible only during a fire sign in a new moon or a full moon—but there's an exception: the realm jumpers have found that by some mysterious coincidence, you can travel during a new moon in Virgo or Scorpio. I would have been forced to wait until September 25, but the goddesses must be on my side because there's a new moon in Virgo on September 9. I'm just praying the Royce family doesn't roll through our village with arrows blazing when Louella doesn't show up next week and we can keep the peace until I get her back.

Ten

Louella Aponi Delphine

Kailani Bay, Gemcove Island

My wedding was supposed to be four days ago, and I don't know how I feel about that. Usually when I have trouble sorting through my emotions, I talk to Chester or work in the fields or take Shea out for a nighttime ride to ease my mind. But I can't do any of those things right now. I've been completely cut off from everyone back home, and it's left me feeling isolated. Even my limited hours with Shea are difficult because she's grounded while we're here. Counting down in my head, I realize I still have . . . four more weeks until I can fly back home.

Ugh! Time, why won't you speed up?

So I opt to watch the sunrise on the beach this morning. Following a narrow path from the backyard of the house, I walk down a not-so-steep hill to sink my toes into the sand. I face the bay as the sun's rays crest over the water, slowly bathing me in warmth in an attempt to melt away my guilt, confusion, and crippling fear.

Lately, when I'm not sulking in Knox's room, I've been bothering Lloyd almost daily for a ride to the library. I've been too afraid to go anywhere else, and I've ended up becoming somewhat of a hermit. It doesn't help that Lloyd is working long shifts most days . . . and it's the same with Knox. When I do see Knox, he barely even acknowledges me. We are like two ships passing in the night.

I dig my toes deeper into the sand. The squishy feeling relaxes me; it's a weird sensation, but it reminds me of all the times when Chester and I would wander down to the shore near the castle grounds and watch the tide roll in and out. Most of the time, we would sit in silence, but other times, we would talk about dragons, combat training, or heavier topics, like what it would be like when we got married and couldn't see each other as much anymore. We always promised we would visit as much as possible be-cause, at the end of the day, siblings stay with you forever.

A powerful gust of wind tugs little strands free from my braid, and I can almost convince myself I'm riding on Shea's back. On instinct, I close my eyes and spread my arms out wide. I hear the wind whip past my ears and feel its warm caress against my face. I listen to the waves crashing as the smell of jasmine mixed with salty air invades my nos-trils—for a moment, it feels like I'm home on Kapu Island.

"What are you doing?"

My eyes fly open and I slam my arms down to my sides. I spin around to see Knox standing a few feet behind me.

He shoves his hands into his front pockets, and one eyebrow is cocked high on his forehead. He's amused—I can tell by his devilish grin.

"What does it matter to you?" I snap, facing the bay once again. Why does it matter? He's done a good job avoiding me, so what makes him so interested in what I'm doing now, right at this very second?

Out of the corner of my eye, I see movement as Knox now stands beside me on my right.

"Just wondering what the weirdo that's sleeping in my bed and staying in my house is doing outside looking like a full-on crazy person."

"Technically, it's Lloyd's house," I grumble, crossing my arms over my chest defensively.

"Hmm, well, I pay half of the mortgage, so it's my house too." He's soft-spoken now, which is a change from his usual cold harshness.

I twist slightly toward him, keeping my arms crossed. "What's your issue with me?" I blurt out.

"I don't have an issue with you. I just like to watch you squirm." Knox flicks his eyes from the water to me.

In the morning light, his eyes are a rich shade of chocolate with swirls of lighter brown—not a flat black like I had thought the night we met. The dark brown and caramel intertwine, creating something unique I've never seen before. For the first time, I notice three tiny scars on his face: one above his left eyebrow, one on his chin, and one on his left cheekbone. I want to ask him about them, but I bite back the question. I don't realize my observation of Knox's face is lingering a bit too long until he clears his throat, and the flush of red-hot embarrassment consumes my face. I quickly turn away as the thought of what I did on his bed the other night plays back in my mind. I mimic his action and clear my throat to pretend I wasn't just sinking deep into his eyes at the thought of him between my thighs.

"How did you get here?" I can hear the curiosity in Knox's tone.

"You know how I got here: on a dragon," I state.

"No, how did you get here?" he repeats, this time his voice is firm.

I look down at my bare feet, my toes now buried beneath the sand, as I contemplate how to describe to him what I went through when Shea and I realm jumped.

Meeting his eyes again, I shake my head. "I don't know how to explain this any differently, but I was taking my final ride with Shea before I was supposed to move to Castle Hana and get married. Instead of taking our normal route, she headed toward Maka Mountain, which is in the center of Kapu Island. I knew something was off because dragons never fly up the mountain with their riders; they only ever travel there alone. I don't remember much after that, but it felt like I was sucked into a hole in the sky. Then . . . I was

here. I can't tell you anything else because that's all I know."
I shrug my shoulders, waiting for Knox's reaction.

He nods as if he understands, but I don't think he does—I don't think anyone does.

"Weird. Do you think Shea knew what she was doing?"

"Yes. Shea always knows what she's doing. She's calculated and stubborn," I say, unable to hold back a snort of laughter. "It seems so silly because she's just a dragon, but Shea's always been different." My voice is wistful as I think about how much that bullheaded beast means to me.

"She sounds a bit like you," Knox teases.

"You know nothing about me," I scoff.

He turns suddenly and it startles me, grabbing my attention so I'm looking in his eyes again. He presses his lips together and squints at me as if he's thinking, or studying me . . . Before I can ask what he's doing, he speaks again. This time, his tone is back to cold and stern.

"You know what I think, koa? I think I do know quite a bit about you. When I look at you, I see a girl who wants adventure. A girl who wants to feel the sun on her skin and have fun. She wants to ride dragons because she loves the thrill of it, and she's searching for that thrill in her everyday life because it's so boring. She wants someone to show her how to feel—and not in a cute, in-love kind of way, but the feeling of ecstasy and pleasure, the kind that makes your legs shake and takes away every thought in your head to the point where you can't remember your own name. But you're too afraid to say no to Mommy and Daddy.

You're too afraid of what your family might think, or what your village will think of the princess who turned down the ever-so-charming prince she was destined to marry, because it seems like reputation means everything where you come from, and you're too scared to actually have one."

Knox's words are harsh, and I feel completely deflated . . . because he's absolutely correct. He read me like a book and doesn't even know me.

"How do you know that?" I rush out.

"Ahhh, so I'm right. That is what you want," Knox says, acting very pleased with himself.

"I don't know what I want. I've never had a choice in my life," I reply tonelessly.

"Well, you do now. You might as well make the most of it before your time is up." Knox lightly nudges his elbow into my arm, and it tingles where our exposed skin briefly touched. I pray he doesn't notice as my body breaks out in goosebumps.

Silence stretches between us as we continue to stand side by side, looking out at the waves pushing and pulling at the sand before us. I don't know how to respond to him, or if I even should. I could embrace this adventure while I'm here, but I'm scared to. I'm afraid I will get caught for being from another realm and be killed or something equally terrible. I'm afraid that if I do let loose and have fun, I'm betraying my family back home, who are probably going through hell trying to find me.

I'm torn.

Knox interrupts my internal battle. "Get your shoes and meet me at my bike in the garage. I want to show you something."

I hesitate, "I don't know if I should trust you."

A chuckle rumbles low in his throat. "Other than Lloyd, I'm the only person here you should trust, koa," he warns. Without hearing my argument, he turns away and walks toward the hill and up to the house.

Why does he keep calling me that?

I watch him for a while until he disappears from view into the backyard, and slowly I drag my feet to follow. I want to know what koa means . . . I make a mental note to ask Lloyd.

Knox doesn't notice when I enter the garage. He's kneeling on the ground, working on something at the front wheel of his bike, and I watch his arm muscles pump with the motion of the tool he's holding. Looking more intently at the tattoos along his forearm, I notice that they sort of resemble mine, but not quite. And that makes me wonder if his have meaning like ours do back home. No one here has asked me about the designs on my arm, but tattoos seem very common in this realm, so why would they?

Knox rises to his full height and does not look surprised when he sees me standing completely still by the door watching him. He grabs the helmets off a bench, walks over, and hands me the one I've worn each time we've ridden together. I gingerly slide it on over my braid, tugging it over my face and down to my neck. Once it's on, I wobble my head back and forth a bit and huff in frustration.

"Why do I have to wear this thing?" I ask Knox as he pulls his helmet on.

He smirks and then reaches his hand out to flip the black-tinted shield over my eyes. "So you don't die." He does the same motion with his helmet, and I can no longer make out his facial features through the darkness of the shield.

"Oh. All right." My response is muffled by the helmet, and I think that was Knox's intention when he closed the shield over—so he didn't have to hear me complain any longer.

Knox straddles the motorcycle seat and begins to move the bike backward with each step he takes. It looks so odd to me as he waddles down the driveway that I bite my lip trying not to laugh. When he has the bike facing the road, he turns the little knob between the handlebars and then twists the handle, bringing the bike to life as its roar echoes through the neighborhood. I've seen him go through the motions a few times now, but I don't think I'll ever get used to the ferocious sound of his machine.

He turns to me and points at the space behind him. Following his command, I walk over, place my right foot on the small peg, and grab on to his shoulders for support. I gently glide my left leg over the seat to sit down behind him.

As soon as I'm able, I snatch my hands back to maintain the distance between us—like I've done every time we've shared this small seat—and hold on tight to the strap in front of me. There's not much room between our bodies, but I do the best I can. Knox twists the handlebar some more, the bike growling louder in response, before we take off down the road.

I have no idea where he is taking me, but I lean back and enjoy the views as we cruise along the coast. Knox explained to me that we'd be riding on a highway, which is like a road but bigger and busier—but he said that means we can go faster. The highway is winding, and I'm in awe of the breathtaking landscapes, of the cliffs that overlook the sparkling water below. The tinted shield over my eyes makes the water look black and gray, but I know how beautiful it really is—it's etched in my memory now. I'm loving every second of this because this is truly the closest I've felt to riding on Shea in weeks. It's only me and my thoughts—no interruptions.

Knox zooms the bike along tree-lined roads and down into a tiny village littered with people. There's a sign on the right side of the road that reads "Welcome to Opal," and it strikes me as such an odd name for a town. Then again, who am I to say what's odd in a place where I don't belong? Both sides of the street are packed with small markets and pubs. He slows us down and veers into a little alcove beside the road. Once Knox stops the bike, the engine goes quiet.

He yanks his helmet off his head and turns his chin to his shoulder. "You may get off now, princess."

I roll my eyes but do as I'm told, placing my hands on his shoulders again. Unfortunately, my dismount isn't nearly as graceful as when I got on, and I awkwardly fumble off the bike, getting my foot caught on Knox's leg in the process.

"Need help?" he snickers as he offers his hand.

"No, I don't need your help," I sneer.

Knox shakes his head at me, kicks the little stand under the bike, and then hops off. He places his helmet on the handle, and I watch as he runs his hand through his long dark hair, effortlessly flicking his tresses over to the side and off his face. Without looking back at me, he treks down the street lined with markets.

I follow his lead, leaving my helmet hanging on the opposite handle. I walk behind him a few paces and watch as he steps into one of the small shops. Before I open the door to go inside, I look up to read the sign above my head: Relics of the Realms.

What I see when I walk in stops me in my tracks. The air leaves my lungs, and my mouth flops open as I take in the sight of bows and arrows, daggers, dragon saddles, dragon teeth, dragon claws . . . The list in my mind continues to expand as I notice more and more—nearly everything in here is from my home. A whistle jostles me from my shock, and I find Knox waiting for me at a glass counter in the back corner of the shop. I compose myself and walk toward him.

Knox is leaning against the counter as he chats with a man standing behind it. I assume this must be the shop owner. He's large and burly, with long gray hair, which has been pulled back into a bun. He has Kai tattoos down the right side of his face, which throws me off guard. Kai tattoos are worn by the Kaimans from the village of Molokai—on my island.

"Todd, meet Louella. She's a realm enthusiast much like yourself," Knox says as I approach them warily.

Todd smiles at me, and I decide it's best to return the gesture, though I'm still unsure of all this.

"That's great!" he beams, clapping his hands together with excitement. His eyes are twinkling and his toothy grin is broad, almost reaching his ears. That's when I realize Todd is not scary at all, despite my initial impression.

"How did you get all these pieces?" I spin in a small circle, and each time I look around, I spot something else I recognize from Kapu Island.

"Oh, I've got trusted sources who come in claiming they make this stuff or find it online. I trade them laptops, iPods, things like that for whatever they have to offer," he says.

I nod my head at him. "It's amazing."

And it is amazing, but now I'm wondering more about who the "guy" is and where he finds this stuff—which isn't "stuff" at all, and it isn't merely made. These are definitely authentic, handcrafted pieces from my home. Not all of it, but based on what I've seen so far, a good majority of Todd's collection originated on Kapu Island.

"Yeah. My main contact got me hooked on anything and everything about the dragon realm—I'm obsessed. In the last delivery, I got a couple of books. Allegedly, this is all fictional, but man, I'm not so sure. The stories and dragons seem so real." Todd's eyes are wide, and I can tell this is his passion.

I wish I could say, "Buddy, it is real!" But I can't.

Bummer.

"That's interesting. I would love to read them." I wonder if they have any stories on realm jumping that could benefit me, maybe get me out of here sooner . . .

"I lent them to my nephew a little while ago—but once he's finished, I'll call my man Knox and you can swing by and grab them."

Damn—another thing I'll have to wait for.

"Thanks," I smirk at him.

"Look around and let me know if anything catches your eye. Enjoy, enjoy," Todd says, kindly shooing me away to go explore.

I can't stop my feet from taking me straight to the dragon-bone bow hanging on the wall to the right of the counter. The bow is accompanied by a dragon-skin satchel filled with dragon-bone arrows. Inspecting the bow more carefully, I run my fingers along the markings carved into the bleached-white surface, recognizing them as the tattoo on Papa's chin. My eyes burn with unshed tears when Papa's face comes to mind.

I miss my home so much.

"It's beautiful," I hear Knox say from behind me. I could feel him approaching me, so he didn't startle me like usual. Something about the store has me on high alert, and I've been aware of my surroundings ever since I stepped foot in here. There's been an odd prickling feeling on the back of my neck and running down to my legs.

"Yeah, it's made from dragon bone," I state reverently.

"Hmmm." There's a pause before Knox speaks again, "Do you want it?"

I chuckle, "No, I have plenty of these at home." I turn to him, and his brows are high on his head in shock.

"You have plenty of those?" he challenges, pointing to the bow.

Standing taller, I lift my chin slightly before responding, "Yes, me." Then I drop my voice low so Todd can't hear me. "My brother has trained me in combat, and I have a modest stash of weapons I've been gifted over the years."

"Ahhhh, I see. Remind me not to piss you off." He looks at me as he flicks his lip ring with his tongue. Despite his words, Knox doesn't look intimidated; oddly, he looks impressed.

"Ha! You've already pissed me off . . . numerous times, actually, so I think you are safe . . . for now." I waggle my brows at him as I brush past to resume browsing.

I wander around the shop for another twenty or thirty minutes while Knox and Todd chat at the glass counter. I catch snippets of their conversation as Todd explains his face tattoo and how he saw it in one of the books his nephew is borrowing. It must be fresh ink because I sense that this is the first time Knox has seen it, and the two seem to have a good relationship and probably talk often.

While I peruse the shelves, I take notice of some of the items that aren't from my realm—but I don't bother to ask about them for fear of drawing too much attention to myself. The objects are adorned with shimmering crystals and intricate designs, and by the looks of the craftsmanship, I'm guessing these are also made by hand. A dagger catches my eye, and I've examined it a couple of times already. The blade is made from a sharpened red stone, and the hilt is a silver metal, but the cross guard is what keeps luring me back: the metal is shaped into an ornate raven, its wings spread wide. I have never seen anything like it.

"You ready?" Knox asks, still standing across the room with Todd.

I turn and reply with a simple "Yes."

Todd waves and tells me to come back soon. As Knox walks toward the exit, Todd promises to let us know when his nephew returns the books so I can borrow them. I nod in acknowledgment and wave back.

I push open the door to leave, and the warm, humid air hits my cold skin, giving me goosebumps. I didn't realize how chilly it was in the shop until now. Knox follows behind me, but when I get to the bike and turn around, he's not there like I thought he would be. I preoccupy myself while I wait for him by looking in the windows of the other markets in the vicinity of the bike. Several moments later, he finally strides into the alcove holding a small brown bag.

"Did you get something?" I ask him.

He puts the bag into a satchel attached to the back of my seat. "Yeah. I'll show you when we get to the house." He hands me my helmet, and soon enough, we're heading back to Kailani Bay.

***

"Here." Knox hands me the little brown bag as we stand in the garage.

I carefully take it and open it up. Peeking inside, I see the red-stone dagger I was eyeing at Relics of the Realms. My mouth opens and closes, then falls open again because I'm unsure of what to say.

Did he really buy me something?

"This is for me?" I ask Knox with skepticism in my tone.

He narrows his eyes at me. "Um, yeah, it's called a gift."

"Well, I know what a gift is. But why?"

"I guess you can think of it as less of a gift and more of a way to protect yourself." He takes the bag back, and I'm quick to try and snatch it from him, but not quick enough.

"Chill out. I'm just going to show you how to wear it." Knox raises the bag above me and stiffens his arm as I stretch up on my tiptoes and jump to grab at my gift. He shakes his head at me, laughing as I struggle to snag it back. "Are you done?" he asks.

I know he wants me to admit defeat, and I glower at him. Pushing my pride aside for the sake of the dagger, I answer plainly, "Yes." It comes out like a grunt because I'm out of breath from jumping up and down.

He pulls the dagger out, along with a leather harness to sheath the blade on my body.

Knox juts his chin out at me and says, "Lift your shirt."

"I'm not flashing you. I know how to wear it, and I can do it myself."

A muscle in his jaw pops as he clenches and grinds his teeth. My stubbornness is clearly irritating him now. He tilts his head down and maintains eye contact.

"Do. It. Koa." He says the words slowly, with a full stop after each one.

He looks sexy, and I'm forced to choke down a hard swallow. I slump my shoulders and let out a low growl. Grabbing the bottom hem of my T-shirt, I lift it to expose my belly, holding the fabric so it stops above my belly button. I catch Knox staring at my exposed stomach, and he flicks his lip ring with his tongue.

"Fold the top of your leggings down a bit." His voice comes out strained, and I respond with a low cackle.

"Ha, ha. This is hilarious. I told you already, I know how to put the harness on."

Knox doesn't respond as he closes what little distance was left between us, his eyes still trained on my exposed stomach. He reaches around my waist and encircles my back with the leather strap. Working one end through the buckle, he jerks me forward to tighten the strap. I stagger and almost fall into his chest, but I manage to stay on my feet. With the sheath now resting on the side of my right hip, he secures the harness in place. Knox's fingers graze my lower abdomen, and it sends a shock through my body. I can feel the warmth of his hands radiating into my belly, and I have to turn my face away as my desire for him returns.

"Is this too tight?" Knox asks in a low, husky voice.

I fumble over the words before answering, "Uhh . . . No, it feels good." I bite my lip and summon the courage to look up at him.

He's absentmindedly dragging his finger across the top of the harness strap, along my exposed skin, while he stares back at me. His nostrils flare as he looks at my mouth.

I have the urge to push up onto my toes and press my lips to his—but I do the opposite. I shove his hands away and adjust my pants over the dagger as my shirt falls back down, covering the harness. I step back and look down at my right hip.

"I like it. Thank you."

Knox nods once and heads toward a workbench along the garage wall. "I'm assuming you know how to use it, since you have combat training and all. Now you can go places alone, just carry that with you . . . but don't kill anyone."

He doesn't look over at me as he shifts tools and random things around.

"Yeah," I answer, and it comes out as a whisper. The longer I stand here, the harder it becomes to breathe, so I turn away from him and quickly walk into the house, straight into his bedroom. I shut the door and press my back against it as I release a deep sigh that had been trapped in my lungs during our entire interaction. I look up at the ceiling and pray to the goddesses I can keep my libido in check for the next four weeks.

ELEVEN

CHESTER PALA DELPHINE

Castle Waimea, Kapu Island

It has come to the attention of King Victor and Queen Maribeth that the time allotted for Princess Louella Aponi Delphine to be delivered to Castle Hana for her marriage to Prince Malcolm has come to pass as of August 30. Although their majesties do hope the princess is alive and well, they cannot ignore that Castle Waimea has failed to comply with the written and verbal contracts on which the two castles agreed.

Therefore, Castle Hana is left with no other option but to demand that Castle Waimea provide dragons to spawn since its portion of the marital agreement remains unfulfilled. King Victor and Queen Maribeth expect the dragons to be delivered by sundown no later than Sunday, the third of September. Their majesties require King Rowland and Queen Theadosia to send several of Castle Waimea's largest, quickest, and healthiest dragons—along with their handlers. As the castles had discussed prior, these dragons will remain at Castle Hana to care for their offspring until the offspring are of age to survive on their own. If Castle Waimea fails to complete its portion of the agreement (again), the king and queen will have no other option but to seize the village and castle, thus claiming Castle Waimea as property of Castle Hana.

Their majesties trust that King Rowland and Queen Theadosia understand and will abide by these revised terms.

Regards,

King and Queen of Castle Hana

I squeeze the edges of the letter in my hands and angrily crumple it into a ball.

"Argh!" I can't help the frustrated grunt that escapes me as I throw the balled-up letter across the dining room. I shove one hand into my hair and place the other on my hip as I think about our options. "Condescending assholes," I hiss.

"Well, we knew this was going to happen. At least they're giving us more time . . . and a warning," Luke offers in a placating tone.

He is sitting at the dining table to the right of Papa. Mama is across from Luke, with Pop-Pop to her left. I'm pacing the length of the windows next to the table because I'm too on edge to sit down.

I haven't told the chief about my realm-jumping plans yet because I know he won't like it and will try to stop me, but I must do this. I need to see if Louella is on the other side of that portal. I narrow my eyes at Luke as if to say, "Shut the fuck up."

He snaps his mouth closed and flares his eyes at me. Message received.

"What's our plan?" I ask, looking at Papa.

"Son, I know you don't want to give up on finding Louella, but sending them some dragons is our best bet."

"We can't do that. What if they go back on their word and attack us? We can't fight them without Shea; she's the strongest dragon we have. We need all the power we can get." I slam my fist on the table, making Mama jump. Her eyes widen as she looks to my father to put an end to my temper tantrum.

"Calm down. Stop thinking the worst, Chester. I say we send the dragons, but we keep the guards around the perimeter of our land—and in the sky, for added measure." Papa's face is stern, and I know he's tired of the constant back and forth with me. (That makes two of us.)

I break eye contact with him to glance at Luke. He is one of our strongest warriors and rides one of our largest dragons. Luke's face is blank, unreadable, but I'm sure he will let me know how he's feeling when we are alone.

"What does that mean for Zeus and me?" I look back to Papa. My dragon is the second largest and fastest we have, and, respectfully, I'm one of the best handlers and warriors on this island.

Papa sits in silence, but before he can speak again, Pop-Pop chimes in, "He's unhealthy."

My eyes shift to Pop-Pop, who has been quietly staring out a window since I walked into the dining room. I wait for him to elaborate, but he doesn't.

"Zeus is in perfect health. I'm not sure what you're insinuating," I scowl at my grandfather. I glance at Papa to see if he has any feedback.

Papa returns my questioning glare, and then his face brightens with realization. With a smirk and a mischievous glint in his eyes, he explains, "That's how we keep you and Zeus here. In the letter, it states that they want our healthiest dragons. It's simple: Zeus has an ailment."

My shoulders relax at the chance that this little plan could work.

"See? I'm still good for something," Pop-Pop chuckles to himself. His pride is radiating off him as he takes a small sugar cube from a white ceramic bowl in the middle of the table and plops it into the cup of tea that's been sitting in front of him for quite some time now—it's bound to be cold.

I nod and smile as a thought comes to me: "Can Zion have an ailment as well?"

Papa looks to Luke and then back to me, knowing that Zion is Luke's dragon. "No, only Zeus. Castle Hana already has the biometrics of our dragons; if we say two of our best dragons have ailments, they will most certainly be on to us."

I let out a frustrated sigh because I know he's not wrong.

Mama clears her throat. "So what exactly is our plan?" she asks flatly.

"We respond to Castle Hana's correspondence, agreeing to send three dragons that meet their criteria, along with their handlers. The handlers will remain at Castle Hana with the dragons temporarily, since we can't afford to lose our best trainers for an extended period of time. Chester's correct; Castle Hana could still declare war, and we need every last warrior we have." He pauses, tapping his fingers on the table as he thinks. "It's a tight deadline already, but let's prepare for their travel and send them to Castle Hana on September second to arrive a day early. Chester," the chief looks over to me, "give orders to the guards that they are to remain on border patrol and sky duty until further notice."

Mama stoically nods in agreement with my father, satisfied with his answer.

"In addition to Zion, which dragons and handlers should I prepare to send?" Luke asks the chief.

"I'll leave that for you to decide. I trust you, Lucas," Papa replies.

Luke nods in acknowledgment, his face beaming at the chief's comment—and it doesn't go unnoticed by me.

Papa continues, "You'll also need to add Zeus's injury to the reports—be sure to add it today, and make it convincing. Let's say it's a wing injury that occurred during battle practice. That will be all for now."

As he formally ends the meeting, Papa straightens in his chair at the head of the table. The staff begin filing into the room with lunch plates and placing them in front of Papa, Pop-Pop, and Mama.

I exit the dining room to make my way down to the practice grounds so I can inform the soldiers of our plans right away—food can wait.

Luke is following me. I hear his heavy footfalls thumping on the marble floor behind me. It doesn't take him long to catch up and match my stride.

"We should set aside some time tomorrow to go over the realm-jumping plan." Luke's voice is hushed so that no one else can hear him.

"I agree. I'll come to your place tomorrow after-noon—once we have this Castle Hana shit figured out.

"Hey." As soon as our boots hit the gravel pathway out-side, Luke's hand gently grazes my forearm, causing me to turn and face him. "He trusts me . . . We can't let him know I'm helping you. I want there to be a chance for us, and he's the only thing that could stop us."

I purse my lips and inhale deeply through my nose. "Don't worry about it. I will make sure he believes you had nothing to do with helping me."

Luke pinches his brows together, skepticism etched into every line on his face. "All right," he nods reluctantly, then starts walking again.

I follow him toward the practice grounds. Luke is right; I'll have to make sure he has an alibi for the night I jump—and I know just the right people.

TWELVE

LOUELLA APONI DELPHINE

Kailani Bay, Gemcove Island

Highway: a giant road where cars travel really fast.

Car: a large (often loud) vehicle for traveling long distances.

Motorcycle: my favorite vehicle because it <u>almost</u> feels like I'm flying; also called a bike; also very loud.

Restaurant: like a pub, but you sit at a table and people bring you drinks and food—lots of food.

Knox: the guy I always daydream about even though I should be thinking about my home and my fiancé . . .

I sigh, leaning back in my chair at the kitchen table. I slam my journal shut and drop my pen next to it.

I'm determined to document my findings while in this realm so I can remember my time here when I go back home in less than a month. I've played with the idea of writing a book about this realm when I return home. My people would be able to read it centuries from now, when I'm long forgotten (which wouldn't matter anyway because I would have to write under a pseudonym). It's a fun thought . . . Not the dying part, but leaving a legacy behind other than just being a docile, adoring queen.

Maybe Knox is right and I should live it up a little while I'm here, even if only for the sake of my book. If I don't, people will read about how I sat in a house all day, pacing around like a lost chicken that snacked on grilled cheese sandwiches and canned soup.

How exhilarating.

But what does "fun" even consist of? Goddess, now that I think about it, I'm not sure if I've ever had genuine fun apart from riding Shea and combat training. Maybe I should con Lloyd into doing something fun with me—or maybe Knox? I snicker to myself and shake my head. That's a funny thought. I haven't seen Knox since our trip to the Relics of the Realms shop on Tuesday, and after our awkward exchange with the dagger, I'd bet he's had enough Ella time to last up until I realm jump home. But I remind myself that Lloyd said it's normal for Knox to be scarce. I keep hoping if I stay out in the kitchen long enough, we will eventually bump into each other—but that hasn't happened yet and it's Friday. It's like he can sense my intentions and whereabouts, so he completely avoids the areas I'm in until I leave, and only then does he magically show up.

Regardless of what Knox is up to, I have plans tonight. Lloyd invited me to go to something called the "movies." I'm not exactly sure what I agreed to, but he managed to get a wary yes out of me. He told me that the movies are when people watch other people who pretend to be other people on a giant screen. Sounds strange, but could this be the fun I'm looking for?

I open my journal back up at the thought and jot down another entry.

Movies: when people pretend to be other people, and people watch them.

Maybe it'll make more sense when I get there.

Scooping up my journal and pen, I head back to Knox's room to change out of my leggings and black T-shirt into a more presentable outfit. Then again, this is all I really own, so I'll have to rummage through the top drawer of the mostly empty dresser, which I claimed as mine for the time being. Hopefully one of my four other shirts is a bit nicer than my current one, which is oversized—and maybe a bit smelly. I turn and glance at the laundry basket in the corner of the room when I can't find my tightest black shirt (the nicest one I have) and notice the basket's almost overflowing.

I guess I have to do some laundry.

Lloyd has taken the time to show me how to wash my clothes, and I'm grateful that he continues to teach me new things. Laundry was especially confusing because I was distracted, wanting to know how the inner parts of the machines work instead of just the basics of how to get my clothes clean. I can tell when Lloyd is starting to get annoyed, though, because he'll say things like "Louella, focus," or "Let's simplify this." But he has been very patient with me, which has been a welcome change after spending most of my life being taught by Chester and Mama—the most impatient people on Kapu Island.

The shirt I was hoping to wear reeks and needs to be washed—like, reminiscent of the days I shoveled dragon shit for Chester. I cannot go out of the house smelling that bad, so I settle on a simple white tee that, after a sniff test, is the cleanest-smelling option that isn't wrinkled like a balled-up piece of paper.

When I'm swapping shirts, I hear a light knock on the door. "Louella, it's Lloyd. If you still want to hit up that movie, I'm good to go whenever you are."

I finish putting my arms through the sleeves and throw open the door. Lloyd is standing in front of me with an uncertain smile on his face.

"Yes. Yes, please get me out of this house," I beg him.

He laughs and jerks his head toward the kitchen to usher me out. I brush past him and dart through the kitchen to the door, practically running to Lloyd's car outside.

We drive to the movies in comfortable silence with the windows down. The sun is setting in the distance, making the sky look like a painting splashed with light blues and pinks. I rest my head on the edge of the open car window as I take in the sight. My right arm hangs outside, and I try to grab the wind that passes through my fingers.

It starts drizzling, so my bare arm gets wet, but I don't care. The feeling is calming—a simple reminder that I'm still alive—and I'm trying to capture this moment. I know when I get back home to Kapu Island, this will all feel like a dream. Even though I miss my family and riding Shea, and even though this realm can be overwhelming and scary, being here is a nice break. I hadn't realized how routine my life had become and how much I craved control over my future. Here, I can make my own decisions. It's odd to simultaneously miss the comfort of my home but also find happiness being uncomfortable in a place so different from my home—it feels like my head and my heart are misaligned.

Still leaning against the window frame, I twist to glance at Lloyd beside me. He's mindlessly humming a song that's quietly flowing through what he explained are the car's speakers. I take in his handsome face with full cheeks and lips, which are surrounded by a short dark beard. He has a brilliant smile that's contagious, which pairs nicely with his sense of humor.

I imagine what it would be like falling in love with Lloyd—it would be easy. He's thoughtful, caring, and inter-esting, and our conversations flow naturally; nothing ever feels forced between us. But my heart doesn't ache and yearn for him. Rather, it feels content, like how I feel with

Chester. It's a comforting and reassuring relationship, and he never pushes for more.

I turn to look out the window again as I realize that I don't want easy love. I want the kind of love that keeps me on my tiptoes, guessing and wanting more. The kind I've been reading about in the books from the library—which I quickly snatch from the romance section because I'm too embarrassed that Lloyd or Knox might see me reading them. I want to banter like the main characters do, which inevitably leads to confessions of true love and then passionate, steamy lovemaking in some random location, which only adds to the sultriness of the chapter . . . And I just can't see that with Lloyd. If I'm being honest with myself, I can't see that with Malcolm either. Not anymore.

Thoughts of true love drift from my mind and out the window with the humid breeze as we pull up to a brick building with blinding lights on top that read "BAYSIDE CINEMA." The lettering is so bright, reminding me of the diner we went to. A visual from the diner comes to mind of Knox with that girl, and I can feel the flush of red spreading up my neck and cheeks. Dammit, I was doing so well not thinking about him tonight.

Lloyd is kind enough to buy our tickets and handle all the social interactions since I have no idea what is happening. He also insists on me trying something called "movie theater popcorn." We argue for a bit as I try to tell him not to bother because we have popcorn at home—and I hate it; it's dry and weird—but he claims it's for him and I can have a bite if I want. He grabs a drink for us to share and some weird roped red candy. The bag says licorice, but that doesn't quite fit with how Lloyd pronounces it.

Some things in this realm just don't make sense.

I carry the drink as I follow him down the narrow red hall lined with posters of people with beautiful faces and bodies. Lloyd holds open a door for me, and when I enter, I'm shocked at all the seats facing me. There's only us in the massive room, but I see multiple levels of seats to accommodate a couple hundred people.

My jaw is practically on the floor, and I think my eyes might pop out of my skull. "I've never seen anything like this," I gasp.

Lloyd laughs, "I've heard you say that a lot since I've met you. This is getting fun for me." He points to a row a few steps above us, and I slowly make my way up and slide in, shuffling along until Lloyd signals for me to sit down. He's got us in the middle of the room, directly in front of what looks like a stage.

"So, like, what do we do now?" My nose is scrunched wondering what happens next.

Lloyd grabs a handful of glistening bright-yellow popcorn and pours it into his mouth. "Now we wait for the movie to play on the screen, and all we have to do is sit back and watch it," he manages to say between chewing. I'm impressed with myself that I can make out what he said.

I sit back in my seat, as instructed. "These are comfortable," I say, nodding with surprise.

"Well, yeah, we are going to be here for over two hours—they better be comfortable."

"TWO HOURS!" I shout.

"Damn, quiet down! You're not supposed to be loud in the theater."

"Two hours?" I whisper-shout to Lloyd.

He always wears an amused smirk on his face, and I'm starting to wonder if he ever gets upset.

"It goes by fast. That's why we have snacks!" He waves his hand out, gesturing to the drink and licorice placed between us. "Oh, and bathrooms are back out the way we came, across the hall. Ladies' bathroom is the figure with the skirt." He shoves another handful of popcorn into his mouth as some of the pieces roll onto his chest and land in his lap.

The ladies' bathroom has a skirt. Got it.

Suddenly, two older women burst through the theater doors with their hands full of treats. They make their way up toward the back of the room, laughing with each other after almost tripping on the dimly lit steps they couldn't see over their Maka Mountain–sized pile of food in their arms. I snort out loud as I listen to them plop down into their seats, still giggling and hushing each other.

The bright lights above us dim, and the screen on the stage flickers to life with moving images. A booming voice fills the air, causing me to jump and grab the armrests of my seat. I wasn't expecting it to be so loud, which gives Lloyd another good chuckle.

My mouth is watering from the wafting smell coming from the bucket of popcorn Lloyd is holding, and I remember that I haven't eaten yet today. I give in and scoop up a handful, then sink back into the plush seat to get comfortable.

He was right: this popcorn is delicious and so addicting. The butter, the salt, the crunch . . . I keep digging my hand in and grabbing more. I take a sip of the drink and shut my eyes tightly as the weird sensation of bubbles bursts into my nose and down my throat. Quickly, I swallow it down before I spit it out.

"Ick!" I cough, sticking out my tongue. "What the fuck is that?" I ask more to myself than to Lloyd.

He smiles, still entertained by my movie theater antics, and responds quietly, "It's soda."

"Oh, I see." I shudder and frown at his response.

I won't be drinking soda again anytime soon.

Loud music plays, and the screen flickers before us as people's names appear and disappear in black and white, followed by the words Some Like It Hot. It takes several minutes for the actual movie to begin, and once it does, I can't take my eyes off the screen. In no time at all, I am on the edge of my seat in anticipation of what will happen to Sugar, Jerry, and Joe. I mindlessly paw at the popcorn bucket, taking handful after handful, and I find myself sipping on the disgusting soda because it's within arm's reach and this movie is too incredible to walk away from.

After what feels like only an hour has passed, the screen turns white again and the lights gradually brighten around us. I'm still sitting upright, never having settled back into my seat, and for the last few minutes of the movie, I've been gripping the sides of the plush cushion.

Lloyd clears his throat, "So . . . what did you think?"

I slowly turn to him, my eyes wide. Lloyd looks worried—but there's no need for him to be.

"That was fucking amazing." I cackle to myself. I can't wrap my head around what I just witnessed.

Lloyd lets out a deep sigh, "Oh good. I thought you were mad at me for making you sit here for two hours."

"So that was all fake? Those people were pretending to be in those situations? None of it was real? And their outfits—I have never seen clothing like that before."

"Yup—all fake. But that really is what they used to wear back in the old days. You ready to go?" Lloyd stands and starts sliding out of the row and back toward the door we entered through.

I follow him out in silence as my mind recalls scenes from the movie. I want to remember as many details as possible of the story that just played out before us.

"That woman with the breathy voice and the . . . the . . ."

"Big tits?" Lloyd interjects.

"I wasn't going to say that. I was going to say the mole on her face, but sure. She said her name is Sugar."

"Her character's name is Sugar, but she's actually known as Marilyn Monroe." Lloyd walks ahead of me to the car and opens my door for me.

"Yeah, her. She is beautiful."

"Was beautiful," he says before closing my door and making his way around to the other side to get in.

I eagerly wait for him to get settled in the car so I can ask him my question. Finally, once he has the car started, I say, "What do you mean by 'was'?"

"She's not alive anymore. I don't think those two guys are alive anymore either. That movie is pretty old."

"That's sad," I state.

Lloyd doesn't respond as he drives down the dark road, his car lights guiding us through the wet night. I use the silence of our ride to replay the movie in my mind. I giggle to myself when I think about how silly the men were when they pretended to be women. Lloyd just squints at me as if I've gone crazy.

I think about what it would be like to have men look at me the way they looked at Marilyn in the movie. I glance down at my body and wonder if anyone would think I'm sexy, but I don't get far in my thoughts because Lloyd pulls over to the side of the road and turns off the car.

"I'll wait for you here. I don't want to get wet," he says with a slight grimace, like he feels guilty for not offering to come with me to check on Shea. Large raindrops thud against the windshield, and what was a drizzle when we left the theater has turned into a downpour—so I understand why he doesn't want to get out.

"All right, I'll be quick!" I grab the flashlight from the cup holder between us and jump out of the car. I jog gingerly down the trail toward the caves, dodging branches and being careful not to slip and fall. Raindrops plunk on my head, and soon enough, my hair is soaked and sticking to my face and neck.

When I reach the cave entrance, I shine my light on Shea's face. She's sitting on her haunches waiting for me, but something in her facial expression is off. I approach her slowly.

"Hey, girl. What's going on?" I ask. I move the beam of light down to her feet. Right when I notice that her legs are bound with rope, a hand cups my mouth from behind, and I drop the flashlight in shock. Another arm snakes around my waist, pressing my back flush against the unknown visitor's chest.

"Don't fucking move or scream, or we will kill you." The guy's voice is sinister as his hot breath fans across my ear.

My mind is racing, but I've been trained by Chester to calm myself and think of a plan in situations like this. I nod in acquiescence.

"Good girl," he growls, and the suggestiveness in this creep's voice has my skin crawling. He releases his hand from over my mouth, then he jerks both my arms behind my back and holds my wrists tightly. He starts to push me toward Shea, and I stumble forward but remain on my feet.

An alarm triggers within me when I realize he said we. My eyes roam the darkness for any trace of another person—but there's not enough light, and my wet hair is hanging in front of my line of sight.

"Hey, Soho! We have company!" my captor shouts. I can smell his rotting breath, and it makes my eyes water.

A girl, who I assume is Soho, appears from behind Shea. It's hard to discern her features through the curtain of my wet hair, but I can make out that she's a tiny thing with her hair in pigtail braids and barely any clothes on.

Why are they here, and what do they want?

"Bring her over here and tie her up," Soho says as she rummages through something I can't see at the edge of the woods. "Did you remember the tape so we can cover her mouth?" she asks the man behind me.

"Yeah, it's in the toolbox." He continues to shuffle me toward Soho.

Once we are fully behind Shea, Soho tosses the man a length of rope, and he gets to work wrapping it around my wrists. Before he can finish the job, I quickly turn and step back from him, shaking free of the rope. He's surprised for just long enough that I manage to slide my hand under the waistband of my leggings and unsheathe my dagger from my hip. I jerk forward and grab one of his wrists, twisting his arm around as I position myself behind him, much like how he just had me. With my dagger in the other hand, I bring the blade to his throat, and I hear him gasp.

"Now it's your turn not to move."

He squirms a little against me, and I see Soho making her way toward us.

"Don't come any closer, or I'll slit his throat," I command, poking the skin under his jaw to make my point.

Soho stops and puts her hands up with her palms facing me. "I told you this wouldn't be easy, Marcus," Soho squawks in frustration. "The dragon was way too complacent."

I glance at Shea, and she's watching us intently. I'm not sure what her plan of action is; honestly, I don't think she has one.

"I want you both to leave here and never tell anyone what you saw."

Marcus's laugh is ominous. "Fat chance, girlie." He grabs my arm that's holding the dagger and swings my body around, slamming me to the ground.

I land on my back but recover instantly, jumping to my feet and shifting into a defensive stance as I face both of them. My arms are out in front of me; the dagger is pointing toward Marcus, and my free hand is open toward Soho. With my back to Shea, I can hear a low growl rattling inside her chest, but she holds it back.

Focusing on Marcus and anticipating him to lunge at me, I hear a short but loud click echo off the trees. I drag my attention to where the noise came from as my eyes find Soho through the darkness and rain. No longer standing with her hands up in surrender, she now has her arms extended in front of her, gripping something small. Her hands tremble as she points the weapon in my direction.

"Looks like you brought a knife to a gunfight, honey," she says with feigned confidence.

Marcus laughs at Soho's snide comment.

A lump forms in my throat, and I try to swallow it down as I realize she's holding a gun. My efforts to swallow only make my stomach roil with the feeling of wanting to puke. We don't have guns on Kapu Island. They were banned after a realm jumper brought some back and a man was murdered with a single shot to the head. The chiefs of all four castles saw how powerful yet deadly guns could be, and they unanimously vowed to ban them—guns have disappeared from the island ever since.

Logic seems to escape me as I take a step toward Soho. But I stop in my tracks when she jerks the small weapon mere inches to the side and pulls the trigger. A loud bang erupts from the gun, and I gasp and hop back.

"Don't move, or next time I point the gun at your head."

I remain frozen as I grip my dagger tighter, calculating my next move.

Think . . . Think! What can I do now without getting killed?

"Marcus, go get her again!" Soho demands.

Marcus slowly walks toward me, his face menacing with a promise of violence, but I keep my eyes on Soho and the gun.

Suddenly, my attention is drawn to a black figure lurking behind Soho and coming our way. The bile in my stomach rises as I wonder if there are more than just these two. I blink rapidly, trying to clear the raindrops from my lashes. I frantically smack my hand across my forehead to clear the hair from my eyes, making sure I don't lose sight of Soho and the mystery guest descending upon us.

As the figure approaches, I squint my eyes—and I realize that it's Knox. I faintly recognize the tattoo on his forearm. The rain has created a steady thrumming noise, which is masking Knox's footsteps; Soho and Marcus have no idea he's here.

Knox looks at me and lifts his pointer finger to his lips, gesturing for me to stay quiet. Relief lights up my face for a moment before I school my expression so as not to give him away.

He unsheathes a dagger from under his shirt as he gets closer to Soho's back.

"Put her here." Soho points with the gun to the ground in front of her.

Marcus grabs my wrist that's holding the dagger and jerks it behind my back, and my other arm follows. He's squeezing my wrists together so tightly that my grip on the blade loosens. Unfortunately for me, Marcus notices and purposefully shakes my hands until the dagger tumbles from my fingers and onto the ground behind me. He doesn't bother to grab it as he pushes me forward.

I attempt to resist his shoving by planting my feet firmly on the ground, but it doesn't take long for Marcus to freeze in place when he notices Knox snake his way behind Soho.

Knox presses his dagger against Soho's throat and grips her waist to prevent her from escaping. If he says anything to her, I can't hear it.

She lowers the gun but keeps it in her hand at her side.

"Oh, fuck," Marcus mutters. "It's Knox Campbell." He still has my wrists pinned behind my back, but he's no longer trying to force me to move.

Soho doesn't flinch, and a sinister smile forms on her face. She grinds her ass into Knox's hips, and he immediately jerks back.

"What's wrong, baby? This doesn't turn you on?" Soho asks Knox in a sultry tone. The sound of her voice is grating, irritating; it's repulsive and makes me want to gag.

Then it dawns on me: Soho was the girl sitting in Knox's lap at the diner. My head begins to swirl with questions—so many questions—but one rings the loudest in my mind.

Is Knox with me, or is he with them?

Before I let myself spiral, I take a calming breath. Right now, I don't care what side Knox is on; all I know is that Shea and I need to get the hell out of here. I wiggle my arms in Marcus's grip and realize he's loosened his hold on me. This could be my last chance to get away, and I'm taking it. I snatch my hands free, my wrists slipping through Marcus's fingers.

"Hey!" he yells, but it's too late.

Like Chester taught me, I plant my foot behind me and then slam my shoulder as hard as I can into Marcus's chest.

We both hit the ground with a thud, which is shortly fol-lowed by a sharp POP as the gun goes off again.

Soho screams, but my attention remains on Marcus. I sit up, straddling him and pinning him on his back. I try not to look into his eyes as I pummel my fists into his face. He reaches for me, clawing at my throat and digging into my skin. I let out a panicked squeal as his hands circle my neck and his fingernails pierce deeper into my flesh. I grab at his wrists as I feel my windpipe narrow and my breathing becomes labored.

I don't know where my dagger went, so I've got no weapon to help me. I attempt to stand up, but Marcus's chokehold keeps my head and neck locked low to the ground. With my legs free, I lift my right knee and drive it into what I'm hoping is Marcus's crotch. It's a short, swift, and slightly awkward movement since I can't lift my leg all the way.

Marcus expels a deep grunt on impact and releases his hold on my neck to clench his groin and writhe on the ground.

I scramble away from him and look for my dagger in the darkness and wetness of the night. I can see silver glinting a few inches from Marcus's head. I dive for it on my hands and knees, but I'm not quick enough as Marcus realizes what I'm after. Just as my fingertips graze the hilt, he catch-es my right hand in his left, squeezing tightly. With his other hand, he lands a punch to my eye, and I'm momentarily stunned by the pain. But I'm not giving up. I yank my arm back as hard as I can to get out of his hold. Then I lurch forward and snatch the hilt of the dagger.

Marcus grabs my wrist once again and shakes my arm in hopes that I'll drop the blade—but I've got my grip locked firmly on it. He maintains ahold of my wrist while he pushes us to standing and twists my body around, slamming his chest to my back.

I thrust my free elbow up and into his nose.

"UGH!" Marcus shouts, and he lets me go. His hands gingerly touch the bridge of his nose while he winces. Blood pours down to his chin.

"You fucking bitch. You broke my nose!" he yells as spit and blood sputter from his mouth and into the air.

I turn without a second to lose and take off toward Shea. When I get to her, I anxiously rub the skin under her eyes.

"It's okay, girl. It's all right," I whisper to her repeatedly, but it sounds more like a mantra to myself. "Are you hurt, Shea?" I ask, and she gives a low snort. "I'll look you over once I get you somewhere safe."

I crawl between her two front legs and work the dagger through the rope binding her back legs. It's wrapped around three or four times, but the rope easily drops to the ground when I cut through it.

With my hand still clutching Shea's back leg, I feel the vibrations from her growling. The gnashing of her teeth warns me that someone is approaching, and I know I'm about to be attacked again. I quickly crawl out from underneath her wet, dirt-covered belly, and drops of her saliva land on my shoulder from her vicious snarling. I wish Shea could intervene and end this quickly, but she knows she must keep a low profile or our cover in this realm would be blown. Sighing deeply, I prepare for the hit.

When I stand up, I'm immediately grabbed by the neck from behind, and I can already tell it's that fucker Marcus by the stench of his breath. I flip the dagger in my right hand so it's pointing behind me and waste no time jabbing it into Marcus's right side, just below his rib cage. I yank it back out ferociously, and he sucks in a gasp of air. I turn and face him as he clutches the open wound, which is gushing with blood.

His eyes are wide as realization hits him.

On impulse, I stab the dagger into the side of Marcus's throat and pull it out.

His eyes grow impossibly wider as he stares at me. Even in the darkness, I can see the unnatural amount of white surrounding his irises. Marcus slaps his left hand over the gash on his neck, but it does nothing as blood leaks through his fingers. His face goes slack, his knees give out, and then he slumps over, landing hard on the ground.

Shea bends and sniffs at him, and I imagine his blood must be tantalizing to her, but she doesn't act on her impulses.

I spin around to see where Knox is. I'm still not sure whose side he's on, but I have to know if he's all right. Several yards away, I catch sight of some movement, so I conceal myself in the trees and sneak my way over. With all the stealth I can muster, I try to stick to the shadows and snap as few twigs as possible. I don't know where the gun is, and after Marcus's punch to my eye, which I can already feel swelling, I really don't need a gunshot wound as well . . . or to be killed.

I find Knox walking in a circular direction—but I can't work out what he's doing. When I get close enough to him, I realize he's tying Soho to a tree with rope. He has bound her hands and feet, and there's a thick piece of tape over her mouth, stifling any sounds she might be making. She spots me as I emerge from the trees, and her eyes are wide with anger, her nostrils flaring.

"Are you in on this?!" I shout at Knox. My heart is beating heavily as tears prick my eyes.

Knox finishes tying Soho up, cuts the extra rope with his dagger, and tosses the remaining length of it to the side before facing me. "Why would I be in on this, Louella?"

"Because you were with her the other night. I saw you! How did she know Shea was here?!" I scream at him. I point my dagger, which is dripping with Marcus's blood, in his direction as I try to steady the tremor of my hand.

"Louella, I"—Knox aggressively jabs his finger into his chest—"would never tell anyone about Shea. Either people would think I'm insane, or this would have happened. And why exactly would I want this to happen? Shea is your way out of here. Do you think I want to prevent that from happening?" Knox's voice is fierce and seething, reiterating his point that he wants me gone.

I know that's what he wants—I've known since the night he and Lloyd found me in these woods.

He wants me gone, but not dead.

I shake my head as the tears spill down my cheeks, mixing with the rain, which has turned into a light mist falling from the sky.

"Then how did she know?" I croak out. My shoulders start to quiver, and I can't tell if it's from my cold, wet clothes, which are sticking to my body, or the adrenaline, which is beginning to wear off.

Knox moves closer, and I let him. He carefully lifts my forearm and takes the dagger from my hand. With a quick drag along his pants, he wipes most of the blood from the blade. Gingerly, he slips the dagger back into my harness—with no lingering caresses this time. He looks at me, and his face appears almost pained.

"Let's get you back to the car, koa. You're freezing."

"But what about her?" I point behind him to Soho, who is now slumped over, and her eyes are closed. "Is she still alive?"

Holding my arm, Knox glances over his shoulder at Soho. "Yeah, she's alive." He looks back at me, and his forehead is puckered. "Go back to the car. I'll take care of all this. Tell Lloyd to take you straight home."

I'm too tired to fight, ask questions, or help him clean up this mess, so I turn and walk toward Shea. I give her a quick pat down to check for any injuries, and she nudges my face with her snout to let me know she's fine.

I place my forehead to her snout. "I love you, Shea. We will get home soon," I whisper. She nods in acknowledgment, and I let go of her. I slowly trek back to Lloyd's car. My body is numb and my mind is blank as I push forward through the brush and trees. I have nothing left inside me.

THIRTEEN

LOUELLA APONI DELPHINE

Kailani Bay, Gemcove Island

Lloyd drives us back to the house on the slick road and through the dark abyss of the night sky. He keeps apologizing for not getting out of the car with me, to which I haven't responded because I can't get my mouth to move. No coherent thoughts are coming to me, and the muscles in my body are mush.

He has also asked numerous times if I'm okay, and I think I nodded in response at one point—even though I'm still not exactly sure if I am okay. I'm so exhausted that I could sleep the entire ride home, but instead I sit here in shock and stare out the windshield in front of me.

Right before we pull into the driveway at the house, a single truth dawns on me: I murdered someone . . . And that cold reality isn't sitting well with me.

I finally come to as I trudge through the kitchen and head straight to the bathroom to shower off the dirt, blood, and remorse that's consuming my body. Before tonight, I had never killed anyone. Although it was the right thing to do in that situation—I know it was self-defense—I still feel like a terrible person.

I guess I would have had a hard time being a warrior.

Maybe that's why I am who I am . . . because I was never meant to be a fighter.

The water is scalding hot as I aggressively scour my body with the hope that if I scrub violently enough, I can wash away the doubt and apprehension I'm feeling. But when I'm out of breath and my skin is flushed red, tender to the touch, I realize that it's not going to work.

I wash my neck delicately, flinching when I find the scratches from Marcus's attempt to strangle me. The ache around my left eye from his punch will definitely transform into a black eye soon. I scan my arms and legs but don't find any serious injuries—just small knicks and cuts from the debris on the ground of the woods, but I'm sure I'll spot more bruises and soreness tomorrow.

I place my hands on the shower wall in front of me and let the stream of water glide down my hair and onto my back. My mind abruptly springs to life with thoughts of what Knox is doing with Soho. Did he help them? If he didn't, then how did they know where Shea was? If they knew about Shea, then who else knows? Are the caves safe for her anymore?

I clench my fists until my fingernails cut my palms. I need to calm down. Forcing myself to inhale deeply, I then let it all go: the tension in my fists, the questions, the worry, the doubt, my breath.

When I return to Knox's bedroom, I can't seem to summon up any energy to get dressed, so I toss my ruined clothes in the small trash bucket next to the door and set my dagger and its harness on top of the dresser—I'll care about cleaning it properly tomorrow. I shut the door and crawl across the soft blue blanket. All I can manage is to scrunch my body into a ball and lie on my side, facing the door. Without even realizing it, I doze off to sleep.

"Louella?" I faintly hear Chester's voice calling my name.

Has he found me? Has he come to take me home?

"Louella?" Chester says again, slightly louder this time.

I must be dreaming because Chester can't possibly be here in this realm. But this voice sounds so much like my brother's . . . Then I feel a weight on my hip, his hand nudging me.

As I awaken, I realize it's not Chester's voice; it's Knox's. Burying my face in the pillow, I keep my eyes shut a bit longer, but the reminders of what happened flood my memory. I begin to rub my eyes before I open them but yelp as pain radiates across my face from where Marcus punched me. Instead, I lightly tap the swollen skin above my cheek and around the socket, frowning as I think of how terrible I must look. Slowly, I ease my eyes open. The light from the bedside table is so bright, making me squint. When my eyes finally adjust, I find Knox sitting on the edge of the bed by my legs. I look toward him and then down at my body, noticing that I'm still in only a towel curled up in the same spot I lay down in.

I try to sit up, but he turns toward me and places a hand on my bare shoulder, gently pressing me back onto the bed. His hand is warm and soft, and it feels comforting against my cold skin. I shiver, and chills break out along my body. The soggy towel is doing nothing to keep me warm, and now I'm feeling self-conscious and uncomfortable.

"You don't have to get up. I'm going to get these wounds covered, make sure you don't get an infection," he says as I hug the towel tighter to my body. Knox's chest is bare, but he's wearing green-and-blue plaid pants that look soft and comfortable. His dark hair is wet and slicked back into a long braid that trails down his bare back.

Knox grabs a roll of white tape from beside him on the bed, alongside a small yellow tube, a white bag with a picture of green peas on the front, and gauze. He gets to work ripping small strips of tape from the roll, lining them along his forearm, where they dangle for easier access.

"Is everything all right?" I hesitantly ask. My words come out as more of a croaking noise from the soreness in my throat.

He coughs lightly before answering, "It's taken care of." He keeps his eyes down as he removes the cap from the yellow tube and smears some clear jelly along his fingertip.

"What did you do with them?" I whisper, a tinge of fear creeping into my voice.

"I let Shea handle them." He shrugs his shoulders as if to say he had no other option—I would have done the same thing and let Shea indulge in her most basic instincts. It's rare that she has the opportunity to hunt anything larger than cattle.

He shifts closer to me and holds up the finger that's smeared with the goopy substance. "This is Neosporin; it's an ointment that will help your cuts heal without any infections. I'm just going to rub this along your open wounds and then cover them with some gauze. I'll leave all of this in the bathroom for you."

"Okay," I say as I lie completely still, stiffening every muscle in my body with the anticipation of his touch.

Knox smears the cool ointment on my neck first. Instantly, my skin prickles from the contact. He presses a small gauze pad to my neck and tapes it in place.

"How is Shea? Did you move her?" I ask, just as his knuckles brush the bottom of my chin.

He looks up at me. "She's perfectly fine, like nothing happened—not a scratch on her. I can't really move her, so she'll have to stay at the caves." He sits up straighter and tilts his head to ask, "Is the tape too tight?"

I shake my head no, and he nods with satisfaction. As he squeezes more ointment onto his finger, I find the courage to ask the most important questions I have for him.

"Who were they? How did they know she was there?" My voice is stronger now, accusatory.

Knox sighs, "Marcus and Soho are brother and sister. They are known around the bay for being cons. I suspect she must have followed me there one night, and then they concocted this plan."

I sit still as he dabs the Neosporin on small cuts I acquired on my shoulder. I think about the times we've visited Shea together.

"But you have only been with me once to see her. My first night here."

With a shrug, he answers, "It must have been that one time."

Knox quickly scans my body for any other cuts, but he must not notice anything because he wipes his hands clean on a spare gauze pad. After gathering up the materials from the bed and placing them in his lap, he grabs the white bag with the picture of peas on it.

"Here, this will help with the swelling around your eye." He leans in toward my face and carefully presses the bag to my cheek.

I inhale sharply at the freezing cold.

"Frozen peas make the best ice pack, I swear. Keep it on there for thirty minutes, leave it off for thirty minutes, and repeat," he instructs. His eyebrows are raised to the top of his head and he drops his chin, as if he's reading my face to make sure I understand the directions.

He takes my hand and brings it to the bag, holding it against my injured eye. I shiver once again, but this time, it's from the freezing-cold temperature of the bag and not his delicate touch. He twists away from me so that I'm looking at his back again.

My brows knit together, and I can't stop myself before I ask, "Why would you hook up with someone like Soho?" I spit her name in disgust.

Knox's shoulders bunch up, and I can tell he flinched at my accusatory tone, as if he's also repulsed at the thought of being with Soho. He pinches the bridge of his nose while I wait for his answer.

"We had a good time. We hung out once or twice, and that was it. The guys kept telling me to stay away because she was no good, so I kept her at a distance. Sarah never asked questions, and it seemed like we had a good thing going . . . It was nice."

"Sarah?" It's the only response I give, and I realize that Knox is being open with me about his life . . . kind of.

"Yeah, Soho's her 'crew' name." His hands are gripping the edge of the mattress as he stares at the floor.

"A crew?" I snort. "Does she work on a ship?"

"No," Knox huffs out a small laugh. "A crew here means her group of friends she hangs out with. They all have nicknames, and that was hers."

"Oh." I look at nothing in particular for several seconds, deep in thought. "But I still don't understand what she and Marcus were trying to do with Shea. It doesn't make any sense to me."

I look to Knox, and his molten eyes meet mine with something that looks like sadness, but I can't be too sure.

"The people in this realm aren't like the people where you come from, koa. They will do anything to survive and make a quick buck. Dragon skin, bones, and teeth are traded for thousands of dollars here on a shady black market, so when they found Shea, they didn't care that they would be killing what most people believe is a mythical creature—and they especially didn't care that someone loves her. It didn't faze them that they were about to kill something period. They saw dollar signs and got to work."

Dropping the bag of frozen peas onto the mattress, I prop myself up on my elbows and scooch back. Knox doesn't try to stop me from getting up this time, and I carefully move my legs around his body to place my feet on the floor. We are now sitting side by side, our bare arms nearly touching, and the warmth radiating from his skin is like electricity humming between us. Thinking through his explanation, I still don't understand how or where he got this information.

"How do you know so much about dragons and the black target?" I ask, still unconvinced.

A slight grin tugs at the sides of Knox's lips. "Black market," he corrects me, shaking his head like I told him a joke.

If it wouldn't hurt so much, I'd roll my eyes because I just want clarification on the situation . . . and maybe because I'm a bit embarrassed.

"I learned everything I know from Todd at Relics of the Realms. He wants so badly to believe the dragon realm is real . . ." Knox pauses before continuing, "But I never ever believed him until I saw you and Shea. Then it all made sense; everything Todd told me over the years was true. But he doesn't even realize it! He acquires his merchandise from these mystery dealers who for sure hop between realms. And Todd knows all the rumors swirling around about the scavengers trying to access the dragon realm so they can slaughter dragons and bring back the parts to sell for thousands of dollars. Luckily, not many people realize the portals are real, and even fewer know their locations. Those who do have kept it to themselves."

Knox's words bounce around in my mind, and I search for reasons not to believe him or why he would lie to me—but I come up short. He's not very fond of me, but he did help me. Multiple times now. Following my heart, I decide that it is best to trust him and move on.

Minutes pass with neither of us speaking as we sink into the severity of our actions tonight. We both have blood on our hands, and if we ever get caught, it could be bad . . . I may never make it home.

I sigh, "I feel terrible about what happened to Marcus. I fucking killed someone. But at the same time, I can't afford to get in trouble."

Knox releases a dark chuckle, "Don't feel guilty—he was a fucking asshole."

"Well, I mean, I've met a number of assholes in my life, but that doesn't justify killing them," I argue.

Knox shakes his head, "Nah, this dude was more than an asshole, he was fucking scum. He's been in and out of jail for assault, rape—I mean, the list goes on and on. Don't feel bad about him. Plus, no one will be looking for them, I can assure you. The cops will be relieved not to hear anything about them for a while."

My shoulders sag as I relax just a bit. My remorse begins to wane, but it still feels wrong.

"Why were you there?" The question pops into my head and slips off my tongue before I can even decide if I want the answer.

Knox rubs the back of his neck and itches his scalp under his braid before letting out a long sigh, "I . . . I tried calling Lloyd to see where you two were. It was getting late, and usually, you haven't been out that long going to see Shea. Lloyd didn't answer his phone, so I figured I'd take a ride to double-check that everything was okay. As I got closer, I saw Marcus's car parked about a mile from the caves. I've never seen him around the woods before, and it seemed suspicious."

He turns to face me, but I can't meet his eyes. I don't want to do or say anything that might shatter this moment—he's being so honest and unguarded. Silence hangs in the air, and then he looks away.

"When I pulled up next to Lloyd's car, I was surprised to see him in the driver's seat. I asked why he was in the car and not with you, and he said he 'didn't want to get wet,'" Knox scoffs. "I was so fucking pissed at him because we had agreed that we were not going to let you go alone into the woods."

My heart skips a beat at the thought of Knox being concerned about me. The blood rushes to my face, rising all the way to the tips of my ears. I tilt my head down so that my hair hangs over my face like a curtain in hopes that Knox won't notice my blush. Through the curls of my hair, I can see him glance at me again and then back to the floor.

"Sure as shit, when I went out there, I saw Marcus had you with your arms pinned behind your back, and I knew Sarah was close. They're always together when bad things are about to go down. I crept around through the trees and finally found her, right as she pulled the gun on you. And . . . well, you know the rest."

"Hm, yeah, I do," I sneer.

"Does that answer all your questions?" Knox stifles a yawn, and I know it's time to let him go.

My thoughts are consumed by images of everything that happened tonight. A specific moment stands out, other than my moment with Marcus: Soho standing in the rain with the gun in her trembling hands.

"Just one more: What did you do with the gun?"

"I took care of it. Don't worry."

"That's a less-than-satisfying answer, but fine . . . and . . . and thank you," I mumble.

I look at Knox now and catch that the whites around his dark-brown eyes are bloodshot. He hitches up one side of his mouth, and my stomach flutters at the sight. I want to reach out and trace the outline of his lips, but I fight the urge. Instead, I cautiously rest my free hand on top of his. My pulse is pounding, and I hold my breath, praying he can't tell.

Knox looks down at our hands and then back to me. His expression is pained, like he doesn't enjoy the sensation of my touch. He slides his hand out from underneath mine, gathers the medical supplies from his lap, and then stands up, leaving my hand feeling cold and lifeless on the bed.

I can't look at him as I fight the embarrassment and anger that swell inside me. Thankfully, the room plunges into darkness once again when I hear the chain of the bedside lamp.

"Don't mention it, koa. And remember: thirty minutes on, thirty minutes off," he whispers into the now-dark room.

I try to watch him exit, but my eyes haven't adjusted yet, and I'm unable to see anything. I hear the door click shut, and the sound snaps me back to the reality of Knox's icy interactions and distant stares.

Standing up from the mattress, I yank the towel off and toss it to the floor. Groping around in the pitch-black room, I find a T-shirt to pull over my head, put my panties on, and dive back into bed, tucking myself in under the covers and holding the bag of peas to my swollen eye. I lie still, facing the wall for what feels like hours—surely, it's only been minutes—waiting for sleep to come, but it doesn't.

It was stupid of me to assume Knox was opening up to me; I should have never thought he would respond to my touch. I feel icky thinking about how stupid I am for putting myself out there and being rejected. It makes me angry. A frustrated growl escapes my throat, and I flop onto my other side, facing the door.

I think about Kapu Island and wonder if there's a war happening yet—but I feel silly thinking a war would start because of me. There won't be a war over me. I chuckle into the quiet of this lonely room as I compare myself to Helen of Troy from a book I once read. It's comical to think that awkward, naïve me could ever be compared to the beauty and elegance of "the face that launched a thousand ships." . . . There's also that small, minor detail that a man has never even loved me to think I was worth the hassle of defending my honor or fighting for me. The only guy I'm pining over doesn't even want to breathe the same air as me.

I wrap an arm around my stomach, embracing myself in a hug. There's a sinking feeling in my chest, like my heart is drowning, and my stomach feels hollow—or I could be hungry . . . I'm not sure at this point. But I think the feeling is hopelessness. This realm is fascinating to me, but it's also so lonely.

Trying to ignore this ache in my chest, I force myself to think of happy memories from back home. Of the family that loves me. The last thought that flickers through my mind is how excited I am to tell Chester all about the new things I've experienced during my time here, but before I can enjoy the slight burst of happiness the thought brings, sleep overcomes me.

That night, I dream about visiting Castle Hana as a child with Papa. I'm eight years old, watching an eight-year-old Malcolm play-fight with his friends in the training arena on the castle grounds. Malcolm watches me when I walk by, but the look he gives me isn't what I expect—it's as if he hates me. He has a wooden practice sword dangling limp in his hand and a stern look on his face—my consciousness recognizes it as the same expression he wore when I saw him last. The boy Malcolm is sparring with is slightly taller and slimmer standing next to him, and he flashes a smile at me, which quickly fades when Malcolm turns toward him. Another boy is standing with them, and this one playfully shoves Malcolm to lighten the mood, and soon all three of them are laughing and play-fighting once more.

In my dream, I am overcome with jealousy that Malcolm has friends and I don't. Whining to Papa, I beg him to let me make friends. Instead, he tells me that I have my brother, and that Chester will always be my best friend—which is true. But I want a girlfriend. I want to chat about boys, style each other's hair, and giggle over our little secrets and jokes. Chester is a great brother and friend, but he could never really fill that void.

Gradually, the scene at Castle Hana fades away, and the rest of my sleep is dreamless.

The next morning, I wake up to the familiar scent of Knox . . . and a bag of mushy, warm peas under my head. I slide the bag out from underneath me and, without looking, slap it onto the bedside table. The sun's rays beam in through the cracks between the curtains hanging over the windows. I lie still on the bed as my eyes roam around the room.

Contemplating my dream, I think about how odd it is to have conjured up this scene with Malcolm . . . But it wasn't a dream—it was a memory. Everything that happened in my dream happened in real life over ten years ago. The loneliness I'm feeling and the guilt over my attraction to another man must be seeping into my subconscious. Everything is weighing so heavily on me lately, and I wish I could jump on Shea's back and fly away from it all . . .

Shea . . .

The instant I think of her, I shoot out of bed. I need to see her to ensure she made it through the night unharmed and is still hidden. This is my top priority—the first and only thing I will do today. Well, that and toss the peas back in the freezer to use on my eye again later.

FOURTEEN

CHESTER PALA DELPHINE

Castle Waimea, Kapu Island

Lucas and two of Castle Waimea's top handlers, and their respective dragons, were sent to Castle Hana yesterday morning, thus fulfilling the request (or rather, demand) of Castle Hana for breeding dragons. Just as my father wanted, the selected trio was delivered a day early. My family and I breathed a sigh of relief when we received confirmation of their safe arrival last night. That should quell Victor and Maribeth's desire to siege our castle and village—at least for now.

It's before dawn, and I'm taking stock of our equipment shed now that three dragons have moved out—temporarily, at least. It's mindless work, and I'm distracted wondering how Luke is handling the Castle Hana royals. The thought of him being stuck there for months makes me shudder, and I force myself to focus on the task at hand.

Suddenly, I hear the swooping sound of wings in the sky above me. Glancing up, I spot Luke and his dragon, Zion, flying toward me. The two other dragons sent for cross-breeding, along with their handlers, follow closely behind them.

Zion hastily lands, digging his talons deep into the soft earth and tearing it apart from impact. Before the dragon can even come to a complete stop, Luke is dismounting him, the pair of them heading straight for me at the mouth of the dragon caves.

The expression on Luke's face is hostile, and he looks grim under the dim lights of the caves. Wordlessly, he ushers Zion into a cavern and sets off in a furious march toward the castle, ripping his riding gloves off his hands and throwing them to the ground. I tail him, hustling to walk at his side. When I appear next to him, he doesn't even face me.

"You need to wake the chief when we get inside," he demands. His demeanor is authoritative—I've never seen him this way before, so I don't ask questions.

We enter the castle, and I go straight to Papa's room and tell him Luke is requesting an urgent meeting in the dining room.

Once we're all assembled, Luke recounts what happened. Apparently, Castle Hana is looking for a specific dragon to crossbreed, and that dragon just so happens to be Shea. When Luke explained to Maribeth and Victor that Shea had disappeared with Louella, they called off the arrangement. Even Luke's attempts to appease them with the selected dragons failed. Castle Hana is accusing Castle Waimea of lying and falsifying documents; they claim we knew that Zeus did not have an ailment and that he should have been one of the dragons standing before them—but he wasn't. Because of this, they no longer believe Shea and Ella are missing; instead, they think we have the two of them hidden within our castle. They told Luke that we are trying to deceive them and that it appears we have no intention of fulfilling the contract or honoring the treaty.

Soon after this conversation with Victor and Maribeth, the king called his guards to see our dragons and riders off Castle Hana's land immediately. Before Victor left them, he told Luke to alert Castle Waimea that we should prepare for war.

Papa holds his composure as Luke delivers the news. Mama, however, isn't as composed, which is odd for me to witness. She is seething with rage. Her fists are clenched so tight at her sides that she's trembling. I am worried that at some point she will begin to draw blood from her nails cutting into the skin of her palms. Mama's face is so red that it looks as though she has a brutal sunburn.

Finally, she puts her anger into words. "Let's attack first," she snarls.

Papa looks at her with a confused expression. "Theadosia, I don't think that's wise. We have an advantage if they come to us because we have ample supplies and won't need to travel anywhere. I know yo—"

"I'm not going to stand back and let Maribeth and Victor besiege us—that's absurd!" The veins in her neck are straining against her skin as her voice bellows throughout the room.

Papa stomps his boot down, and our eyes snap to him.

"Thea, please. Let me do my job, and you do yours." Despite how loudly his boot hit the ground, his voice is calm and even.

He glares at Mama, and she returns the look. They stay like that for several seconds before Mama throws her hands in the air and storms out of the room.

***

Over the past couple of days, news of Castle Hana's threat has spread throughout our castle and into the village. As a result, the castle guards, the military, the villagers, and everyone in between are understandably frantic. Those under my command have their instructions and are working together to secure the castle and village, but the possibility of war is unprecedented for our time. Not since the Algonquin Battle has there been serious fighting on our island.

Today, I have done nothing but rush around without actually getting anything done. The anxiety is crushing. I have less than four days to prepare for my realm-jump rescue mission to find Louella, and the pressure to succeed in bringing her home just got more intense. I've been praying to the goddesses that the war holds off until Louella and I safely return. We can bring her to Castle Hana and clean up this entire mess of a situation we've found ourselves in—we can call off this war. This will all be over.

I have about five minutes until I'm due to meet Luke down at the dragon caves to finalize my flight details. Since the declaration of war, I've been in a frenzy gathering food, clothes, daggers, and pretty much anything I can carry in my satchel, which is the only luggage I'm taking. At this point, I've forgotten what is even in the satchel—but I'll keep adding more until I can't latch it closed.

I will be stashing the bag in the equipment shed for when I leave Saturday night, so I just need to take inventory of the contents and bring it down with me today. We figured it would be best not to have the prince walking toward the dragon caves with a large bag in the middle of the night. Instead, we agreed it's much less suspicious if I'm carrying the satchel with me during the day. The last thing we need is for people to think I'm skipping town like their princess—and certainly not with threats of a war about to take place.

Camilla will be joining Luke and me at the caves today to go over last-minute details and prepare me for the actual jump. She mentioned that the portal is essentially a suctioning black hole that some don't survive if they aren't prepared. This is the part that scares me the most—not what's on the other side of the portal, but going inside it. If Camilla's goal is to scare me into not going, she's almost succeeded by the stories she has been telling me. But I'm not going to say that to her—nor will I back down.

I shove some sort of jarred vegetable and a single unripe banana into the satchel and am barely able to secure the flap. Then I dodge out of the kitchen, briskly walking out the castle doors and onto the gravel path. None of the castle staff even notice me because they're too busy worrying about the impending war. I'm thankful I don't have to pass through the village today like I did yesterday while on my way to Camilla's for supplies. When I took the road through the village, I was stopped every few strides. Some villagers are concerned about Louella, some are ready to fight for our castle and our village, and others are confused and angry about what is happening. The tension within the village is growing, but today, I want to focus solely on the mission ahead of me.

Picking up my pace into a light jog, I approach the caves. Luke is standing at the shed with Camilla, and they are deep in conversation. Luke notices me first and beams, then he taps Camilla's shoulder. She is slouched on her wooden crutches with her ankle still wrapped. Standing next to Luke, she looks even tinier than usual and so young, but she's actually a few years older than him. Camilla perks up when she sees me, giving me a hesitant smile. I can tell she is not entirely happy about what we've roped her into, but I'm eternally grateful for her help.

"Hey, sorry I'm late. It's crazy in the castle," I say in between deep breaths.

"Oh, I bet. The village is the same way. People are so distracted that I was knocked over twice yesterday while working the market stall with Tallulah." Camilla shrugs, and her short black bob scrunches on her shoulders with the gesture.

I hate that she has to work while still recovering from her injury, but I know nothing I say will convince her not to. I give Camilla a sheepish grin because I have a little surprise for her, and she doesn't know it's coming: I've put a large chunk of change aside to repay her and Tallulah for helping me, and Luke has offered to bring it to the sisters while I am away. This should help them not to have to work so hard, and maybe they'll even take some days off. My hope is that they will be able to live more comfortably—as long as we can avoid this war.

"Camilla was just asking me how you plan to find Louella once you get to the other realm," Luke tells me. "I was explaining how dragons form bonds within their bloodline, and with that bond, they can communicate with echolocation. Almost like they are speaking telepathically."

"And you are certain that Gabriel is strong enough to find Shea?" Camilla asks with her eyebrows pinched. She lifts a hand above her forehead to create some shade as she looks up at me to inspect my facial features.

"Gabriel's our best bet. He's a dark-enough brown that he will blend in with the night sky, and he's quick, which we need. No one except Brynlee rides him because he's not fully grown and ready for combat yet, but his bloodline bond with Shea is strong," I reply assuredly. Knowing how much Luke has agonized over these details, I have to appear confident if we're going to get through this.

Camilla gives a satisfied nod and brings her hand back down to grip her crutch.

"I'm going to toss this satchel inside the shed under Gabriel's saddle. You two find some shade, and we will go over the 'hell hole' logistics once I'm done," I joke.

"Oh, stop! It's not that bad," Camilla chuckles.

I snort in response, "Suuurrre."

Luke points to a shaded spot under the nearby willow trees and says, "We'll be right over there."

I nod at them and push open the door to the shed.

The air in the small structure is always stuffy during the day, and I don't want to linger in here any longer than I need to. I find Gabriel's saddle and tuck my satchel underneath it, then I scurry out of this oven. Looking back, I make sure that the bag is not visible to anyone who might poke around in here.

Back in the bright sun, I take a deep breath of fresh air, clearing the thickness from my lungs. I spot Luke and Camilla under the tree where they said they would be waiting and saunter over to them.

Camilla is sitting with her legs stretched out in front of her, the wooden crutches lying beside her. Luke is next to her, sitting cross-legged and playing with a blade of grass between his fingers. I plop down on the other side of Luke, reclining into the grass and leaning my head back. I intertwine my fingers, bringing them behind my neck to use as support. This small moment of peace might be the most relaxed I've felt all week.

"All right, what's the plan?" Luke says as he claps his hands together.

I let my eyes fall closed, feeling the heaviness in my lids. I didn't realize how exhausted I was. My mind is still zinging with the need to be productive, but my body is currently winning out. I could fall asleep right here.

I feel a tap on my leg. Lifting my head, I squint my eyes to see Camilla and Luke waiting for my response. With a sigh, I push myself up to a seated position.

"What's going on with you?" Luke asks. There isn't an ounce of annoyance in his tone, just genuine concern.

"I haven't slept well lately, that's all." I brush away his question by waving my hands in the air.

Luke gives me one last glance before he nods and turns to Camilla.

"Well, you'd better rest up before you realm jump—it takes a lot of energy out of ya. Did you get the rest of the supplies from the list I gave you?" Camilla raises a single brow at me, and I can tell she's still unsure about me doing this—but I'm sure of myself, so she doesn't need to worry.

"Yes. I just finished packing my bag with food, toiletries, the flashlights and lighter you lent me, and clothes."

"Damn, that sounds like an awful lot to bring . . . Is your satchel heavy?" Luke questions.

"It is, but I'm going to strap it to the back of the saddle so that it won't add any extra weight to my body when I go through the portal. I want to minimize the risk of anything knocking me off-balance, and this way, I'll be able to hold tightly to the reins so I don't fall."

Luke smiles and nods at my response.

"I'm on watch for the caves Saturday night, so I'll already be down here. And no other guards will be on duty until the next shift change, when I'll be long gone. The men patrolling the perimeter may catch sight of me in the sky, but hopefully Gabriel will blend in and we will go unnoticed—plus, he's so quiet when he flies that I'm sure no one will hear him." I shrug a shoulder, half believing myself and half doubting. Right now, though, I have no other option. I have to run the risk of getting caught if I want to find Louella.

"I'll meet you down here just before midnight to send you off, but I'll leave shortly after to avoid suspicion that this was planned or that I know where you are," Luke interjects.

"You have the map and coordinates of the sky portal to get back from the other realm, right?" Camilla asks as she grabs her crutches from the grass beside her.

"Yeah, in the satchel," I reply, offering her a hand, but she dismisses it.

"Good. Remember, you only have until four o'clock in the morning to get back through the portal. It shrinks every hour and closes at five o'clock, so four is the absolute latest time when you'll be able to squeeze on through with Gabriel. Shea will be able to fit as well, but barely. So don't dawdle." Camilla clambers upright to her good foot, propping herself on the crutches.

I humph at her warning. "I'll try not to stick around too long, but that doesn't give me much time to find Louella. I can't promise I'll come back with her."

"Well, you'll have tried," Camilla reassures me.

"Any questions for me before I head back home?" Camilla struggles to adjust the crutches under her arms as she prepares to move. She lists to one side, looking as if she's going to fall, which prompts Luke to jump up and assist her with finding her balance.

I scan through my mental checklist, and a question bounces forward, begging to be asked. Even though I've already interrogated Camilla and Tallulah about it countless times, I want to hear the answer again.

"What do I do if we don't make it through the portal in time?"

"You gotta wait until September twenty-fifth, so I suggest you get your ass in gear once you get there." Camilla assesses me with a look that says I'd better not fuck this up.

I get to my feet and watch the two of them for a moment. "Thanks for all the help, Camilla. I appreciate it," I say earnestly.

Camilla shuffles on her crutches over to me. "Just bring our princess back," she whispers.

I dip my chin and give her a solemn smirk. "As you wish."

FIFTEEN

LOUELLA APONI DELPHINE

Kapa'a, Gemcove Island

This morning, while I was reading at the kitchen table, Lloyd asked me to join him and Knox at the beach. They both have the day off from work, and he wants me to come hang with their "crew," which, as I've written in my journal, means "group of friends." I hesitated to give him an answer right away for a number of reasons, the first being that, although people back on Kapu Island surf all the time, I've only ever tried it on Shea's back—obviously, I can't do that here. Another reason is that I'm not quite sure if I want to jump headfirst into Knox and Lloyd's world. It's an odd feeling, but I don't want to waste my time getting to know their friends when I will never see these people again. It may be slightly selfish, but I can't allow myself to get attached to anything in this realm. I fear that I will let myself enjoy it too much . . . and it will be harder to leave.

But I have to leave. Shea and I don't belong here.

Since the attack five days ago, Shea has been her normal self, thank the goddesses. My scratches have healed over nicely and are barely visible, even along my neck. A small yellowish-blue spot on the side of my eye from where Marcus decked me is the only real reminder of the fight and how I mur—

The thought of my dagger puncturing Marcus's neck makes my throat tighten. It's an image I've been trying to erase from my mind, which has been easier to forget when Lloyd's around with all his talking and questions.

Lloyd didn't settle for my initial no, and he didn't give up easily, repeatedly pestering me over my breakfast of toast and strawberry jam. I mentally argued with myself, trying to decide what to do. Several times I had to reread the same paragraph in my book. Eventually, I closed the novel, leaving it on the table beside my plate of crumbs to watch Lloyd rave about how beautiful the beach is, how much fun they always have, how Knox is the best surfer out of everyone in the crew, how all the local girls stop by to ogle him with his shirt off . . .

I agreed to tag along. I mean, what else will I do with my time? Meander around the house alone, drowning in guilt for killing a man to protect myself and my dragon? Not a chance.

After a brief look in the mirror to check my wounds and what felt like the longest car ride I've ever experienced, I'm sitting cross-legged on a sheet draped on top of the sand, intently watching Knox wade in the water with his back to the shore as he waits for a good wave.

This is a new part of the island I haven't been to yet, but Lloyd insists it's the best beach for surfing. Lloyd is the only one of the three of us who did any talking during the drive here because apparently Knox is back to not talking to me. So I sat in the backseat by myself while Lloyd drove and chatted Knox's ear off about the "surf conditions" for the day.

We were the last car to arrive, so the boys were in a rush to grab their gear and get moving. Thankfully, on his way to the water, Lloyd showed me where to sit and promised he'd give me a good show by catching some "sick" waves. I swear, I could create a whole dictionary based solely on my conversations with Lloyd.

Their crew consists of two other "dudes" (as Lloyd calls them) and two girls. All the guys are in the water, and the girls are sitting a couple of feet away from me on a cloth of their own. We're listening to music coming from a small box they brought. Before taking off into the surf, Lloyd whispered to me that it's a "speaker," like how we listen to music in the car. I'm already a bit overwhelmed sitting here alone, but I want to try and enjoy this experience.

Feeling self-conscious, I do my best to avoid making eye contact with the girls. Instead, I've been casually glancing at them from time to time. They talk and laugh loudly over the music as they sip out of flimsy red cups. Occasionally, they playfully push each other and then fall over, hysterically laughing while their drinks slosh onto the sand. It's a kind of banter I've never seen before because, well, I've never had any friends like that.

They resemble the girls from the posters on Knox's bedroom walls: slim figures, plump breasts, and perfectly round bums, with cute tattoos scattered in exactly the right spots on their bodies. Their tight shorts and tiny halter tops are perfectly beachy and perfectly sexy. Unlike me, who opted for a pair of leggings and a long, baggy T-shirt. I tell myself that I don't need to impress anyone, but seeing them makes me feel frumpy, like maybe I could have put a bit more effort into my beach attire. Still, being here in this realm has given me a nice break from having to wear our traditional garb and tight braids and curls, which I'd been stuck in more frequently while I was training to be a queen. If Mama were here, she would make me sit up straight, uncross my legs, and clasp my hands nicely on my lap. Actually, she would probably make me go back to the house to put on makeup, braid my hair, and dress in something fit for royalty. Overall, I'm thankful I get to put on what I want and wear my hair how I like.

I'm comfortable. And I'm happy with my choices.

"Hey!"

My head whips in the direction of the sound, over to the girls to see what they're shouting at. The one with long blond hair is waving at me. She has her other arm raised, a red cup in her hand.

"Wanna come join us? We have spiked iced tea!" she calls.

I gawk at her in shock, with my mouth slightly agape.

They want me to join them?

She pats a space next to her on the sheet, beckoning, "Come on! It's sooooo good!" She's swirling her cup and smiling widely—I can't help but smile back.

Before my mind can process what my legs are doing, I stand up, walk the few paces separating us, and join them on their sheet. I hesitantly sit down next to the blonde who called me over, and I hear a loud rustling noise as she gets to work grabbing stuff out of the blue-and-white box next to her.

She speaks to me while she fills another red cup with various liquids. "I'm Gabby. This is Sage. She's dating Dean, the short surfer out there with the buzzed bleach-blond hair." She briefly stops shuffling around in the box and points to Dean out in the water, who just jumped up on his board to ride a decent-sized wave.

I nod, "Cool. I'm Louella." I smile shyly at both Gabby and Sage.

Sage has shoulder-length red hair—a shade of red I've never seen before. It's so bright that it doesn't even look real. Her brown eyes are kind as she returns a small grin.

Gabby hands me a cold red cup and sits back down next to me. I lift the drink to my nose and give it a whiff. The smell is a weird mix of lemon, sweetness, and something like the rubbing alcohol we use to clean metal weaponry back home. I want to gag and frown at the contents, but I fight to keep my face blank.

"Where ya from, Louella?" Gabby asks.

Hmm, this is tricky. I think about it for a second and decide to make my answer as ambiguous as possible without being rude.

"I'm from another island. Just happened to stop here." I take a sip of the spiked iced tea, and my mouth puckers from how sour yet sweet it is. I let out a little cough and scrunch my face, causing Gabby and Sage to giggle at my reaction.

"The first sip is usually the worst, but after that, it goes down smooth," Sage reassures me.

"Do you vacation here with your family or something?" Gabby probes further.

"Uhhh, no, just making a stop." I'm unsure of what else to say.

She tilts her head in thought. "How do you know Knox and Lloyd then?"

I look away from her sapphire-blue eyes and take another sip so I have time to think of an answer.

"I just met them one night, and we have been hanging out." I lift my shoulders nonchalantly, hoping to change subjects.

"This must be a Lloyd scheme. Knox rarely 'hangs out' with girls," Gabby responds.

"What does that mean?" I ask, trying hard not to sound too inquisitive.

"Knox is a player. He doesn't 'talk' to girls; he fucks them and then is on to the next one," Sage answers.

"We've all been there," Gabby says as she and Sage clink their cups together in agreement.

"I thought you were with Dean?" I ask Sage, feeling perplexed by this conversation.

"Well, yeah, I am. But the island's small so, like, we all get with each other at some point. Ya know?"

No, I really don't know what Sage means by that, but she has made it clear that Knox has been with a lot of girls. An image of Soho flashes before my eyes, and my blood boils as my heart races. I feel nauseous, and I know it's probably visible on my face.

I look out and watch Knox as he straddles his board. My mood takes a turn from enraged to curious when I look at him, and I imagine running my hands along his stomach and feeling the contours of his abs. Caught up in a fantasy about how his body would feel on top of mine, I clasp the red cup tighter in my grip and lick my lips.

"Mmmm, yes, girl. He is so fine." Gabby catches my attention. I shift my eyes over to her, and she waggles her eyebrows with a knowing look.

I take another sip of my drink, trying to hide the blush forming on my cheeks. She's not wrong—he is very nice to look at.

"I'm not surprised he befriended you at first sight—you are gorgeous . . . ," Gabby pauses, turning to look at me. "I'm just trying to figure out why a hot girl like you isn't wearing a swimsuit to the beach."

Sage lightly slaps her friend on the thigh. "Gabby! You can't say things like that," she chastises. "Maybe she's self-conscious."

I look down at my clothing and then at Gabby's and Sage's swimsuits.

"Uh, I don't have a swimsuit," I say, shrugging my shoulders and praying they'll accept my answer and leave it at that.

"Wait. How are you vacationing on a tropical island without a swimsuit?" Sage asks in disbelief.

"As I said, I didn't plan on being here for very long," I rush out. I wish they would stop asking so many goddess-damned questions.

I should have stayed on my sheet.

"Well, I'll come over later and drop off some of my extra suits for you to borrow while you're here," Gabby declares rather than offers.

"Thanks," I answer. I take another swig of my drink because it is delicious after the first sip. When I look back to the water, the boys are making their way over to us, carrying their surfboards as they all share a laugh.

They drop the boards down in front of the two sheets, and then the four of them disperse in different directions. Lloyd is moving toward the blue-and-white box, and Dean has his eyes set on Sage. Knox joins the guy whose name I don't know yet as he plops down onto the empty sheet I previously occupied. He has dirty-blond hair that's short on the sides but a bit longer on top. His wavy locks are effortlessly styled by the salty ocean water, and it looks good.

Tousled-hair boy catches me observing him.

I have seriously got to get better at that.

"I'm Ethan," he says with a quick wave.

I offer a polite smile and respond, "Louella."

"Lloyd was just telling us that you're vacationing here for a bit. How are you liking the island so far?"

To anyone else, it seems like a simple question to answer—but not for me. Gemcove Island reminds me a lot of back home: it has a similar landscape with breathtaking beaches, vibrant flowers, tall palms, and lush greenery. Hell, when Shea and I first emerged from the portal, I thought it was Kapu Island. But this place has a lot more stuff and noise and people, so I wouldn't consider it extraordinary, especially compared to my home . . . But I'm not going to say that out loud.

"It's nice."

"Aw man, you're a tough crowd. Most people who visit Gemcove never want to leave," Ethan responds with a smug look on his face. "Hey, you going to join us at the Shack later for reggae night?"

I look over to Knox and then to Lloyd, who is now standing behind Knox and drinking from a red cup. I have no idea what Ethan is asking me to do, so I'm searching for answers from these two. They look at each other and exchange some kind of glance I can't read.

"We will see. She may have plans tonight," Knox supplies for me.

"C'mon! Take her out. If you don't, I will . . . We could have some fun." Ethan jerks his chin out and winks at me.

From where I'm sitting, I can see Knox clenching his jaw, the muscle twitching.

Ethan is handsome, but in a royal way. He reminds me of Malcolm, except with a slimmer stature and no tattoos. He is constantly running his hands through his wavy hair, and I can't tell whether it's a habit or he's flirting. His green eyes are a muted shade, like the color of Sage's name, with a roguish glint directed at me. Sitting next to Knox, however, Ethan looks like any other boy—nothing special.

"You aren't taking her out. No one is," Knox growls.

Ethan playfully slaps his shoulder. "Already claiming her as your own, like every other girl on the island?"

Knox turns to Ethan with narrowed eyes, and I can feel the aggravation between the two of them intensifying. Knox looks like he may pounce on Ethan at any moment. Everyone else remains silent—the only sound is the low hum of music playing from the small speaker.

After several seconds of no one talking, I decide to break the tension . . . with more tension. "Sure, I'll come," I boldly state.

Knox's eyes dart to mine, and I give him a mischievous grin. No one needs to claim me or coddle me. He's the one who told me to enjoy my time while I'm here, and that's what I'm going to do at the Shack.

"Yay!" Gabby shouts from beside me, and just like that, the unease around us melts away. Gabby places her hand on my arm as Knox and I stare each other down. "I'll swing by with some outfits. We can get ready together!" she squeals.

A wide smile stretches across my face as I turn to Gabby and say, "Perfect."

This is what I had been searching for most of my adolescent life: girlfriends. My heart flutters in my chest, and I'm genuinely excited for tonight.

Knox doesn't say much after the Ethan debacle. He mostly keeps to himself, quietly speaking to Lloyd here and there. I continue to hang out with Sage and Gabby while they sing and dance. They talk to me like I'm one of them, gossiping about people I don't know and filling me in on the latest drama. They share fun facts about the island and things I should eat and do before I go back home.

I feel so relaxed being here at the beach, enjoying Gabby and Sage's company. I have nowhere to be, no one to impress, and nothing to do. My brain starts to feel foggy after finishing the spiked iced tea, so I decide to take a dip in the water to help wake me up.

I head down the shore and stand where the water just barely washes over my toes. I watch the waves in the distance as they crash down, following them until they meet the sand and pull back again as the foamy crests fade into the shimmery blues and greens of the ocean. Closing my eyes, I take a deep breath in. The ocean smells like home. The salt and sand have a way of easing stress I didn't know I was holding inside me. My thoughts waver between wanting to go home and enjoying this new sense of freedom I've found with these strangers.

When I open my eyes again, Knox is standing waist-deep in the water a few feet in front of me. His face is slightly cast down as his eyes bore into mine. He flicks his lip ring back and forth like he's keeping time, waiting for me to say something.

My stomach tightens with anticipation. I chew on my bottom lip as I wait for him to make a move or say something.

He looks intimating right now with the way his face is angled, the sunlight accentuating the little scars on his face. He looks like he could kill something or someone . . . me.

I suck in a deep breath of air as shivers cascade down my spine. Avoiding eye contact, my gaze roves over his body, watching as water droplets slide off his shoulders, down his torso, and back into the water around him. He drags his hands through the water, still waiting.

I can feel the pull between my body and Knox's, like a tether attaching us, and it's tugging me toward him. I slowly stride into the water, digging my toes deep into the sand to press on farther. I stop when I'm only inches away from Knox and the water is at my belly button, the bottom half of my shirt now soaked and sticking to my skin. He dips down, submerging his body but leaving his head above the water. I stand still, but my body sways with each wave that rolls by me.

"What do your tattoos mean?" Knox asks softly.

I look down at my left arm and hand, having forgotten about the markings because I'm so used to seeing them. I gulp, trying to bring moisture to my throat before I speak. "They are Wiki tattoos. You receive them when you come of age. It's a special design for the people of my village."

He nods in acknowledgment.

I can't really make out any of his tattoos when most of his body is obscured by the water, but I feel compelled to ask anyway. "What about yours?"

Knox stands up so that the water is at his waist once more. His long dark hair is slicked down his back. My eyes rake over his broad shoulders and sculpted torso, survey-ing the ink on his skin. The design on his arm looks akin to mine but distorted, in a way, with large dark circles, stars, and squares sporadically breaking up the traditional-look-ing swirls. He also has little random tattoos of things I've never seen before . . .

My gaze lands on his face again. He's watching me, a playful smirk dancing across his face, but then his eyes burn with what looks like . . . hate. I can't tell if he wants to let his guard down and be real with me, or if he truly despises me and this inexplicable connection we have. His conflicting emotions are so extreme that, with every glance, smirk, and cold shoulder, I feel like I'm swirling through the portal once more, being whipped around as the air is stolen from my lungs. I guess it's good practice for the trip home.

"Nothing. I just liked them, so I got them." His voice is smooth like butter now, as if someone snapped their fingers and his attitude has instantaneously shifted back to being soft and seductive.

I know I should loathe him for the way he makes butterflies flutter deep in my stomach, but I don't. If it weren't for the ocean around me, I would be able to feel the wetness between my thighs I know is there. The way my body responds to him is like torture. I want him so badly, but I know he doesn't feel the same way. Besides, I would only be another conquest for him.

Malcolm, my fiancé . . . That's the other reason why I can't have Knox.

We are staring intently at each other, which is making me uncomfortable. I'm not sure if it's the alcohol that pushes me to ask or my brain trying to break the awkward silence as neither of us looks away, but the words fall out of my mouth: "How did you get those scars on your face?"

Knox lifts his left hand and places the tips of his fingers on the raised skin along his cheekbone. The gesture is odd to me, as though he had forgotten the mark was there or he's trying to remember how he got it. He shrugs before responding, "An accident with my brother."

I tilt my head and narrow my eyes in a look of confusion. "You have a brother?" I ask cautiously, attempting to make it seem like I didn't pester Lloyd for information regarding Knox's background.

"Had," Knox bites out.

I look down at the blue water surrounding me as my face falls to a frown. I think of Chester and what might happen to him if I never get out of here. The idea of losing him, of telling people that I "had" a brother . . . It would break me.

Unshed tears sting my eyes, and I keep my gaze focused on the water. A sloshing sound pulls my attention back to the present as Knox starts to move toward the shore. He stops when we are side by side, and I look straight ahead to where he was a moment ago. Our arms touch, and the chill from the water shocks me like a little electric spark. Knox turns his head and leans into me, his lips grazing my ear. I can feel the warmth of his breath on me, causing goose-bumps to spread down my back. Tiny droplets of water drip from his nose onto my shoulder when he speaks.

"You be careful in this realm, koa. The men here aren't like the princes you're used to back home. They will destroy you if you aren't smart enough."

My breath hitches at how seductive he sounds, but his words are a warning. He must have forgotten how well I can fight my own battles, seeing as I've already killed a man.

"Maybe these men should be afraid of me," I growl as I swivel my head toward him so we are nose to nose.

Knox snickers at me before breaking eye contact and swishing through the water back to the beach. I watch him until he spins around to sit down on one of the blankets again, at which point I turn back toward the vast ocean. A new sensation of anger bubbles inside me, quickly overtaking the sorrow I had started to feel for him.

He has no idea what I'm capable of.

***

Gabby has strewn a handful of garments across Knox's bed, and at first sight, I'm scared about the kind of clothing she is forcing me to wear. I keep hearing the two girls call our outfits "dresses," though these are unlike any dresses I've ever seen, including the ones Tallulah sells from her stall. But with each outfit I've tried on, I find that I can't stop observing myself in the mirror behind the door in Knox's bedroom. I am fascinated by how interesting and appealing they make my body appear.

I choose a dress that is less formfitting than the others so that my dagger and harness aren't visible from under the fabric like they were with the others. It's a simple white dress with a pink floral pattern and thin straps that rest on my shoulders. The front dips down into a simple scooped neckline. It's tighter across my breasts and stomach but flares out to flow around my hips and thighs, and the bottom hem rests just above my knees.

Before Gabby and Sage showed up at the house tonight, I braided my hair into three sections, which now hang down my back. My braids make me feel secure—not the kind of tight styles Mama likes to see me in, but the kind I would wear for combat training or riding Shea. I can't explain it, but I feel stronger and more confident when my hair is braided this way.

Sage insists on doing my makeup, and I begrudgingly agree. We make a deal, though: she can apply my makeup, but it must be light—I want it to look and feel natural, not caked on or greasy. I want to still feel like myself and be comfortable because all I've felt since I landed here is out of place.

Sage stops moving the blush brush around my cheeks and pulls her body back to study my neck and eye.

Shit. I forgot about the fight . . . and the whole mur-der-in-self-defense thing.

"What the hell happened to you?" Her tone sounds con-cerned, not accusatory.

I catch Gabby's reflection in the mirror as she peers over at us from the bed. She's been lying on her belly, next to the discarded garments, staring at a little black device in her hand while Sage has been applying my makeup.

"I fell while walking in a wooded area. Lots of rocks and things, and I fumbled down a small hill. Got my eye good on a rock, and some branches tore up my neck." I take my time explaining what didn't happen to me, hoping that they believe me.

Gabby squints her eyes, probably wondering if I'm being honest, but she stays silent.

Sage's facial expression eases as she leans toward me and gently strokes the brush against my cheek. "Ugh, did Knox take you on one of his adventure hikes? He's constantly trying to get Gabby and me to join him and the guys. But they just walk into the woods and then, like, find a clearing to lie down, get high, and watch the clouds. The things he thinks of are so beyond me." She rolls her eyes and slightly shakes her head.

"Yes, yes! That was it. Too high, and I just, whoops! Fell down." I nervously laugh and check to see if Gabby has caught on to me, but she's looking at the device again.

"Well, I'm going to add some foundation over the scratches on your neck and that bruise by your eye to cover those up," Sage responds.

"Okay." I think I used that term correctly. The people in this realm seem to say it frequently when they agree with something and, well, I agree.

She carries on with my makeup, and I find this experience much more enjoyable than any time the royal stylist worked on me. And it was work—I made sure of it.

When Sage finishes applying a light-pink color to my lips, I move closer to the mirror to examine my reflection. I can't believe how pretty I look, like I'm glowing.

"Wow," I say in astonishment as I tilt my face at different angles in the mirror. There's shimmery gold powder brushed on my eyelids, just above my darkened and elongated eyelashes. My cheeks have a bronze tint to them, coupled with a subtle sheen to accentuate my cheekbones. I look at Sage in the mirror, and I can tell that she's ecstatic about her work.

"You like it?" she asks in a high-pitched squeak.

"Like it? I love it. You are so good at this!" My eyes are wide in amazement as I tap my pointer finger along my bottom lip. I pucker my lips together and make them pop, and Sage giggles at me.

"I take it you don't usually wear a lot of makeup?" she guesses.

I shake my head, "No, and when I do, it's slathered on and I look . . . well, I look ridiculous."

Sage laughs and then cocks her head in contemplation while we continue looking in the mirror.

"Wait, you don't do your own makeup? Someone else does it for you?"

"No, and yes. I mean, I can apply my own makeup, but I hate how tedious it is. I would rather be in my natural state. Plus, I'm only expected to wear it for big events, like receptions, rites, weddings, things like that, so the stylist does my makeup for those occasions." I realize too late that I might have slipped up, revealing too much.

Sage scrunches her nose and shakes her head at me. "I don't know what you mean. It sounds like you are part of a royal family or something," she snorts in disbelief.

I clam up, not sure of how to respond. "No," I lie, "my parents are just extravagant, I guess." With a shrug, I turn away from the mirror in hopes of ending this conversation. I make my way over to the bed and sit down to slip on the pair of white sneakers I got from the market the night Knox took me to buy clothes. Sage doesn't ask any more questions, so I think my diversion was successful.

Gabby slides off the bed, still staring at the little black device. It looks like the iPod I once saw back home, but hers isn't playing any music like that relic did—she seems captivated by it nonetheless.

"The boys said they will be at the Shack soon. Ready to go?" Gabby asks as she picks up a small bag, slips the device inside, and hangs it on her shoulder. "Holy shit, you look fucking amazing." Gabby whistles her approval as she takes in the sight of my new face.

I blush at the attention, but they probably can't see it under the thin layer of bronze that's already there.

"We know who Knox is bringing home tonight. Or should I say coming home to . . . already . . . in his bed." Gabby has her eyebrows raised, paired with a devilish smirk.

The heat in my cheeks intensifies and spreads down my neck as I swallow, trying to suppress the memory of Knox's wet body standing in front of me in the water.

"Is he coming tonight?" I ask Gabby.

After we returned from the beach, Knox showered and left with Lloyd, and I haven't seen them since. Considering our interaction earlier, I don't think he wants to be around me—but then again, I don't know what he wants. There's always an element of surprise when it comes to Knox.

"Oh yeah. He's there most Wednesday nights. Wednesday is his 'fun' day. He hangs with the guys all day, heads to the Shack in the evening to find a nice lay, and then we don't see him again until the next Wednesday."

"Where does he go during the rest of the week?"

"He runs a garage in town, so I'm sure that's where he spends most of his time. Other than that, I'm not sure what he gets up to. None of us know his story or anything about his life. I think that's what girls find so attractive about him—that mysterious, broody bullshit. Ya know?"

I smirk at Gabby as I remember Lloyd saying almost the exact same statement. Weirdly, I understand the allure of Knox's mystery. It's the same allure I felt toward Shea and the dragons. I was so infatuated with learning all about the dragons because it was forbidden for me to do so. Eventually, I got what I wanted, and now I like to think of myself as an expert. With that knowledge, the mystery has faded and dragons have become part of my everyday life, but they are something I understand so thoroughly, like an extension of myself.

Chester would most definitely disagree that I'm a dragon expert.

I stifle a snort at the thought, but then my mood shifts as tiny pangs of guilt and sadness hit me thinking of what Chester could be dealing with at Castle Waimea. The chief is probably losing his mind, and Mama is probably stoic on the outside but raging on the inside. I get a little homesick at that moment, and I guess it shows because Sage asks me if I'm okay, which pulls me from my thoughts.

"Yeah, I'm okay. I've just never been to the Shack, so I'm a bit anxious," I force out cheerfully, trying to put on a mask of fake happiness.

"Oh my god, don't be. You'll have so much fun. Plus, the boys are so, so, so hot, it will make your mouth water. They all look like surfer models or gods. Ugh, delicious," Gabby gushes. "You will get so much attention because you're new and damn fine. Free drinks for you all night—and us, since you're our friend." Gabby's face is lit up like the sun. Her excitement is infectious, and I decide there's no point trying to resist it. I return her smile as the three of us leave the house.

SIXTEEN

LOUELLA APONI DELPHINE

Poipu, Gemcove Island

After cruising the crowded lot—circling twice—we finally find an open parking space. Gabby accelerates the car into the spot and then jams the lever into the "P" position, which I've learned means "park." Sage jumps out before Gabby turns the car off, shutting the door with a loud thud. Gabby and I follow, and I'm surprised when I step out and my shoe sinks into sand. It's odd to me that people simply leave their massive, heavy cars on the beach, but at this point, nothing should surprise me about this realm.

The Shack resembles the homes and pubs in the village of Waimea—minus the thumping music and swarms of people. It has a straw-thatched roof and exposed wooden beams and paneling. A large deck along the front of the building is lit up and crammed with patrons. The music from inside the Shack pulses through the open windows, and I can feel the vibrations through my feet as we step up onto the deck.

Walking into the Shack, I follow Gabby and Sage closely as my awareness heightens and I feel like I should be on alert. I stagger back slightly as I take in the sight of so many people clumped together in this small space. Every one of them is drinking—clear cups, brown bottles, green bottles, silver cans. Some people wear serious expressions while they talk, some are laughing and smiling, and some are singing and dancing without a care in the world.

I've never seen a party quite like this.

There's a cluster of people playing instruments on a stage, but the only instruments I recognize are the ukulele and the guitar. The sounds flowing from the band are similar to the music Knox's crew was playing on the beach earlier . . . I'm going to assume this is the reggae they were talking about.

"Louella!" I hear Sage shout over all the noise.

I hadn't noticed that I had stopped walking to take in the sights, and Gabby and Sage are now standing across the room, waiting at the bar. Sage is waving at me to come join them. Glancing around once more, I take a deep breath before I weave my way through the crowd.

"What do you want to drink? The first round is on me. Well, actually, it's on Dean," Sage says right as Dean strolls over to us from behind the bar. He tosses a white rag over his shoulder and gives Sage a sultry smirk accompanied by a wink. In response, Sage hoists herself onto the ledge of the bar, stretching her neck out as Dean meets her halfway to lock their lips in a long, passionate kiss.

I can't look away; I've never seen such intimacy before. I've seen innocent stolen kisses, but nothing so long and . . . hot.

"Ugh, young love. It's gross," Gabby moans beside me, loud enough for Sage and Dean to hear.

Sage breaks the kiss first and laughs, but before she lowers herself back down, Dean grabs the nape of her neck and forces their lips together once more in a deeper kiss.

I catch little glimpses of their tongues as they intertwine. I keep watching as I suck on my bottom lip, imagining what it would be like to kiss someone like that, passionately and deeply. My heart feels like it's bubbling with anticipation at just the thought of kissing . . . kissing . . . well, Knox.

I'm in disbelief at my own admission, and I try to shake the image from my brain.

Finally slipping free of the embrace, Sage drops down, her heels hitting the ground in front of Gabby and me—and at that, the thought of Knox drops out of my brain. Dean licks his lips and winks at Sage again. Her only response is a small giggle as her face flushes pink.

"All right, I'll take a . . . Sex on the Beach," Sage says to Dean suggestively. She wiggles her eyebrows at him as her tongue works the inside of her cheek.

Dean's amber eyes glimmer with heat, and he bites his lip before pivoting to Gabby and me.

"What can I get you?" he asks, nodding his head toward me.

My mind begins to race as I survey the people around me to see if I can read the labels on their drinks. Most of the time when I drink at home, it's wine or some kind of ale, but none of these drinks look like what we have at our pubs.

At a loss, I shrug my shoulders and lift my hands. "Ummm, ale?" I ask Dean.

He tilts his head at me like he's waiting for me to elaborate.

"We have lots of those. What ale are you thinking?"

Before I can respond, Gabby finally jumps in to save me. "We will take two bottles of Kona Lite with lemon. None of that icky lime stuff," she orders confidently.

Dean nods and moves around behind the bar. He grabs a metal cup, swirls it in the palm of his hand like some sort of magic trick, and then sets it on the rubber mat in front of him. I watch in wonder as he spins around, grabbing bottles and combining liquids in the cup. He slams a second metal cup onto the first one, then vigorously shakes them together over his shoulder. With a smack of his palm, the second cup releases from the first, and Dean pours the contents into a glass filled with ice in front of him. Adding a final splash of red juice, he completes the drink with a tiny green umbrella and a cherry. Next, he grabs two clear glass bottles and pops the tops off, jamming lemons through the tiny opening. Dean masterfully picks up all three drinks in his hands at once and places them on the wooden bar for us to take. I've never seen anyone move and shake and hustle with such steadiness in my life. He's faster than most of the soldiers back home.

He'd be a great warrior.

Once we collect our drinks, Sage gives Dean one last kiss and tells him she will tip him later—even I can pick up on that innuendo—and we squeeze past everyone, making our way over to where the band is playing and people are swaying to the beat.

"Let's dance!" shouts Gabby.

I violently shake my head because I don't dance, and if I do, I don't dance well.

"No, no, no!" I shout in protest over the music, but Gabby takes my free hand, turns her back to me, and drags me deeper into the gyrating crowd. Looking behind, I try to see if I can squirm my way out of here, but Sage follows closely behind us, sipping her drink as she shimmies her shoulders to the music.

I'm trapped.

Gabby drops my hand when we find a spot large enough to accommodate the three of us. She immediately starts to sway in front of Sage, and Sage follows her lead. I look around, feeling embarrassed for them but also for myself because I have no idea what I'm doing . . . But no one seems to notice us at all.

Sage leans into my shoulder and grabs my hand. "Move to the music!" she bellows as she swings my arm back and forth to the song's tempo. The movement is jerky, but once she releases my hand, I have no trouble finding my groove as I settle into the rhythm—it's a modest effort to start. After several minutes, I close my eyes and lose myself in the strums of the ukulele and the voices of the singers.

We stay like that for I don't know how long, just drinking, dancing, and laughing. At some point, Gabby heads to the bar to grab us another round of drinks. I continue dancing in her absence but suddenly grow extremely thirsty. When she doesn't return after a while, I swish my hips while I scan the room to see if she needs help carrying our drinks. As I turn my body around, I spot Knox leaning against the bar.

Knox's eyes instantly lock on mine, and he watches me intently. He looks good, as always. In a room full of people, Knox stands out to me with his long dark hair and tall stature. Tonight, he's in a black shirt and matching jeans, and he appears to be particularly broody. He reminds me of a folklore I once read about a god named Hades: tall, dark, and naughty. But instead of finding his one true love in the goddess Persephone, Knox's version of her seems to change . . . weekly.

A girl leans into him, whispering in his ear and rubbing her hand on his chest as her long shiny hair drapes across her face, obscuring it from me. He breaks our eye contact to look down at her, and I take the opportunity to turn my back to them, not wanting to see her touching him—but I can feel his stare burning into me again like the sun at noon on a cloudless day.

Suddenly, I feel singled out among the crowd. It makes me self-conscious, and I stop swaying with the music. At a loss for what I should do now, I slide a hand over the braids on the top of my head, grabbing one and placing it over my shoulder nervously. Scrubbing my hands down the front of my dress, I wonder if I look better than the girl Knox is with.

Why am I comparing myself to another girl?!

Finally, Gabby returns with our drinks, and I take an ice-cold bottle from her hand.

"Are you okay? You look a little sick. Do you need some water?" she asks, her brows pinched together.

"I'm good." I plaster a smile on my face and begin dancing again.

This round of drinks goes down smoothly, as I've become accustomed to the taste, making me borderline drunk. With the mix of the mellow tones coming from the band and the buzz that I have going, I'm feeling . . . sexy. Seductively, I move my free hand over my body and roll my hips a bit harder as I imagine my hand is someone else's.

I slowly turn and press myself back-to-back against Gabby, grinding my hips and flicking my gaze to Knox.

His eyes narrow at the movement and his nostrils flare. Knox gently removes the girl's hand from his chest and shifts a bit against the bar, putting some distance between them and crossing his arms over his chest.

I smirk at him and tip my chin down in hopes that he notices I'm inviting him over.

"May I?" a male voice says impossibly close to my ear. There's so little room between us that I can feel the heat from his breath tickle my neck. I really must be tipsy because I didn't even notice anyone approaching me.

When I glance over, Ethan is standing at my side with his hand outstretched, waiting for me to take it. Before I make my decision, I peek over my shoulder at Knox, feeling disappointed that he never took the bait. But the disappointment is quickly replaced with irritation as I spot him locking lips with the blonde, his fingers laced in her hair.

I turn back to Ethan and nod—all thanks to liquid encouragement and this newfound envy I have toward anyone I see with the guy I barely know—placing my hand in his.

Ethan moves his other hand down to my lower back and brings my hips close to his as we synchronize our movements to the music. His leg is between my thighs, and his mouth is close to my neck. Enjoying how our bodies feel pressed into one another, I tip my head back and close my eyes. Ethan's lips graze my neck, sending chills down my spine. Moving my arms from gripping his biceps, I wrap them around his neck, bringing us impossibly closer. Every so often, the leg he has positioned between my thighs grazes the bundle of nerves that are now pulsing with desire. Instinctively, I squeeze my legs together, and I feel Ethan let out a breathy laugh on my neck.

He pulls back a bit to look me in the eyes and says, "God, you're sexy. You have no idea." Then he leans in and places his lips on mine.

My eyes widen in shock, and I still my body from dancing. My back stiffens, as I wasn't expecting him to kiss me.

Ethan pulls away, and his expression oddly resembles anger, but I can't understand why he would be angry with me.

"Is something wrong? I thought you wanted this," he says sharply, like he's accusing me of something.

A gasp of disbelief escapes from my mouth, and before I can fully respond, Ethan is sent flying across the room. A black shadow passes before my eyes, taking Ethan with it as he crashes into the group of people beside us.

I'm frozen in place with no idea what to do. My normal instinct would have been to fight, but all the Kona Lites have impaired my nervous system, making me slow to react. Instead, I watch as Knox picks Ethan up by the shirt collar and thrusts his back into a wall.

When Knox's face is close to Ethan's—their noses nearly touching—he mumbles something only the two of them can hear. Ethan's reaction to whatever Knox said is to pound his fist into Knox's jaw. The impact is so hard that Knox's face thrashes to the side, but he keeps a firm grip on Ethan's shirt.

More people have noticed the scuffle, and the whole room has gone still. The band has stopped playing, and we're all watching to see what will happen next.

Knox spits a gob of thick red liquid on the floor and wipes his mouth on the shoulder of his shirt.

Seeing that makes me snap out of this haze, my mind calling my body to take action. I slink toward the bar as Knox winds his right fist back and slams it into Ethan's nose. But Ethan isn't deterred for long, throwing his fists again and breaking free from Knox's hold as they fall to the floor. Turning my back to them, I look to see if behind the bar is vacant. If I move far enough away from the group of people, then I can get my dagger out from under my dress—I just need some privacy to do so. In hindsight, strapping a dagger under a dress was probably not the smartest idea I've ever had—but right now, I'm glad I did it anyway.

This is why I don't do sexy.

Lucky for me, the bartenders have made their way toward the skirmish to try to gain control of the situation. I take the opportunity to scurry behind the bar, looking around to make sure that everyone's eyes are on Knox and Ethan. Crouching down, I lift my dress, carefully and quickly jerking the dagger out of its sheath and pushing the skirt back in place.

I grip the weapon in my right hand and hoist myself onto the bar, swooping my legs over the slippery wooden surface and hopping down next to a stool. My feet clunk loudly on the floor, but people are shouting as the fight carries on, so I remain unnoticed.

Slipping through the crowd to get closer to Ethan and Knox, I clutch the dagger tightly behind my back in a feeble attempt to hide it. Ethan now has Knox shoved against the wall, and smears of blood are everywhere. Knox grunts loudly as he overtakes Ethan, spinning so that Ethan's back is against the wall once more. Carefully, I flip the dagger in my hand, the blade resting in my palm. I gingerly inch the blade down my hand to pinch it between my thumb and pointer finger.

When Knox dodges out of the way of Ethan taking a swing, I chuck the dagger through the air toward the mental target I've made on the wall. Holding my breath, I watch the weapon twist through the air. The blade penetrates the loose fabric of Ethan's shirt, pinning him to the wooden paneling. Both boys stop wrestling and look at the dagger and then at each other—while the entire bar is now looking at me.

Knox drops Ethan's shirt and glances back at me. With a livid expression veiling his features, he jerks the dagger out of the wall. Then he grips the hilt in his fist and drags the back of his hand across his mouth, attempting to clear some of the scarlet-colored blood and sweat, but all it does is smudge up his cheeks.

He strides toward me, looking insane with blood smeared across his face, but as he shoves past me, he mumbles, "I didn't need you to save me." He doesn't wait for my response as he storms out of the Shack.

I survey the room as everyone continues to stare at me: some people have their mouths open in shock, some are whispering to each other with looks of disgust on their faces, and some look horrified. My feet are glued to the floor, and I'm unsure of what to do next. Should I go to Ethan, who's slumped on the floor now that the fight is over, and make sure he's all right? Do I follow Knox outside to make sure he's all right? Do I stay with Gabby and Sage? Or help clean up this mess and apologize to Dean for disrupting his place of work? In this split-second decision, I find myself dashing out the doors of the Shack and chasing after Knox.

Frantically, I jerk my head left and right to scan the parking area for any sign of Knox or his car. I spot glowing red lights from a vehicle at the edge of the lot as it begins to turn onto the main road. I sprint to the back of the car, drawing closer to the red lights and praying they don't pull away yet. As I approach, I recognize Knox's Pontiac Trans Am.

I shout his name over the roaring of the engine, but I know he won't be able to hear me. The car doesn't budge, so I scramble over to Knox's door and yank on the handle, but it won't open. My fingers slip, throwing me off balance, and I stumble back. Debating whether I should make another attempt, I pause and steady myself. Once I've regained my footing, I approach the window and peek inside to see Knox's blood-smeared face and narrowed eyes piercing through me.

If looks could kill, I would be in my grave right now.

I gesture for him to open the door so I can explain myself, but he turns and looks straight ahead into the darkness. My heart sinks as I assume he's going to speed off down the road and leave me behind. After a few stressful moments, he stretches across the empty seat next to him and pops the other door open. Instantly, I run to the other side, grabbing the doorframe and sliding onto the leather seat.

Without acknowledging me, Knox keeps his face forward and turns the wheel to the right, peeling out of the Shack parking lot. My body lurches back into the seat, and I reach out to grasp the handle on the panel in front of me for support. He speeds down the road and aggressively shifts the knob in between our seats. My heart is racing the faster he drives, and I don't dare to tell him to slow down. He catches sight of my white knuckles gripping the handle in front of me, and when he shifts again, the car bucks back with a roar and slowly decreases velocity.

Thank the goddesses.

I can't sustain the silence much longer—it feels like it's been hours.

"What the fuck happened back there?" My voice comes out loud as I try to compete with the incessant rumbling of the car.

Knox twists his hands back and forth on the steering wheel, and I see his jaw move as he grinds his teeth. I watch and wait for him to speak.

"I told you to be careful," he spits out.

"And you already know that I can handle myself." My voice is shaky but fierce.

"If I hadn't found you that night with Shea, Marcus would have killed you. You needed me," Knox claims.

"I did not. Regardless, Ethan and I were innocently dancing. And he tried to kiss me, not kill me!" I shout.

"Ethan is a bad guy, Louella. You have no idea what kind of person he is."

An evil cackle escapes me. "Oh, like you're any better? Hanging with people like Soho, and screwing different women every week?"

"Have you ever thought that maybe people lie? That maybe the women I've 'been' with were cleanup jobs from Ethan's messes?" he growls.

I scrunch my face as my brain tries to process what he is insinuating. "I'm not following," I admit.

Knox dispels a loud breath. "Ethan tends to get carried away with girls when he drinks. He gets handsy and sometimes forces them into doing things they don't want to or aren't coherent enough to object to. I caught sight of it happening once, and ever since then, I've kept a close eye on him, and I . . . Well, I try to intervene—help the girls get home or let them crash at my place if they are too shaken up."

I grip the hem of my dress, idly rubbing the seam, because I don't know what to do with myself or this information. Every time we are alone together, Knox surprises me. He's not the guy I once thought he was.

"But what about Sage? And—and Gabby?" I ask, suspicion worming its way in again.

"I've only been with Sage—before she was with Dean," he stresses. "I've never been with Gabby. She just pretends we have been together because she doesn't want everyone to find out that she was almost another of Ethan's victims . . . and that I helped her."

"Then why do you all still hang out with Ethan?"

"We don't intentionally hang out with him. He's Dean's cousin, and wherever Dean goes, Ethan follows. We hate it, but Dean feels responsible for him since Ethan's parents died when he was young and his aunt and uncle pretty much raised him."

"But what about the new girl you were with tonight?" I think of where she might be now . . . and if she's stuck without a ride home.

Knox snorts as if I said something funny. "She's a friend. That's Ethan's ex."

"Soooo, you were . . . ?"

"Making Ethan jealous? Bingo. Winner, winner, chicken dinner, babe. It's not a crime to have fun, you know? You should try it sometime."

I roll my eyes at that little jibe, but then I worry my lip as I contemplate what Knox is telling me. My stomach clenches at the thought of all the assumptions I had of him that he has since proven wrong. I feel like a terrible person for not trying harder to get to know the man who has helped me since we met—the man I'm utterly attracted to.

Still, losing someone doesn't give you the right to be a shitty, mean person like Ethan. But is Knox like that? Or is he just serious and intense, and I mistook it for being mean to me? My theories are interrupted as we pull into the driveway of the house and the car stops.

Knox turns the key to cut the engine, and the silence is immediately overwhelming. He throws open the door and jumps out, leaving me dumbfounded.

I stay seated in the car, my eyes fixed straight ahead at the open garage door, and I can't seem to bring myself back to the present.

My door opens, and Knox's hand enters my line of sight. I tap my fingers on my exposed knees as I stare at his palm, agonizing over whether I should take it.

Ultimately, I do. His hand is warm and comforting, and our touch feels like it has a pulse. He curls his fingers around my hand and helps me out of the car. I focused my eyes on my feet until I'm standing in front of Knox. I look up at him, really seeing him for the first time since the fight, and it startles me. He still has blood smeared across his face, which is gross, but it's also oddly attractive because the blood is a result of protecting me.

A smile creeps on my face, and I suck in my lip to try and hide it.

"What's so funny?" Knox's deep voice sends shivers down my exposed arms.

I glimpse into his eyes, and instead of the simmering anger I used to find there, I see lust hidden in his dark-brown irises. I've seen a similar look before from Malcolm, but instead of shrinking into myself like I used to, this time I feel beautiful and courageous. The thought of Malcolm comes and goes, not lingering as I watch Knox's tongue flicking that damn lip ring from side to side, waiting for my response. No longer afraid of him, I hold his gaze with confidence. I know I'm about to cross so many lines tonight, but this is what I want.

"You look like a crazy person." My voice comes out breathy, almost inaudible.

"I am a crazy person." Knox smiles at me, and it's the first time I've seen him look like that, exposing his teeth in a wide grin. It's gorgeous.

He nods his head toward the door. "C'mon, let's get you inside."

Without a word, I follow his lead as we step over the threshold and into the house hand in hand.

SEVENTEEN

LOUELLA APONI DELPHINE

Kailani Bay, Gemcove Island

Leisurely, Knox guides us through the kitchen, down the hallway, and into the bathroom. He releases my hand, closes the door behind us, and then moves to turn the shower on.

Something about the sound of the droplets trickling and bouncing off the tiles makes me squeeze my thighs together, only now realizing the overpowering sensation of want building below my belly button. Maybe it's the steam beginning to billow around us . . . or it's Knox, casually and slowly undressing himself mere inches from where I stand.

He pulls his shirt over his head and tosses it to the ground. My eyes slowly roam the contours of his body, noticing a smattering of fresh cuts on his ribs and a large bump on his clavicle that will surely be black and blue by tomorrow.

Knox unzips his pants, shoving them to his ankles. Gingerly, he lifts one leg at a time, removing his jeans entirely and kicking them to the side, on top of the discarded shirt.

I squeeze the hem of my dress in my fists as the anticipation of him removing his black boxers has me frozen in place. My heart is hammering in my chest, making it hard for me to take a normal breath—I think I might be lightheaded . . .

My attention is brought back to Knox's face when he releases a small chuckle. "Have you ever seen a naked man before, koa?" His expression is a mask of amusement, but his eyes dazzle with excitement.

I shake my head vigorously as I keep clenching the fabric of my dress, wringing it in my hands.

"What are you doing?" I breathe. My voice doesn't sound like my own—it reminds me of Marilyn's from that movie I saw with Lloyd.

Knox smiles, "Getting cleaned up. You can join if you want." He winks at me, and without waiting for my answer, he pinches the sides of his boxers and slowly brings them down. His erection pops out from the pressure of the waistband, and I gasp, clenching my thighs together even harder and creating a blissful friction.

Knox steps out of his boxers and enters the shower, closing the curtain behind him and leaving me reeling with my thoughts in a cloud of thick steam.

I came in here confident and ready to take what I wanted, but now that confidence has quickly faded. I argue with myself, knowing how much I want this, but also knowing full well that I shouldn't do this. For so many reasons. I think of Malcolm and how I would be betraying my husband-to-be again . . .

What if he didn't find out?

No. I banish that thought and decide that sex with Knox is out of the question. But maybe he can show me how to do the other stuff I've read about?

I yank my dress over my head, promptly discarding it along with my bra and panties. After some calming breaths, I shake my hands out, hoping to rid myself of the jitteriness surging through me. Then I straighten my shoulders so that I'm standing taller, and I carefully climb in to join Knox in the shower.

His eyes are closed as he leans his head back into the running water. Soap suds mixed with bloody water trickle down his face and onto his body. I watch the reddish rivulets trail along the planes of his chest, and I swallow hard as I take in the sight before me. He slicks back the water from his long hair, and I don't miss the way the muscles in his arms flex with the movement. Crimson blood is still smeared across his face, so I grab a cloth hanging from a towel bar beside me. I bring it to Knox's face while his eyes are still closed, but he senses my proximity and they fly open.

Knox stands completely still, his heated gaze fixed on me as I wipe away the blood with delicate strokes. When I meet his eyes again, something has changed. There's an understanding between us that no one else knows. We have secrets with each other and a newfound appreciation for one another. I trust him, and he trusts me. It heightens the attraction I feel for him—and I can tell he feels it too. The memories of all those arguments and frustrated glares melt away as I finally let myself fully embrace my desire for him.

After a moment, he softly clasps my wrist and takes the cloth from me. I place my arm back down at my side, standing completely bare before him. Knox grips the cloth harder as his smoldering stare rakes up and down my body. He licks his lips, and I notice his erection twitches.

Knox places a hand on my hip and spins us so that he can study me from where I once stood. Now it's his turn to watch the water as it splashes against my skin, gliding down over my breasts. I catch his nostrils flaring and pupils dilating. Ever so tenderly, Knox washes my neck, shoulders, and arms with the cloth. He moves it deliberately around my hard nipples, halting the air in my lungs. My legs shake, and I tip my head back into the stream of hot water. Knox wraps his hand around the back of my neck, lifting my head again. His face is close to mine, our breath mingling.

He nuzzles my nose with his, as if he's asking for permission. I close the small gap between us, and I take his bottom lip along with his lip ring between my teeth. I swipe my tongue across the gash he got from one of Ethan's punches. Knox doesn't flinch, but instead, a small groan escapes him. I lightly suck, drawing blood from the wound, but neither of us cares about this strange act while the tension intensifies between us. He tosses the cloth to the shower floor and tightens his grip on my neck as we finally collide.

Our tongues frantically move and twirl together. I circle my hands around his back, pressing his chest to mine as I concentrate on kissing him. It's messy and hot, and I'm not even sure if I'm doing it correctly, but it feels good, so it must be right. My clit pulses, begging for his touch.

Boldly, I reach between us and gently wrap my fingers around his erection. He inhales sharply and then smiles, and I can feel it against my lips. I slowly pump my hand up and down his length. Knox moans into my mouth. We break our kiss and place our foreheads together, staring at each other with fiery heat. Unspoken words pass between us—we both know that this is wrong, but it's too good to stop now.

I continue to stroke him, drawing another low moan from him, and he closes his eyes.

"How are you so good at this?" he asks incredulously.

"I've read about it," I say breathlessly.

Knox laughs and presses his nose to mine again as he sucks on my bottom lip. He moves my hand away from him and bends down in front of me, lifting my right leg so it sits on the ledge of the shower. He looks up at me.

"Please," I beg him.

Knox holds eye contact with me as he slowly swirls his thumb around the bundle of nerves aching for him.

"Yes," I gasp as my head drops back.

He drags his thumb from my clit to my pussy and plunges it inside me. I whimper loudly. Then I feel his mouth on me and his tongue swirling. Knox slides his free hand to my ass, pushing me firmer against his mouth. My heartbeat picks up with each sensual touch—every nerve is tingling, and my body jerks a few times from this heightened sensitivity. Knox presses his lip ring to my clit as he sucks, and it creates an odd sensation of pain mixed with pleasure. I wonder if that's why he has the stupid thing.

He slowly inserts a finger inside me and begins to pump while he continues to lick and suck. It's sloppy, and I can hear the motion of his finger, and it's loud and embarrassing but it feels euphoric. My moans come out louder now, and his name falls from my lips over and over again. He curls his finger, and I feel the pressure intensifying. I open my eyes and watch him as he works my body like his car or bike—knowing which buttons do what. My legs quiver and I feel like I might fall, so I grab on to his shoulders to keep myself steady.

Knox looks up at me. "I've always wanted you," he rasps out. He licks his lips, and I nod enthusiastically in agreement because I've always wanted him too—since the night I landed in this realm, I wanted him to be mine.

Knox closes his mouth around my clit again, and everything inside me explodes.

I hold his head to me as I buck against his face. "Yes, Knox, yes, yes!" I chant, like they are the only words I know.

My body violently twitches as I come down, the explosion gradually wearing off and my breathing returning to normal once again. My legs are trembling from the lingering pleasure pulsing from my clit down to my toes and up into my belly.

Knox stands back up, and without another second passing, I kneel in front of him. I take his erection in my mouth because I want to taste him as thoroughly as he just tasted me. I hold the base of his cock with my hand, and suck and swirl my tongue around the head. He runs his fingers along my braids, grasping either side of my face. I can feel him pulse in my mouth, which makes my lips widen in a smile around him—I've never done this before, and the movement feels odd.

"Louella, baby, yes. I've wanted this for so long. I've always wanted you," Knox purrs.

I bob my head faster, and Knox groans louder.

"Just like that, baby," he says, his voice deep and raspy.

My eyes water from how fast and hard he is moving, but I couldn't care less. I want to make him feel good.

He lets out one last moan of pleasure as he holds my head still, and I feel him twitch against my lips, spilling inside my mouth.

Breathing heavily, Knox steadies himself by bracing a hand on the shower wall. He reaches down and helps me back to my feet. "Mmm, my koa," he murmurs, smiling at me with hooded eyes. He rubs his thumb across the side of my mouth and between my lips.

I suck on it and then playfully bite down, which makes him laugh.

"Will you ever tell me what that means? Koa?" I ask lazily.

"Hmm, maybe someday. Now let's actually get you clean." He snakes his arm around me and smacks my ass.

I yelp in response and shoot him a withering look, but I know he's not fooled.

The rest of the shower, we bask in the afterglow without saying much. He washes my hair and my body, and I soak in the bliss. It feels like I'm floating on air.

We reluctantly turn the knob of the shower and leave its steaming heat. After wrapping a towel around his hips, Knox grabs another for me and places it over my shoulders—the sweet gesture makes me weak in the knees all over again. With his wounds now clean, he takes a moment to tend to them with gauze, tape, and Neosporin like he did for me the night we fought off Marcus and Soho.

I sit on the edge of the tub with my towel wrapped around me as if it were Knox's embrace. Watching as he patches himself up, I'm overwhelmed by a feeling of tenderness toward him. I think about how handsome his profile is, and how I can't wait to feel the warmth of his body on mine again. I don't know what I look like, grinning stupidly at him, but I can't drag my sleepy, sated eyes off him.

That night, Knox stays in his room, in his bed, with me, and it is the best sleep I've gotten in a long time.

***

When I wake up in the morning, I move my hand across the pillow next to me, but it's unoccupied. Sitting up, I rub my eyes and look around the room to see if Knox is still here, just not in bed, but there's no sign of him. Inspecting the bedside table, I notice my dagger lying on top of a folded piece of paper. Beside my dagger are two books, both with dark-blue covers—I don't recognize them. I toss the blanket away, causing a chill to spread along my bare body, and swing my feet over the side of the bed. Slipping the paper out from under the dagger, I see it's a note.

Koa,

Todd gave me the books he had mentioned to you during our trip to the Realms store.

Have fun reading today . . . and when I get home, I'll take you to another realm. Again, and again, and again . . .

—KX

I snort out loud and cover my mouth with my hand. My heart swells in my chest, and excitement bubbles out of me in a giggle. I think about how Knox had my legs shaking from the intensity of my orgasm, and my body shivers from the memory, yearning for him to come back.

I tuck the note back under my dagger, but before digging into the books, I grab one of Knox's shirts from his dresser, pull it over my head, and hurry back to the bed. Sliding my legs under the covers once again, I snatch the books off the table. Shamelessly, I hold Knox's shirt to my nose and breathe in. It smells like the ocean—which I now recognize as his (our) laundry soap—a campfire, and vanilla . . . it's definitely vanilla, not almond. The thought of my first night in this bed and the first time taking in Knox's scent makes me smile wide.

I release the air from my lungs and slump down under the covers. After I fluff the pillow against the headboard so that I'm in a comfortable position, I'm finally ready to start my day of reading. Gliding my fingertips across the front covers, I notice that neither book has a title or author, which seems odd. I slowly open the first book, and the spine creaks. Again, on the inside, there's no title or author.

"Hmm," I say out loud. I shrug my shoulders and flip to the first chapter. "Chapter One: The Dragon Lands," I announce to the empty room. Immediately, I dive into the tomes headfirst, curious as to what has been written about my home—and whether it's true or not.

Eighteen

Louella Aponi Delphine

Kailani Bay, Gemcove Island

I feel a soft touch on my cheek. I lift my hand and rub my fingers along my skin, not finding anything there. Then a gentle, warm hand clasps my fingers. I squeeze my eyes and then rapidly blink them open, noticing that sunlight isn't peeking through the curtains just yet, so it must still be nighttime.

I must have fallen asleep reading one of Todd's books. They have been very intriguing novels—meaning that they read more like folklore than truth—but for these past few days, I've been paging through them every chance I get. A number of the chapters are packed with far-out misinformation regarding what the dragons are capable of and the way my people live, but I can see why Todd reveres Kapu

Island. I guess I never realized how "magical" my home is compared to this realm.

"Hey," I hear Knox whisper in the dark. He brings our interlocked fingers to his soft lips and lays a line of kisses along the back of my hand. My eyes have adjusted to the darkness, and I watch his lips work their way down. He stops when he reaches my wrist and flicks his gaze up to meet mine, our eyes locking for several seconds.

"Yeah?" I respond, but my voice is groggy and full of sleep.

Knox smirks, "It's time to go to your dragon, my princess."

Stretching my body flat along the bed, I let out a small grunt in protest. "Can't we skip tonight?" I whine.

"Nah, I'm not taking any chances after what happened with those two dipshits."

"Grrr, all right." I want to stay in bed, but I don't want another death on my hands in this realm.

I unclasp our hands and grasp the blankets to pull them off me, but before I can get out of bed, Knox speaks.

"Wait, I want to see something," he whispers.

I freeze, wondering what it is he wants to see. Slowly, he shifts the blankets down my shoulders as he keeps his gleaming dark eyes on mine. My breathing grows deeper as I anticipate his next move. Knox pulls the blankets farther down, his attention snared by my exposed nipples hardening as the chill hits me. When he finishes uncovering my nudity, he looks down at the length of my body—his breathing quickens and his nostrils flare.

I don't usually sleep naked, but after feeling nearly every one of Knox's exquisite muscles flush against mine for the first time a few nights ago, I can't seem to get enough. I want to feel his bare skin close to me every night.

Knox bows his head to my stomach and places small, wet kisses around my belly button. My skin instantly responds with goosebumps, and the blood courses through my body as it reaches the apex of my thighs.

"Are you getting wet?" Knox's voice vibrates through me and tickles my belly, forcing a soft moan from my lips.

"Mhmm," I nod.

Knox crawls over me and kisses me hard on the lips. I respond and open for him, edging my tongue out to meet his.

We've kissed a lot over the past several days, but this feels different. He's kissing me like he needs me, like he doesn't want this to end . . . almost as if he cares for me. I've never been in love, so I'm not sure what it feels like. Now that I'm thinking about it, I wonder if Knox has ever been in love. I place my hands on his cheeks to slowly break the kiss. His heavy breathing fills the quiet bedroom as I hold his face in my hands.

"Knox?" I ask, looking into his eyes.

He nods for me to continue as he licks his lips and flicks his lip ring.

"Have you—have you ever . . . have you ever been in love?" I stutter through my question, scared to ask him. A sharp pain pierces my heart. Maybe I don't want to know this answer . . . I don't want to think of Knox loving someone if it isn't me.

His facial expression drops, and so does my stomach as he remains still for several seconds.

Shit, I should have never asked him.

I release my hold on his cheeks and suddenly feel self-conscious. "Never mind, that's a silly question. I—"

"No, no, it's not. I have . . . I think."

"You think?"

"Well, I met this girl once and knew someday I was going to love her. And when that day came to tell her how I felt, I didn't realize she belonged to my brother."

My brows knit together, and I look at him in confusion. "I don't understand," I say, shaking my head.

Knox's smirk returns, and he chuckles. "The answer is yes, but I never had the chance to be with her because she ended up with my brother."

I place my hand on Knox's cheek and run my thumb along his skin. "It sounds like your brother's a fucking asshole."

Knox puffs out a breath, "You could say that."

I lift my head from the pillow and softly kiss his lips; he responds by plunging his tongue into my mouth and pressing me back down to the bed. His kiss is feverish, setting my body on fire, making me burn with want and need. Being with Knox ignites my soul but soothes my heart in a delicate balance I've never felt before. Sighing against his lips, I acknowledge to myself how right it feels to be with him like this.

In this realm, I don't have to hide with Knox. Here, I'm not stuck with the rules and responsibilities of being royalty, obligated to follow through with a marriage I don't even want. What Knox and I have—our relationship—is authentic, and I don't think I want to let this go. I don't think I can let him go.

His sultry voice breaks my chain of thought. "I want to be greedy and keep you naked in my bed forever, but we should get going before it's almost morning," he says, pushing off the mattress to stand.

"Ugh, fine," I pout and reluctantly climb out of bed to get dressed.

Nineteen

Chester Pala Delphine

Castle Waimea, Kapu Island

My hands tremble as I fasten the overstuffed satchel to the back of Gabriel's saddle.

"Ugh!" I growl as I wring my hands in hopes of dissipating the nerves.

Luke moves to stand in front of me and places his hands on my shoulders in a soothing gesture. I take a step back, letting go of the leather straps.

"Here, let me," he assures me. The small act relieves some of my unease, and right now, I'm glad to be with Luke.

As planned, I've been on duty at the dragon caves since the sun dipped below the hill of the castle, setting for the night. Luke snuck down to meet me here twenty minutes before midnight, like he promised. This may be the first time we've spoken since the initial "hey" we whispered to one another when he arrived. I've been so caught up worrying about the trip ahead of me that I hadn't fully registered his presence.

I finished securing the saddle to Gabriel, which was a feat of its own as I kept accidentally knocking against the two large ivory horns on his head. He has yet to grow into them, and at his current size, they're unwieldy. But I managed. Now, however, my hands have decided to start shaking uncontrollably, making it impossible to grab the clasps of the satchel to secure it in place. It's the last task before I take off.

Standing back, I watch as Luke buckles it up. He works his way around Gabriel, shifting and tugging to thoroughly check that everything is secure. When his inspection is complete, he pats Gabriel's haunch as a thank-you for being such a good boy while we've pulled, pushed, and tightened every inch of his riding equipment to the point where he will be sore tomorrow.

In response, Gabriel lets out a low snort—nothing ever seems to faze or hurt him. I'm pretty sure his personality is a perfect match to the woman who works with him in the clandestine militia Ella and I created. Brynlee and Gabriel pair so well together, and she's the only rider he's ever had. Now it's up to me to make sure Gabriel gets home safe so he can reunite with Brynlee . . . and we can reunite this island.

Luke turns toward me, reaching for my arms and gently squeezing them. He pulls me close to place his forehead on mine, and we both close our eyes. Leaning into one another, we remain quiet. The only noise I can hear is my deep, choppy breaths as I try to slow my heart from beating so erratically. I must get my nerves under control before I take off—I can't leave any room for errors.

"Breathe. It will be all right. I know it's scary, but Louella could be waiting for you on the other side. Just think of Louella and seeing your sister again." Luke's voice is calming.

I flush the rest of the air from my lungs, making a shaky whooshing sound as I exhale. Instead of focusing on what could go wrong, I begin to think of Louella. Our time together, our jokes, her smile, her laughter, childhood memories of us annoying Mama to no end . . . a smile stretches across my face from ear to ear.

I'm going to find her. I can feel it in my heart.

"Thank you," I whisper.

Luke places a kiss on my forehead, and then he steps away.

I open my eyes at the feeling of his warmth withdrawing and give him a lopsided grin. Studying his face, I see his lips are pressed in a thin line and his molten blue eyes are swirling with worry. He doesn't like what I'm about to do, but he knows it's our only hope, and he will always support me.

Luke rapidly blinks, breaking eye contact, and his small sniffles don't go unnoticed—especially when he swipes the back of his hand along his nostrils. "I'm going to double-check the strap around Gabriel's chest to make sure it's tight enough, and then you'll be ready to fly. Did you bring the canteen of water for him?" Luke asks.

"Yes, it's packed." I tail Luke to act as another set of eyes as he circles his way around Gabriel in case we missed anything the first time. I've been so goddess-damned forgetful these past couple of days, I wouldn't be surprised if I had only dreamed of putting Gabriel's saddle on instead of actually doing it.

Examining every inch of the dragon, Luke ducks under and around his belly, which elicits a loud snort from Gabriel. Undeterred, Luke gives each buckled strap around Gabriel's chest and head a scrupulous yank. I'm sure Gabriel's tolerance is waning, and he's probably ready to get up in the sky at this point.

"All looks good and snug." Luke nods at Gabriel, who lowers his head and crouches down to allow me to mount—but not before sending a low guttural grunt in annoyance in Luke's direction.

Poor guy.

"Let's get you up and strapped in." Luke looks down at the pocket watch hanging from his black work pants. He nods and announces, "You have ten minutes to get to the portal."

Without hesitation, I place my foot in the stirrup and hoist myself up and onto Gabriel's back. He returns to standing and shifts slightly to adjust to my weight.

"Strap me in," I gently command Luke—before I back out of this crazy plan. He and I designed a makeshift harness to secure my hips and legs to the saddle in case I lose consciousness or can't hang on tightly enough when passing through the portal.

Luke grabs a thick leather strap hanging down the right side of Gabriel and tosses it into my lap. He jogs around the dragon's backside and says, "Move your foot from the stirrup so I can get up to thread this through."

I do as he says and observe him as he hoists himself up, grabs the leather strap from my hands, and slides it through a tension tightener next to my left hip. I watch his tanned face in the glow of the dim lights that fill the dragon caves. He's laser-focused on the task at hand as he pumps the lever, making the strap grow tighter around my hips.

Luke glances up at me, "Shift back for me."

I follow his direction, and he tightens the lever some more so there's no remaining slack.

Finally, Luke blows out a quick, audible breath and hops back to the ground. "You're good to go," he whispers, anxiously running a hand over his bald head.

"Thank you for everything," I breathe.

Luke looks down and unclips his infamous pocket watch from his belt loop. Lifting it up for me to see, he says, "I'm sending this with you. To keep track of the time and, well, to have a little piece of me with you."

The gesture is so kind that I almost want to call the whole thing off and stay here, safe with Luke. I swallow down my emotions and nod at him.

He leans to the back of Gabriel, and I can hear the satchel clasps clank as he tucks the pocket watch inside. When he's done, Luke rights himself and runs his fingers over his trimmed goatee. With a deft movement, he steps up in the stirrup and leans his face forward.

I meet him the rest of the way, and he places his lips on mine in a tender kiss. We remain like that for a moment until Luke pulls away and steadies himself on the ground once more.

"Hurry back!" he says with a wink.

I nod and look toward Gabriel's horns as I grab the reins. It's now or never.

I give the reins a small tug, and Gabriel begins to walk forward and out of the caves. He saunters in the direction I last saw Louella fly with Shea the night they disappeared. I don't look back at Luke for fear of changing my mind if I do.

Gabriel's promenade is gaining speed, and soon we are running toward the edge of the landing grass as his wings vigorously flap. With a powerful leap, we shoot off into the night sky. Gabriel keeps soaring straight toward Maka Mountain, and I twist the reins around my wrists like manacles. Once I have the straps secure, I hold on tight to the jade horn at the front of the saddle.

As we approach the mountain, Gabriel emits a low squawk that sounds like a warning . . . but there's no stopping me. I grip the horn firmly in my hands and direct Gabriel to climb higher in the sky. The momentum makes me slip back in the saddle, so I squeeze my thighs against his sides for extra hold. Hunching down, I attempt to block the rushing air pelting my eyes and making them water, hoping that Gabriel's head will do the job.

After several minutes of hanging on tightly, I start to wonder when we will enter the portal. Suddenly, the world around us goes black—blacker than the night sky. We are spinning and twisting around as my body jerks and flops, but I maintain my hold on the saddle. I can't see a fucking thing, which creates the sensation that I'm falling from the sky, even though my body and Gabriel are still flying upward.

My stomach begins to knot with sickness, and I feel like my head may explode from the pressure of the air sucking us through this hole. Gabriel's grunts and shrieks are swallowed up by the dark abyss—it's an eerie sound. Closing my eyes, I take deep breaths, begging for this madness to end soon, but it doesn't. It persists for several more seconds until finally I hear a loud pop! and the world around me rights itself.

Opening my eyes, I scan the sky. Nothing looks as though it's changed. Then I lean over Gabriel's side to see dozens of lights twinkling below me, as if all the stars in the night sky have plummeted to the ground. I try to find my voice to tell Gabriel to search for Shea, but it comes out as a hoarse whisper. I can't tell if he heard me, but he shoots downward, and we dive toward the fallen stars.

I open my mouth wide to pop my ears from the pressure of the portal, and I loosen the reins, giving my limbs a break. Already, I can feel the soreness setting in from how tightly I fought to hold on to Gabriel. As we drop altitude, I squint to see if there are any signs of life around . . . but the only real movement I can identify are long lines of faint red and white lights slowly meandering about.

What is this place?

Midflight, Gabriel shakes his wings out, and the spikes along his spine make a crackling noise I have never heard before. The sound is akin to someone smashing two rocks together repeatedly. I've known about the dragons' echolocation abilities for years, but I've never witnessed them performing it.

Gabriel turns his head slightly and veers to the right. My sight is drawn to a dark, wooded spot, which, at first glance, looks like the dragon caves we have back home. Based on how Gabriel is acting, I'm confident that Shea must be down there. His body is vibrating, and the way he knows exactly where he's going? This must be it.

When we are about ten feet from the ground, Gabriel juts out his hind legs. Soon after, I'm thrown back as his talons dig into the earth and we gallop to a stop. He ruffles his wings back to his sides and lies on the ground, bowing his head. Given his mannerisms, I can tell he flew me right to Shea.

"Nice work, boy," I praise him, leaning forward to pat his neck. I've been around dragons my whole life, but they never cease to amaze me.

There doesn't seem to be anyone in the immediate area, and I'm surrounded by a shroud of trees, which creates a wall of darkness. My eyes are slowly adjusting to the obscurity of the night sky devoid of a moon to provide visibility—but I don't need the moon to notice a large, dark mass prowling toward us.

Two large icy-blue eyes eerily stare at me. Without a doubt, I know it's Shea—but does she know it's me? She gives off two loud warning snorts, forcing me to speak up.

"Shea, it's me . . . Chester." My voice is a low warning, hoping that Shea won't pounce and rip me to shreds.

She slowly stalks around us, and Gabriel remains stoic, not lifting his head or even making a sound. Shea approaches us, craning her neck so that her face is next to mine. I carefully extend my hand toward her with my palm facing out. She inches closer and pauses for an agonizing moment. After releasing a low sigh, she touches her rough, wet nose to my hand, and I can't help but chuckle as I release the breath I've been holding.

This worked—I fucking knew it.

I relax my muscles as I scratch the bumps on Shea's nose and pet the top of her head. Her response is a loud purr.

"All right, girl, step on back." Quickly, I release the lever to loosen the belt around my waist. With more wiggle room now, I can push off the saddle horn to climb down from Gabriel. My feet land with a thud on the uneven ground, sticks and leaves crunching under the weight of my boots.

I walk around Shea to inspect her condition and see if her saddle is on. Though she looks to be perfectly fine, her riding equipment is nowhere to be found.

"Where is Louella, girl?" I look beyond her, toward where she came from, but I don't see anyone. There's a rock formation with a dark, hollow hole, and I'm certain that's where Shea has been hiding out. I walk a few steps inside the cave and spot Shea's saddle resting against the wall to the right of the entrance. I snatch it up, along with her bridle lying next to it, and head back out. On my short walk over to Shea, my foot catches on something, causing me to trip and fall. Everything tumbles from my arms, and I land on my knees and palms.

"Ugh, fuck," I grunt.

I jump to my feet and cautiously navigate back to the satchel tied to Gabriel's saddle and poke around for the flashlight. Once I've found it, I retrace my steps to where I tripped and shine the beam of light on the ground so I can locate the equipment I dropped.

"Huh, that's odd." I'm confused to find two piles of dark ash with what I recognize are human bones scattered among them. Fear trickles through my body as goosebumps break out down my neck and spine.

What if the people in this realm burned Louella alive?

Then I remember that Shea would tear apart anyone who tried to fuck with Ella.

Snickering to myself at my silly thoughts, I pick up the saddle and bridle and walk back over to Shea. "All right, lady. Let's get you ready while we wait for Louella."

Shea gracefully bends to the forest floor, and I set to work strapping her saddle tightly around her body.

When the riding equipment is secure, I make my way back to Gabriel to tuck the flashlight away for now and dig out the pocket watch Luke sent with me to keep track of the time remaining until the portal closes.

"Two o'clock!" I exclaim—a bit too loudly. "Holy shit. That whole time-warp thing felt like only fifteen minutes at most," I whisper-shout to myself, and Shea gives me a knowing look. But we still have plenty of time . . . as long as Ella hasn't wandered too far from Shea . . . and isn't injured somewhere in need of help . . . and isn't—

My belly grumbles with hunger pangs, yanking me free from my spiraling thoughts. Might as well eat something while I wait for Ella to show up. Rummaging through the bag, my hand grazes what I think is a banana, and that will make do for now.

I rest my back on a large boulder nearby and peel my banana, surprised it's not entirely brown and bruised from sitting in my bag for so long. Intentionally not agonizing over what could have possibly happened to my sister these last weeks, now I can't stop looking over toward the piles of ash, wondering how that happened.

Why would someone burn human bodies? So strange.

Finishing off the banana in less than a minute, I tuck the peel back in my bag—I don't want to leave behind any traces of my existence. Before I close the satchel, I notice the map Camilla drew up, and I pull it out to study for the thousandth time for our return flight. I memorize every detail until I can close my eyes and all I see are the coordinates etched into my memory for a quick departure.

Unexpectedly, the spikes along Gabriel's spine curl and straighten, clicking in warning. His head lurches forward, and he begins snorting and growling, like he's anticipating a fight.

I look at Shea, but she hasn't moved from the position she was in when I strapped her harness on. She doesn't look scared or even concerned.

I hear a girl giggle from the tree line in front of me, and I know for a fact that it's Louella. My heart starts racing as I realize I fucking found her. I'm elated—but that quickly falters when I hear the low vibrations of a man's voice talking to her. Turning my ear toward them, I try to get a better listen of what they are saying, but it's no use. I can't make out his deep voice obscured by the sounds of them passing through the brush. Warily, being careful not to make any noises of my own, I move to Gabriel's side to get a better view of the direction they seem to be coming from. Another male voice pierces through the forest, and I discover that she's with two guys.

I can see lights bobbing through the trees the closer they approach. Before my heart rate can climb any higher, I take a steadying breath and try to form a plan. Suddenly, I wonder if I should have grabbed my dagger from the bag—but it's too late. Peeking out from behind Gabriel, I spot Louella as she steps into the clearing and abruptly comes to a halt. The two guys haven't noticed that she has stopped, so she stretches her arms out and blocks them from walking any farther. They both jerk backward with bemused looks on their faces.

"What's happening? Are you all right?" the taller one asks Ella.

There's a beat of silence as Louella remains completely still, and I can tell she's assessing the situation just as I taught her. I stay in place as well, in case the males with her have weapons . . . I can't trust anyone after seeing those piles of ash close by.

Finally, Louella gradually raises the light in her hand and aims the beam at Gabriel.

"Oh, FUCK!" the short guy bellows.

Louella doesn't respond to him as she staggers over to Gabriel in shock, her eyes wide.

"Calm down. It's going to sense your fear. Just chill," the taller guy says to the shorter one as he pumps his hands down in a placating gesture.

"Gabriel! How in the hell did you get here?" Louella's tone is bewildered.

When he hears Louella's voice, Gabriel's spikes lose their tension and become soft again. He snorts like he's answering her, and she reaches to rub his snout.

With Louella standing so close to me, I figure it's time to reveal myself. The guys seem safe enough—they haven't attacked my dragon, at least—and we've got to get moving if we want to make it back home tonight.

Stepping out from behind Gabriel, I pull my shoulders back to puff out my chest a bit, raising my chin. Knowing my sister, I can sense she may fight me on this. I want Louella to understand that I'm serious, this whole situation is serious, and she's coming back home with me . . . now.

My foot snaps a twig on the ground, and Louella shines the light directly into my eyes. Instinctively, I hold up my arms to shield my face, but it's no use. All I can see are giant white spots speckling my vision.

"Chester? Chester?! Is that you?" I can hear the disbelief ringing in Louella's voice.

"Ugh, can you put the light down, Ella?" I ask her, annoyed.

"Oh my goddess, yes! Yes!" Louella starts squealing and laughing hysterically. In a split second, she dashes toward me and engulfs my chest in a tight squeeze.

I return the hug and close my eyes. I take a deep breath.

I can't believe I found her.

TWENTY

LOUELLA APONI DELPHINE

Kailani Bay, Gemcove Island

"**D**ude, he died in the book, so he has to die in the show," Knox firmly states to Lloyd. For the entire ride to check on Shea, they've been arguing about a television show they watch. Lloyd tried to get me to watch it with him, but I prefer movies at the cinema. Regardless of my lack of interest in the show, I've been their captive audience in the car, stuck listening to them both try to be right and assert their opinions over the other—it's been quite comical.

"Nah nah nahhhh, no. They should have never followed the books verbatim. He should have lived to slay and rule the kingdom with his wife!" Lloyd counters.

Knox slows the car down and parks in the usual spot on the side of the road, near the trail into the forest. He and I open the doors and jump out. I hesitate, wondering if I should help Lloyd on my side but not knowing how. Before I can ask, Knox reaches toward his seat, and with a flick of his hand, the top half flops down. He stands back, and Lloyd climbs from the car. I walk around the front to join them but stop short when I notice I forgot our flashlights.

"Oh shit, hang on," I call so they don't leave without me. I hustle back to the car door, pull it open again, and reach under the seat, stretching my fingers among the bits of debris on the carpet until my fingertips graze one flashlight. I slide it out and reach back under for the second, snatching it up quickly.

"Got them!" I slam the door once more and jog to meet up with Knox and Lloyd, handing Lloyd the other flashlight before we duck into the dense brush together.

"Look, dude, here's the thing: Louella's a real-life dragon queen, and you're offending her by saying she needs a husband to defend her and her castle," Knox jokingly quips to Lloyd.

"Oh, real cool, dude. Now you're making me feel like a dick for liking a character in a show!"

Snickering to myself, I shine the light in front of me to make sure there's nothing in the way of my footsteps.

As we approach the caves, I see Shea standing at the edge of the tree line . . . but it doesn't look like Shea. Her form appears slightly smaller than usual, and it looks like she has horns on her head . . . which, last I checked, Shea does not have.

Knox and Lloyd are trailing behind me, and they don't notice when I slow my gait. I tap my right hip, double-checking that I came prepared with my dagger. My feet enter the clearing, and a loud gasp escapes me as a dragon—who is decidedly not Shea—hunches in front of us with a snarl on its face. The spikes along its spine are flexing, telling me to back off. Instinctively, I jolt my arms out to stop the guys from getting any closer to the mysterious and on-edge dragon standing before us.

"What's happening? Are you all right?" Knox asks.

I raise the flashlight to illuminate the dragon's features so I can get a better look. I can tell its skin is a brownish hue, but when I get to the head, with those horns . . . it's—that's Gabriel! Brynlee's dragon is here in this realm.

"Oh, FUCK!" Lloyd shouts, and I can't really blame him. I'm shocked to see another dragon here too.

"Calm down. It's going to sense your fear. Just chill," Knox advises Lloyd.

"Gabriel! How in the hell did you get here?" I ask him. Carefully, I edge closer.

Once Gabriel recognizes me, his agitation dissipates. He snorts in response to my question, and his spikes slacken and lie back down along his body.

The boys are bickering behind me, but my heart is beating so loudly, wondering how another dragon could have possibly gotten here. Brynlee is the only person who rides Gabriel, and I can't see her realm jumping . . .

He drops his head to look at me, and I run my hand along the side of Gabriel's face, my fingers tracing over the bumps and small spikes on his snout. He closes his eyes and leans into my touch.

A twig snaps on the other side of him, and I point my flashlight to the left. I'm taken aback when I think I see Chester standing in front of me. My eyes must be playing tricks on me because there's no way it could be him.

"Chester? Chester?! Is that you?" I can't believe what I'm seeing. My chest tightens, and I gasp for air. It feels like I'm on the brink of a panic attack, my eyes brimming with tears, which spill over and trickle down my face—I realize I'm so fucking happy.

My brother is wearing his military attire, which is an all-black ensemble consisting of a leather vest with a tight-fitting black T-shirt underneath and baggy pants with the cuffs tucked into his combat boots—he's ready to fight if he needs to. His molten-chocolate hair is in a loose braid, with errant strands wisped around his deeply tanned face.

"Ugh, can you put the light down, Ella?"

My breath catches in my throat when I hear Chester's annoyed tone. I don't waste a second longer and run to him, shrieking with joy.

"Oh my goddess, yes! Yes!" I wrap my arms around his body and squeeze his torso as tightly as I possibly can. I feel him release what I imagine was a long-held breath, and we stay like this, hugging and smiling and laughing.

"I can't believe you found me. I can't believe it's you! How did you know I was here? How did you know how to get here?" I squeeze Chester even tighter, afraid that this is another dream and he's not truly here with me now . . . But this is real. He is real. I'm holding him in my arms at this very moment. I rest my cheek against his chest, hearing his heart thump against my ear, his warmth engulfing me—he feels like home.

Chester attempts to chuckle, but it comes out more like a strangled exhale.

"Louella, what's going on?" Knox asks from behind us.

I reluctantly release my hold on Chester and glance at Knox and Lloyd.

"It's my brother. It's Chester," I answer with a beaming smile.

They remain rooted where they stand, sharing a wary glance.

"It's okay. Gabriel won't do anything to you," I say, gesturing with my hand for them to come forward. With my other hand, I aim the flashlight down in front of them so they can see where they are walking.

They take a few hesitant steps toward Chester and me, but Knox stops several feet away, refusing to get any closer—and Lloyd stays with him.

Knox gets to meet my brother! It's a thrilling thought that two of the men I care about most in my life are here at the same time. I wasn't sure something like this would ever be possible. I'm still grinning stupidly, but I falter when I get a better look at Knox's face.

He's angry.

A frown replaces my smile. My heart is beating in a weird, slow rhythm, and it hurts—like it's splintering. I clutch my hand to my chest as though I can soothe the pain, but it does nothing.

Why do I feel like I'm dying?

But I already know the reason why Knox is angry and why my heart is breaking: Chester's here to take me home.

Looking at my brother, I step back from him and notice that he's angry too.

"What the fuck is he doing here?" Chester's voice is taut as he squares his shoulders.

My face scrunches in confusion. "What's who doing here? Who are you talking about?" I'm baffled by his question.

"Don't fuck with me, Louella. Why are you here with him?"

Shock radiates through me at Chester's cold and accusing tone.

"Ches, I don't understand what you are getting at, but these guys found me when I landed here and helped me. These are my friends, Lloyd and Knox," I tell him, trying to salvage this.

Chester lets out a sinister cackle, and chills ripple down my spine at the sound.

Knox steps closer to us, his eyes locked on my brother as they glower at each other.

I move out from between them and cross my arms. "Do you two want to explain to me what the hell is going on right now?"

The tension is building around us—even the dragons have become uncomfortable, both of them raking their front claws along the ground in front of them.

After a moment of strained silence, Chester shakes his head. "Let's go, Ella," his voice cuts through the air. "Get on Shea right now. We don't have much time."

"I'm not going anywhere until you tell me what is going on," I retort with a stern voice of my own.

Chester crosses his arms and flicks his eyes back to Knox, who hasn't moved an inch.

"You wanna tell her who you are, or do you want me to?"

I can see the muscles in Knox's temples pulse. His fists are clenched at his sides. He doesn't answer Chester but turns to face me instead. The severity of his features softens as his somber brown eyes clash with mine. He licks his lips and then flicks his lip ring.

"Louella," he says, his voice breaking. "My name isn't Knox."

Shrugging my shoulders, I answer, "That's all right. So what? You lied about your name." I can handle this kind of lie.

Knox closes the gap between us, stopping a couple of inches away from me. "My name is Sebastian Ahiga Royce."

Royce . . . Royce . . . Royce.

My heart plunges to my stomach . . . and continues to fall all the way down to my feet. The blood drains from my face, and breathing is impossible once again. I grip my neck because it feels like my throat is closing.

"What are you saying to me?" I gasp.

Knox—or, Sebastian?—releases a deep breath and wipes a hand across his forehead.

"I'm Prince Sebastian Ahiga Royce, and my brother is Malcolm Dasan Royce . . . you're fiancé."

My head is spinning, making me dizzy. Squeezing my eyes closed, I slump to the ground. I want to throw up, I want to punch him, I want to scream, I want to cry . . . but most of all, I want to go home.

Sebastian rushes to me as my knees slam onto the hard forest floor. He tries to take my hand, but I yank it away from him.

"DON'T!" I shout. "Don't fucking touch me." I hold up my quivering hand, making sure he keeps his distance.

"Come on, Louella, we've got to go." Chester's voice reaches me, but it sounds like I'm under water. Nothing is making sense, and I can't stop the tears that pour down my face.

"What the fuck is going on?" I hear Lloyd ask in the distance, but no one reacts to his question.

Chester gently tugs on my arm to pull me up and then leads me toward Shea. I can hear footsteps behind us, and I'm guessing Knox is following us. Fuck! Sebastian. That liar!

"Wait, Chester, just let me talk to her. Don't take her away yet. I can explain, please," he pleads from behind us.

Chester doesn't stop to acknowledge Sebastian; he proceeds to guide me toward Shea. He helps me jump in the saddle, and from my periphery, I notice him reach over to Gabriel and pick up some sort of leather belt I've never seen before. He begins to strap me down with it, and I feel pressure across my lap as he tightens it, trapping me in place. There's nothing left in me to fight him off or argue with him that I want to stay here—because I don't.

"Sebastian, I don't have fucking time for this. Your parents have waged war with our castle while you've been here dicking around with my sister like she's just another conquest to you."

"She's not a conquest—wait, a war?"

"Yes, a war. You heard me. Louella disappeared, and your parents are pissed, so they declared war on Castle Waimea. I have to get her back before shit gets worse. You've been gone for six years and now you care about what's happening back on Kapu? Give me a break. You always were the irresponsible brother, and you still are."

The two of them are still squabbling beside me, but my ears are ringing too loudly to hear their words.

Chester finishes strapping me down. I'm numb, and it's consuming every inch of my body. I can't feel a thing. I don't want to look at Sebastian—I can't bear to see his beautiful face, knowing that he lied to me. Bile keeps rising in my throat, and I keep swallowing it back. My mind feels like scrambled eggs, jiggly and wet. I drop my chin to my chest as a fresh batch of tears spills over my cheeks. I lick the salty tears off my lips.

"Ella, I need you to look at me." Chester's voice booms through the clearing, catching my attention, and I side-eye him. He is studying me. "Grab the reins and hold on like I taught you. Just let Shea follow Gabriel—but remember to hold on tight. Can you do that?"

I can't verbally respond.

"Blink if you understand." I can hear the panic lacing Chester's words. I blink twice for him.

"Louella, please. Please let me talk to you before you go," Sebastian begs.

He knew I was engaged to his brother, and he hated Malcolm so much that he wanted to hurt him by being with me first. I was a pawn in a game between feuding brothers, and I landed right in Sebastian's lap for him to win. Another sob is bobbing inside my throat, but I force down the tears and the sadness as I grab the reins, straightening my back and lifting my chin in defiance.

I refuse to let this impostor see me break apart because of him.

I glare down at Sebastian, holding my head high. "You don't deserve another minute of my time. Everyone was right about you," I spit out.

As Chester settles down in the saddle atop Gabriel, I nod to him, signaling that I'm ready to go. He nods in reply. I pull back on the reins, and Shea stands. Gabriel strides forward, and in a few quick steps and powerful beats of his wings, he and Chester lift off into flight. Shea follows close behind them.

I watch as Chester and Gabriel lead the way, and I never look back at the man I fell in love with—

The man who lied to me.

My fiancé's brother.

Now, my enemy.

Twenty-One

Louella Aponi Delphine

Castle Waimea, Kapu Island

The ride back to the portal feels like nothing because my inner world has already tipped on its axis and spun out of control. My thoughts have been spiraling down a black hole well before my body even entered one.

The leather strap is cutting into my abdomen since I can't be bothered to use my muscles to hold myself upright, nor can I even hold myself together. My torso sways and jerks around, tempting me to lay my head on Shea's neck and wrap my arms around her tightly . . . But I can't; Shea needs to concentrate, and hugging her would only distract her. I really try to focus ahead on Chester and Gabriel to make sure that Shea follows their lead, but as they disappear within the clouds and I follow, not a flicker of fear crosses my mind about not making it out—I don't even care. I'm not sure I have the energy or mindset to remember to blink because this numbness has blanketed all my senses.

Finally, I summon some strength to grip the reins, but I lurch side to side with the motions of the passage. I utilize the eerie silence as an opportunity to examine every moment and conversation I had with Sebastian, gathering details I must have missed, signs that he was Malcolm's brother . . .

They hit me like blows to the gut. I had been amazed that he could read me like a book: "You're too afraid of what your family might think, or what your village will think of the princess who turned down the ever-so-charming prince she was destined to marry, because it seems like reputation means everything where you come from."

Shit, I'm stupid.

The memory-turned-dream about Malcolm and the two boys I had seen him playing with while I visited Castle Hana with Papa—the one who had smiled at me was a young Sebastian Royce. He was so cagey when I asked him about his brother . . . "Had."

And then wondering why he had said this: "Louella, baby, yes. I've wanted this for so long. I've always wanted you." If he knew me for only a few weeks, why did it sound like he had wanted me for years?

Ugh, do I even have a brain?

The air around me whips my hair against my face and slaps me back to the reality of what is to come now that we have entered the realm of Kapu Island. I push my memories of "Knox" to the back of my mind and prepare for the trouble I'll be in when I get home to Papa and Mama. They probably won't believe me when I tell them it was an accident and that I had no intention of running away. My punishment won't matter anyway because I'm going to be living in hell for the rest of my life, married to Malcolm Royce.

I'll have to make amends to the Castle Hana royals, which will just be lovely since Queen Maribeth and King Victor are the most understanding of people in all the realms of however many other fucking realms out there.

Chester had mentioned a war, but at the time, I was lost in the haze of my heartbreak. However, as we descend from Maka Mountain, I notice a fleet of ships sailing in the ocean below us and dozens of dragons flying from the south.

I started a war. Louella Aponi Delphine, the girl who launched a dozen dragons.

It doesn't take long for Shea to hit the landing grass. Launching her legs out in front of her, she claws the ground, ripping it up and releasing the scent of fresh dirt into the air. Shea stalks over to the dragon shed, then bows down and lies as flat as she possibly can to let me hop off.

I rip the constricting harness-strap contraption off my body and leap to the ground.

Chester rushes over to me as Gabriel and Shea amble over to the caves to rest for the night. "Did you see all those ships and dragons?" he exclaims.

"What does this mean? What is happening?" My eyebrows are furrowed as I study my brother's features. He looks tired, worn down, and a bit older since the last time I saw him in this exact spot.

Chester clears his throat, "Louella, we must get you in front of the Royce family. You must marry Malcolm, and Shea needs to be with you. This is the only way to stop this war."

I pinch my lips between my teeth, tears springing to my eyes again. Forcefully, I shake my head. "No. No . . . I can't marry Malcolm. I can't!"

Chester grabs my shoulders—not in an aggressive way; more like desperate—and it jostles me.

"What were you doing with Sebastian? I need you to be honest with me. Did you run away to find him?" His voice is low and he speaks deliberately, as if I'll have a hard time comprehending what he's saying.

I shove his hands off me forcibly. "What the fuck, Chester? Do you honestly think I wouldn't tell you what my plans were? Do you think I would want to leave my home like this? I was scared and lost. I worried I would never see you again."

Chester raises his hands, gesturing for me to remain calm. "No, I'm sorry. I shouldn't have asked you that . . . But you were asking me about realm jumping right before you disappeared, and I thought it could have been a possibility."

My shoulders are shaking as I struggle to hold back my sobs. "I never intended to leave. I had no idea who Kno—Sebastian was . . . or is," I croak out.

Chester nods, and I can tell he believes me. We remain quiet as I take gulps of air, trying to catch my breath. Everything is catching up to me, and I feel like I'm cracking apart bit by bit. Soon, I won't be able to keep my emotions in check.

"You don't remember Sebastian?"

I blink the tears free from my eyes and let out a loud huff.

"No." My answer is barely audible and broken. My knees buckle, and I start to sink forward.

Chester catches me in his arms before I hit the dirt. He sits down on the damp, hard ground with my crumpled body in his lap. We don't say anything for a while as he swipes the thick strands of hair that cling to my wet face.

I sniffle loudly, breaking the silence. "I thi—I think I fell in love with him, Chester."

His hand stops moving through my hair, and he sighs. "As your brother and best friend, I wish I could tell you that everything will work out, but . . . to be honest, you have to marry Malcolm. It's our only way out of this mess."

Stillness shrouds us once again as I work to steady my breathing so that I can ask him all the questions I have.

I clear my throat to strengthen my voice. "How did you find me? How did you know how to get to me? How are we here right now?" I sit up and scoot out of Chester's lap, plopping myself cross-legged in front of him. One light above us glows a soft orange to illuminate the cave entrance; it's not bright, but it's enough for us to see each other at this predawn hour.

"Phewwww," Chester blows out.

I tuck my legs into my chest and hug them tightly, resting my cheek on my arm as I watch Chester talk.

"I remembered you being interested in realm jumping, so . . . so I thought, 'Shit, it's worth a shot to see if I can do it and find you.'"

"You thought I ran away?"

"Well, yeah. I would have fucking tried too if I had to marry into the goddess-awful Royce family, so I figured, 'Why wouldn't Ella?' I wasn't mad at you for it . . . I was mad at the thought that you would do it and not tell me. I love you, and I thought we shared everything." Chester chews the inside of his cheek, and I can see the pain in his eyes. The same pain that I felt when I thought I might lose him forever.

"You found me. I'm glad you did." I flash him a halfhearted smile. "But how did you know where to go and what to do?"

"There are some things that you actually don't know about dragons, Little Sis," he scoffs and rolls his eyes.

"Impossible," I mumble.

"Mmm, nope, possible. Dragons have their own form of communication. They can communicate with each other through echolocation—it's like their spikes can send and receive high-frequency sounds like messages, and they can sense one another. If they are blood related or have mated, then they are bonded and the currents between them are stronger."

I tip my head back in astonishment as I put the pieces together. "And since Gabriel and Shea are from the same bloodline, the bond is super strong. It probably took Gabriel no time to find Shea."

"Correct. I mean, if Shea were farther from the portal, it probably would have taken a smidge longer to find her." A smug smirk dances across his face, and I want to slap him for being so cocky and knowing something I didn't.

"That's the fucking coolest thing."

Chester nods in agreement.

"Moving forward, you are obligated to tell me every detail about the dragons. I want to know all the secrets."

I hadn't realized I wasn't even thinking about that traitorous prince Sebastian for these few minutes we've been sitting here chatting like we used to, and I felt normal . . . But the sadness is creeping back in, making my stomach feel hollow.

Right on cue, as if Chester can feel the emotions radiating off me, he picks up the conversation again.

"Anyway, I've got some gossip for you."

I perk up. "Oh yeah? What's that?"

"Let me just say, Camilla and Tallulah have a lot of secrets, and the other-realm clothing Tallulah has been selling isn't from some mysterious broker she deals with in the shadows. Turns out, Camilla has been jumping to the other realms for years. She filled me in on everything she knows—that's how I found you."

My mouth is hanging wide open. I can't believe Mama's best friends would risk realm jumping despite knowing how Papa feels about it—and how Mama feels about it too. She hates hearing about the realm jumpers.

"Wow. I don't even know what to say."

Chester stands up and extends his hand out to me. "Well, you aren't going to say fucking shit because our king and queen cannot know about the Belmonte sisters' antics. I promised them both I wouldn't say anything, and I'm keeping my word. They are good people, and they're like aunts to us."

I grab his hand, and he pulls me to standing. My knees wobble a bit, and I'd prefer to blame it solely on the strenuous ride, but I know my body is drained and weak because of the truth about Sebastian. I inhale as deeply as I can, but it's more like a big stuffy sniff, and the air goes nowhere. I don't even want to think about how awful I must look from crying so hard—I can feel the snot drying on my face and the faint wet tracks down my cheeks from the tears.

I lift my arm to use the cuff of my sweatshirt sleeve to wipe my cheeks, but before I do, I realize that this is his sweatshirt . . . It doesn't stop me from wiping all the snot and tears away. I am tempted to hawk a big wad of spit in it, but it's chilly, and I still have to trek back up to the castle.

Fuck him.

Tapping the side of my hip, I remind myself to ditch the dagger when Chester's not around. I don't want him asking questions—and I absolutely don't want him to know that I killed a man. I'm not ready for that conversation just yet.

Lengthening my spine, I'm able to take a deep breath that fills my lungs this time. I inhale the familiar scent of plumeria, which reminds me how much I love my home and would do anything to protect it. I push my shoulders back, confident that whatever comes next, I can handle. I allow my mind to envision Knox one last time before I begin the process of letting him go. He's nothing to me now, and we will always remain a realm apart. I face Chester and announce, "Let's go stop this war, shall we?"

I thrust my hand out for Chester to take once more. He briefly looks me over as if I've gone mad and then places his hand in mine.

"I'm not going to lie; you look a tad deranged," he chuckles. "Your time away has changed you, hasn't it?"

"I guess we will find out," I answer as we begin to walk.

Not another word is exchanged between us after that, and the silence is welcome. I want to savor this last moment of peace with my brother before I'm peppered with questions . . . and scorned for disappearing . . . and forced into a life I'm not sure I can bear to live. There will be so much shit to sort through not only between our two castles but also in my mind, and most importantly, in my heart.

We stroll back toward the castle hand in hand. Halfway up the hill, Chester squeezes my hand, and I return it with a firm squeeze of my own as we both acknowledge that our lives will never be the same after today.

ALSO BY KRISTIE PRICE

Prepare to cry, smile, and fall in love with this debut novel from indie author Kristie Price.The Restrictions of Cora is about a good girl, Cora Mitchell, who falls in love with a swoon-worthy punk boy, Jeremiah Novak.Cora is a senior at Rock Point High — but Cora can't wait to graduate and leave her parents and hometown far behind her.

Cora's plans change when she meets Jeremiah, the alluring bassist of a local punk band called The Restrictions.Cora has been struggling with her parents' divorce, and figuring out her future; plus, she has never really felt like she fit in at school – but when she's with Jeremiah, she feels free to be herself.

What starts as a friendship, quickly turns into a heated and loving relationship.The Restrictions of Cora will have you swept away into Cora's world of falling in love with an older boy, and the ebb and flow of childhood friendships –

all during the coming of age of flip phones, MySpace, and pop-punk/emo music.

Being a "bad girl" has never felt so good.

ABOUT THE AUTHOR

Kristie Price

Kristie spends most of her time reading (shocker!), chasing two toddlers around, cuddling with her two golden retrievers, and deep-diving into romance and mystery-binge-worthy shows.

When Kristie's not reading, mom'ing, and solving mysteries – you can find her podcasting (That Scared the Crap Out of Me), attending concerts, running, and baking.

For more information, follow Kristie on Instagram (@author_kprice), TikTok (@author_kprice), and Facebook — or visit www.kristieprice.com